Reid and the Ripper

A novel exploring the mind of
Jack the Ripper and the detective
who hunted him

By

PAUL KENNY

Copyright © 2020 Paul Kenny.
Cover design and maps Copyright © 2020 Adrian Newell.
www.adriannewell.co.uk

All rights reserved.

ISBN: 979-8-6455-9018-5

Dedication

To all the victims of Jack the Ripper; may they be remembered.

Authors Note
The crimes of Jack the Ripper form the basis of this novel. It contains a lot of bad language, particularly from Jack the Ripper. There is also graphic sexual violence concerning the Ripper's crimes. Some people will find the content disturbing, but they were gruesome crimes.

A note on dialogue and language: The book uses some local slang and dialect to reflect how people spoke. Explanations of these are in appendix 1. (*You'll soon get the 'ang of it*) Please read this appendix first if you are unfamiliar with Cockney pronunciation.

Contents

Introduction 1

January 1888 The White Swan and the Princess Alice 9

February 25th The attack on Annie Millwood 25

February 29th Inspector Reid investigates 31

March 28th The attack on Ada Wilson 37

April 3rd The killing of Emma Smith and a surprise attack 43

April 7th Inspector Reid's enquiries 49

April 10th The patient and the policeman 53

May 7th The London Hospital resident 57

July 15th The stalking begins again 61

August 6th The predator stalks his prey 69

August 7th The killing of Martha Tabram 73

August 9th Questioning Pearly Poll 83

August 16th Further police investigations 87

August 23rd Inspector Reid's discussions 91

August 31st The killing of Mary Ann Nichols 101

September 3rd Abberline's investigations 119

September 8th The killing of Annie Chapman 125

September 9th The killer is arrested 139

September 10th The return of Inspector Reid 143

September 21st Police investigations 153

September 29th The *Jack the Ripper* letter 163

September 30th The killing of Elizabeth Stride 165

September 30th The killing of Catherine Eddowes 175

October 1st A postcard to the police 185

October 2nd Police investigations 193

October 3rd The Ripper and a woman 201

October 5th A missed opportunity 207

October 6th Another letter and a glimmer of hope 211

October 19th The Lusk kidney and the *From Hell* letter 219

October 26th Inspector Reid's deliberations 225

November 2nd Revelations in the Ten Bells 229

November 9th The killing of Mary Jane Kelly and the police investigations 233

November 10th Doctor Bond's profile of the killer 247

November 11th The Ripper's demise 253

November 12th Inspector Reid's final investigations 259

November 13th Inspector Reid's analysis 267

Appendix 1 Translation aid 279

Appendix 2 Inspector Reid's noticeboards of the victims 283

Appendix 3 Police officers and officials 297

Appendix 4 Sources of information and permissions 303

Acknowledgments 305

Introduction

In the East End of London in 1888, a series of brutal killings took place. To this day the killer has not been identified, and probably never will be. The police of the time generally accepted that he was responsible for killing at least five prostitutes. However, this figure could have been higher. There is also a reasonable possibility of him carrying out at least two non-fatal attacks before his first killing.

For anyone reading this book with very little knowledge of Jack the Ripper or the East End of London, there are a few facts that may help. Whitechapel and Spitalfields are directly East of the old City of London. It was a working-class area, with a large Jewish population. Much poverty and overcrowding existed; prostitution and alcohol-related crimes were rife. The East End was a much-neglected area of London with a low life expectancy and unhealthy living conditions. An unknown killer murdered five prostitutes between the 31st of August and the 9th of November 1888. The killer, who was later called *Jack the Ripper* by the press, was never caught. Each one of these five women was killed by her neck and throat being deeply cut. Detective Inspectors Fred Abberline and Edmund Reid led the police investigation into the killings.

The Ripper killed his victims while they were lying on their backs. Four of these five women were mutilated, after death, at the crime scene. It was these horrific mutilations that were the killer's *'signature'*. This term refers to those acts that give the killer sexual pleasure; they are the purpose of the killings.

The Modus Operandi (Method of Operation) or M.O. of the Ripper involved a rapid attack and part strangulation of the victim, where he forced her to the ground. The Ripper then cut her neck and throat deeply, resulting in a quick death. This M.O. was an advanced and efficient method of killing, and this had evolved as the killer gained experience. So, Jack the Ripper must have started attacking or killing with a less effective M.O. on a victim, before his attack on the 31st of August 1888. Therefore, Martha Tabram could have been his first kill on the 7th of August, and Annie Millwood could have been his first non-fatal attack on the 25th of February. Both stabbing attacks took place in Spitalfields, but without neck cutting or mutilations. These two earlier attacks may be significant for locating where the killer may have lived and worked.

The case remains the most famous unsolved murder case in history. It was probably one of the first documented cases where the police were investigating a *'serial killer,'* and was also one of the earliest murder cases where the victim was photographed at a crime scene.

This book considers what type of person would kill and mutilate in this way and what drove him to commit such crimes. Since the Ripper killings over 130 years ago, other similar killers, such as the Yorkshire Ripper, have shown several abnormal personality and behavioural traits. Some of these traits will have helped to shape his criminal personality. I, like many other people, believe that Jack the Ripper was an ordinary person from the same class as his victims and lived in the same area of Whitechapel and Spitalfields. Most serial killers are ordinary and unremarkable. From the recent UK past, killers such as Fred & Rose West, Peter Sutcliffe, Ian Brady & Myra Hindley, Joanne Dennehy, Dennis Nilsen and Steve Wright will show many of the psychopathic traits that Jack the Ripper had.

From the existing police evidence, which is not extensive, one could build a broad profile of the type of person Jack the Ripper may have been. Information can be gained from the crime scene evidence, the victimology and the environment in which the killings took place. One's personality develops, not only from the genes that a person is born with but also the circumstances in which a person is brought up. Significant other factors are whether they have been subject to neglect, or physical, sexual or mental abuse. A lack of socialisation and positive adult role models will impair a person's ability to interact with society. A physical and psychological injury or disfigured appearance may also severely affect someone's personality. There are too many variables to make up an accurate description of Jack the Ripper as a person. Still, there is a good likelihood, that certain personality traits would have been present in him, and these can be gleaned from the types of crimes he committed.

Jack the Ripper was a psychopath. Psychopathy is a personality disorder, not a mental illness. (not all psychopaths are criminals, by the way). He was not insane and knew right from wrong. Jack the Ripper may have had mental health issues such as anxiety, depression or paranoia and could have harboured many irrational thoughts, possibly as a result of his neglected upbringing. He could have functioned in everyday society to a degree and blend in, but not be a part of it. He would have learned to exist alone.

You will see through this story how the personality of Jack the Ripper has developed and how Inspector Reid starts to understand the killer from a psychological point of view by reflecting upon the crime scene evidence.

The crimes suddenly stopped after the death of Mary Kelly. Something prevented him from carrying on, such as death, incapacitation by illness or injury, or incarceration in a prison or asylum. He would not have just stopped. Suicide appears unlikely because he enjoyed what he did, and he didn't feel guilt or shame. Suicide would have been an option for him had he been caught.

He may well have had an anti-social personality disorder evidenced by the abnormal behaviour of posing and mutilating women. These killings and mutilations struck terror into the streets of Whitechapel and Spitalfields. Maybe in his mind, he was striking back at society because, society had neglected him, punished him and betrayed him.

The Ripper is destined for obscurity and anonymity forever unless some actual crime scene evidence surfaces, which can be linked to a specific person. Unfortunately, there is no crime scene evidence as it has been destroyed. The confession of a person, hidden for 130 years, would also have to identify some crime scene evidence that only the killer and police knew. Again, this is extremely unlikely.

The story describes some of the life in Victorian Whitechapel and Spitalfields, through the lives of the four principal characters, who are Jack the Ripper, his aunt and the two detectives, Edmund Reid and Frederick Abberline. Many of the Ripper's victims, including the non-fatal ones, were middle-aged women and were not particularly attractive. They were poor, and they were all dependent on alcohol to varying degrees. Some of them were dressed in rags, and not all were well nourished. It was a hard, miserable life for many of the people of the East End of London. The affluent West End of London was a million miles away from these people. These East End people were born poor, cold and hungry and lived their entire lives that way. Their solace was alcohol and tobacco, which took away some of the pain and anguish for a brief, few moments.

The area was plagued by hunger, poverty, crime, prostitution and alcoholism. The average life expectancy in this part of London was around 35 years of age, and infant mortality was about 50% for working-class people. The victims and the killer were part of a largely ignored and forgotten class of people who led miserable lives. There are many photographs of Victorian London showing the plight of these poor people. The story tries to reflect some of the hardship of their lives.

The killer has not been given a name; he is anonymous. The story identifies the **type** of person the killer may have been, but not the **actual person**. This book focusses on the psychology of the crimes from the killer's point of view. It also shows that the attention of the police investigation could have been narrowed down by understanding what sort of person would commit these crimes.

I have chosen to focus the police investigation on Inspector Reid, who realises, through his foresight and insight, that they were dealing with a different type of killer. He critically analyses the crimes in every detail from the killer's perspective. The reasoning employed by Reid and his need to understand the killer contrasts sharply with the more traditional, *'local knowledge policing'*, of Inspector Abberline. It is essential to portray the key events as accurately as possible by using the remaining archived police evidence on the case. The chronological ordering of the chapters best reflects the police investigation and its gradual escalation. It was a while before the police discovered they were looking for a different type of killer, who had no connection with the random victims.

The Ripper would have lived somewhere in Spitalfields, close to where his early crimes took place. The Princess Alice public house is an ideal location for his residence. Two of these initial attacks (Millwood and Tabram) are close to his home, and this formed his primary comfort zone.

I have used the Princess Alice pub, because it provides an opportunity to place a relative. In this case, a hardworking woman who can recount the back story of the killer in general conversations with other people. She is also someone the killer is at ease talking to, which helps to portray his personality and his psychology. I have made the aunt a strong character for several reasons that will become apparent. The killer has not had a lot of contact with her; due in part to him being in prison and having an early dysfunctional childhood. I also felt that giving Jack the Ripper a permanent place to stay, was sensible in that he could clean himself up after the crime without being seen; this would be difficult in a common lodging house. At a private address, he can also take off any blood-stained clothing without anyone noticing.

The Ripper's target of prostitutes was neither because he specifically hated women, nor that he was disgusted with a prostitutes' way of life. He targeted prostitutes because they were easy to overcome. They were out late at night with male strangers, in a remote place and usually drunk. Over time he learned how best to attack them, without them being able to fight back or call for help.

Whether the murder of Emma Smith on April the 3rd 1888 was a Ripper murder or not, we don't know. Briefly, she was attacked by someone who inserted a blunt object into her vagina, causing internal damage from which she later died. The victim stated it was a gang of three men, one of whom was about 19 years of age. On the face of it, this would rule out Jack the Ripper. However, if it was a lone perpetrator and Smith knew him but was not willing to identify him, due to reprisals, then this crime would be in keeping with the profile of Jack the Ripper. Inserting a blunt object with force, into the vagina of a woman, is both callous and sub-normal, and you would expect it from a sexually immature criminal, like the Ripper. However, if it were Jack the Ripper, you would also expect poor Emma to be stabbed, but this was not the case. In 1888, many men were callous, and violence was a way of life for many women. Prostitutes endured hardship and abuse from many men, not just Jack the Ripper. Protection gangs also operated in Whitechapel and Spitalfields, so if it was a gang that attacked poor Emma Smith, it was not a Ripper crime. Jack the Ripper would not have been part of a group of thugs.

Two other murders have been attributed, by some people, to be the work of Jack the Ripper. These are the murders of Alice McKenzie in July 1889 and Francis Coles in 1891. For either of these two murders to be by Jack the Ripper, one would have to accept that he had reverted to a less effective and clinical method of killing and that he no longer desired to carry out his signature mutilations. Neither the Modus Operandi nor the signature of these two murders can be compared to the recognised M.O. and signature of the Jack the Ripper murders from August through to November 1888.

Throughout this book, I have tried to keep to the known facts and portray life in Whitechapel and Spitalfields as it was. I use the term 'prostitute', not as a term of abuse or judgement, but because that is the most accurate and correct description of a woman who has sex for money, regardless of the motives. The term has existed for centuries.

Further, it is a fact that these six murdered women became prostitutes not to buy food, clothing, shelter, nor to support their children but to buy alcohol because they were dependent on it. Being an alcoholic and a prostitute makes a woman an even easier target for a man that wants to kill. It is essential to accept and understand this without being judgemental about them.

January 1888
The White Swan and the Princess Alice

"Get the fuck oot of 'ere an' donnae cam back, ye self-righteous twat," the Glaswegian landlord said as ale was strewn across the pub. Ejecting religious people who proclaim the evils of drink in a pub, is all part of the job for a landlord in the East End.

Detective Inspectors Reid and Abberline ignored the commotion and were talking about the year ahead, in the White Swan public house on Whitechapel High Street, which was just around the corner from the north end of Leman Street. Edmund Reid was now the CID officer for H Division. He took over from Fred Abberline, last July when Fred was promoted to central CID at Scotland Yard.

"How long have you been a copper now, Edmund?"

"I joined in 1872; they had reduced the height restrictions that year. Otherwise, me being only five-foot-six-inches tall, I wouldn't have gotten in. What about you, Fred?"

"I joined in 1863, I made clocks in Dorset before that, as you know. It's 25 years of service for me this year, and I am getting old and fat."

"Here's to us then. Let's hope it is a good year for both of us and my moustache gets even better."

"Cheers, Edmund, I am sure it will be. Whitechapel and Spitalfields have crime, but it is mainly tea-leafs, the odd mugging, controlling and protecting the prostitutes, drunkenness and fighting. It's a rough place, but crime isn't out of hand here.

I know most of the locals, good and bad, and most of the time, the local people self-police. If someone's getting too much of a beating in a pub, others will step in to break it up. But there is nothing that we can't handle."

"It has generally been a lower-level crime, and I am sure that will continue."

"I'll get us another drink," said Abberline, smiling as he stood up, his voice being drowned out by the landlord.

"Af ye donnae like it, ye can fuck off an' all, am nae bothered," the large landlord shouted to another customer.

"He's a nice guy when you get to know him."

"I'm sure he is, Fred."

A few minutes later, he returned with two fresh pints of ale and took his seat in the poorly lit and smoky pub.

"How's your Emily and the kids?"

"They are all fine, Fred, Lizzie will be 15 this year, and little Harold, six."

"And your Emma, has she had a good Christmas?"

"Yes, we had a good, relaxing Christmas, Emma is busy as usual and some of her family came round for a day or two."

There was a lot of laughing from a group of men; one of them had his erect penis out and was pointing it at two women, who were also laughing.

"You know Whitechapel better than anyone, Fred; what is it that I need to know?"

"Get to know everyone, and I mean everyone. Information is the key. When there is a jewellery shop robbery, you need to know who the fences are, and you get them that way. Although no-one will admit it, we get a lot of people grassing others up. We have to be careful not to give them up."

"Getting to know everyone is easier said than done, Fred."

"You know, I made it my policy that all the beat coppers had to know and talk to everyone on their beat."

"I don't ever think that I will be as successful as you. I am not saying that to please you; I am saying that because it takes years to build up that knowledge. You have also been a fair copper; people respect you, and that takes time."

"Look around this place, Edmund. You should be able to pick out those that work and have a trade or profession. Those two at the bar are thieves, the three women behind them are bangtails. You possess a very logical mind that works well under pressure, but you have to know where to look. You will be fine, trust me, but local knowledge is the key. Once a crime has been committed, I know who I am looking for and where they will be. If a wife is killed, then it is the husband that did it and vice versa. The crime here in Whitechapel is mundane; you just need to know who the villains are in the neighbourhood and by keeping your ear to the ground. Good old-fashioned policing."

"Things are changing Fred. Just as Mr Darwin said, that all life evolves, well so does human knowledge." Reid's words were lost with the deep voice of the landlord, drowning them out.

"Am gaein' as fest as aye ken, A need mare ale oop 'ere."

"Well, knowledge may be advancing, but science isn't going to catch a criminal, is it?"

"It might, in time. Several people have said that fingerprints are unique to every person. What if we could pick up such prints at a crime scene and check them across the records that we hold to see if there is a match?"

"Edmund, local knowledge catches criminals and a good eye and a good ear."

"I am not saying it doesn't. Look! You've been on a train and so have I. Fifty years ago trains did about 10 miles-per-hour. Nowadays, trains do 70 miles-per-hour; they have been improved. The engineers have found ways of making them more reliable and faster. Who knows, one day they may exceed 100 miles per hour!"

"One-hundred-miles-per-hour, who wants to go at that speed?"

"Maybe they will develop even faster methods of transportation, 200-miles-per-hour or 300-miles-per-hour."

"You're a dreamer Edmund."

"Look at me," Reid said excitedly. "I was the first Englishman to parachute from a hot air balloon at 1000 feet. We must push the limits. Maybe one day someone will find a fast way of flying. We must try new things and not be afraid to fail. Every failure moves us closer to success. We keep changing the things that don't work until they do work."

"You may be right. I don't know what this year will bring, never mind the future in ten years from now. In December we will be sitting here, both saying, *'well not much happened this year.'* 1888 will be confined to history and no-one will remember anything about it, or you and me."

"You never know, Fred, I hope you're right, but you never know."

"A've ainlae wen pair of honds, af ye just gav' us a manit," the landlord shouted.

"Another drink?" Reid asked.

The taller Abberline nodded.

"Nice friendly pub by the way," Reid said sarcastically.

As Abberline was waiting to order two more drinks, Reid was watching two women who have just walked in and started talking to a man at the bar.

"Hello Poll, how are you? Fancy seeing you in 'ere at this time!"

"Well, you know me, John, I like a good time, life is for livin'."

"And this is your pal, Gina, isn't it?"

"That's right; Gina, this is John one of me reg'lars."

"Awright John, you're a friendly fella ain'tcha?"

"I like to think so."

"I'll 'ave two ales and two rums, please," Pearly Poll shouted.

"I'll be wath ye in a manit, hen," a barmaid replied.

Reid noticed that both women were in their mid-forties and neither was particularly attractive. Abberline was now about to be served.

"Whet's ye two gentlemen heving, mare of the porter, as it?" the landlord asked in a friendly tone.

"That's right, thank you."

"Yer the poliss ain'tcha? I knows the poliss were aim fro."

"Why, have you a problem with the police?"

"Nae problem at ail, wa needs sam lae 'n' erder aroond 'ere."

"De ye wanna a whasky tae?"

"Alright, I'll have two whiskies as well, please."

Abberline brings the two pints and two whiskies to the table and looks at Reid, who looks back at him questioningly.

"It was the landlord's suggestion; I didn't want to refuse."

"You're a wise man Fred Abberline, a wise man."

"Those two women that were at the bar near you, do you know them?" Reid enquired.

"Which one? The old one? Or the unattractive one?"

"Are they not both, er ...," Reid was getting lost for words.

"I'm pulling your leg. The one called Poll, is Mary Ann Connolly; don't believe a word she says. The other one I don't know much about, except that they are both bangtails."

Just as they were both sat down again, there was another commotion at the bar, someone shouted, "stop thief!" and the landlord shouted, "Cam 'ere yae bastards!"

Abberline and Reid rushed up and out the door onto the High Street; the two thieves ran across the street into Commercial Street, Reid set off at full speed after the thieves while Abberline shouted "Frank!". One thief was tripped up by a shopkeeper called Frank and collared straight away by Abberline, who had walked over to him and pushed his face into the pavement. Reid, on the other hand, shouted up Commercial Street, then blew his whistle while running. A constable on hearing the whistle caught the other thief with a truncheon blow to his face. This knocked the thief to the ground. Blood was pouring from the nose of the thief who was also now unconscious. Reid caught up with the constable and the criminal, but he needed to catch his breath first.

"You didn't need to take his bloody head off, Constable," Reid panted out.

"Sorry, sir," came the reply. Very quickly, other police were on the scene; Abberline removed the stolen wallet and waited for Reid, who was still panting heavily. The two thieves were handcuffed and escorted (dragged in one case) to Leman Street Police Station.

"See what I mean? Local knowledge. The shopkeeper knows me and helped, as many others would do, they don't like thieves. Let's return the wallet."

"Can I just get my breath back first?"

A short walk from the White Swan is the Princess Alice pub on the corner of Wentworth Street and Commercial Street. It was named after Queen Victoria's third child and not the Princess Alice Ferry disaster in 1878 as some people think. It was a large, grand pub, built in 1883 with decorative brickwork, stonework and glazing and stands five storeys tall if you include the attic rooms.

The imposing landlady, Letitia, was having a conversation with her only close relative, her nephew. He was in his mid-twenties and had just been released from prison. She was born in Kent on a farm and moved to London as an adult to run the Princess Alice. She now tends to drop her 'aitches' like most cockneys. Over time some cockney pronunciation has crept into her vocabulary, mainly when she is talking to cockney people.

"You can stay 'ere 'till you can stand on your own two feet, there's plenty of space in 'ere," the stocky landlady said while re-arranging the bun of her curly brown hair.

"I won't be no bovver, Aunt Letty; I'll start earnin' as soon as I can."

"You can do some work in 'ere, for your board. You'll not be sat on your arse all day while you're with me, I was brought up on a farm, I only know hard graft."

"I can do that. Does it come wiv free beer?"

"You must be fucken' jokin'; you'll work for any beer. The only thing that's free in this place is my fucken' fist."

"Don't worry, Auntie, I'm only jokin'. I wouldn't get on the wrong side of you; you're built like a brick shithouse."

Letty gave him a stern look, which he noticed.

"No offence Auntie, I just wanna' get right. I hated prison, and I hated the workhouse, there's not much diff'rence between 'em, except there are fewer rules in prison. It's good that you can give me a room to stay and fings," he said in a pleading sort of way. "I 'ain't goin' back in the shovel, fuck that," he stated with confidence.

"Well if you kept your 'ands to yourself, you wouldn't be in, in the first place, would ya, me old China?" Letty said with a smile on her face and putting on a cockney accent.

"I know, it's me 'ead, I've just got to sort meself out, know what I mean? I gets picked on in the jail, by some big geezers. But, I pasted one of them, bad like; they left me alone after that. Everyone picks on me, but I hit back 'ard now. I'm used to takin' a beatin', but I can give one and all," he exclaimed, punching the palm of his left hand with his right fist.

"Well, you get them 'ere barrels and glasses beaten first. I'll teach you the bar work in time."

"I'm strong you know, I can lift fings 'eavy and the like."

"Well, you'll get plenty of practise 'ere, my lad. I've got some nice bags of mystery, as you call 'em, for supper, but there's work to be done first. Did you make any china plates in the spade?" Letty didn't always get the rhyming slang correct at times. She usually kept to a few of the more common phrases.

"Shovel. No, I keep meself to meself, know what I mean?"

"I know what you mean, sunshine. You may come in 'andy yet."

"I don't get on well wiv people, except you. I gets down when I fink of what's 'appened to me, in the past."

"Your mother, my sister, was a waste of fucken' space. You didn't deserve her, no-one did. Still, you can get yourself sorted out now."

"I know you are right, but I don't like 'earin' bad fings about 'er. I don't understand why that is; it just makes me angry."

"I'm sorry, she was my sister, but I shouldn't call her to you."

"I'll do the jobs you ask; I won't piss you about."

"No, you'd better fucken' not. You'll be alright, give it time."

"How tall are you Auntie? There's not many as tall as you."

"What are you sayen' that I am odd or somethen'?"

"No just askin' I wish I were as big as you, I'm just av'rage height and av'rage build."

"Well, about six-foot tall, if you must know, and nearly as that fucken' wide as well," she replied with a laugh. She could joke about her physique but would not have tolerated anyone else making such comments.

"You're well-built, not fat. I 'ardly see many people fat, except them that's rich. There's loads of 'em, a lot finner than me, though."

"Well, so long as you are not taken' the piss. My dad was a big bloke and my mother, there's a lot of fucken' work on a farm, so you need a lot of food to build yourself up. Plenty of meat and potatoes, that's what you need."

"I did plenty of exercise in prison, building me muscles up, they come in 'andy in a fight. 'sides, you're betta lookin' than me, you've got a nice face and big brown eyes. Me eyes are diff'rent fuckin' colours and me nose is crooked from when I got it broken."

"There's plenty worse than you, deary. Don't start feelen' sorry for yourself. I've no fucken' time for them that's always wailen' and wanten' some other sad fucker to show them some fucken' pity. Pull yourself to-fucken'-gether and get some fucken' work done, that's what I say."

"I didn't know you worked on a farm," he said sarcastically, smiling with his head down because she mentions it all the time.

"Don't take the fucken' piss. I'd better get back to the bar now."

Reid and Abberline returned to the White Swan. Abberline spoke to the landlord, "who had the wallet, nicked?"

"At was ham wath tha bag sideburns," came the reply.

Abberline took the wallet over, and the man offered to buy them a drink, to which they declined.

"I see someone has taken our ales and whiskies," Abberline said with dismay. In an East End pub, it is common for an unguarded pint or dram of whisky to be digested by someone else, with exceeding rapidity.

"Nae problem, ye deserve a drank on the 'oose, baethe of ye."

The two detectives gladly accepted, under the circumstances. They then sat down again with their refreshments.

"There is a lot of poverty here in this part of the East End," said Reid, still out of breath and sweating. "The doss houses and the workhouse are nearly always full, especially in winter. The sheer poverty of the place makes me wonder why there isn't more crime than there already is?"

"I've been in the new workhouse at South Grove, and I've seen others. It is a hard life in there, but it's better than starving and sleeping out on the street. The alcoholics can't manage in the workhouse without a drink, so they must go hungry and walk the streets at night. It's possibly one of the reasons why there are so many pubs. They're the only place where you can go to get warm; it's no wonder so many people turn to drink, what else have they to live for?"

"You're right Fred, and there is no easy solution. The workhouse has got to act to as a deterrent, so the argument goes. But for some who are starving, and especially those with children, the workhouse is their last refuge, without it they would die. There are just too many people for the Government to give poor relief to everyone. There are not enough jobs for the increasing population. It is a terrible indictment on our society and our country, which is the richest in the world."

"And for all that, most people strive for a better living. Many people work all hours for a pittance and keep going but don't get involved in crime. There are a lot of good people here Edmund, and through no fault of their own, they are poor."

"We sound like social reformers, Fred, maybe we should go into politics."

"Now, I know you are joking. Politicians are not ordinary people like us. There are only a few men that get the vote, and they are the rich men. Look at the likes of Sir Charles Warren, our boss. He knows nothing of policing, neither does the Home Secretary Matthews nor even the Prime Minister himself. They live in a different world."

"I agree. I see the absolute misery on the faces of so many people as if they have given up all hope. Life for them is painful, both physically and mentally. Some haven't got the strength to stand up anymore. It is sad when there are so many others who are well-fed in other parts of the country."

"If someone is born here in Spitalfields, to a family in abject poverty, where you live between the workhouse and the common lodging house, it's almost impossible for them to climb out of poverty. They are destined to a life of hunger, pain and abuse. We fish bodies out of the Thames daily; they have had enough and can't go on."

"We are lucky, Fred; I couldn't live in the workhouse."

"Come on we had both better get back home."

"Am just gaein' for a pash!" the landlord said to the barmaid as they left the premises.

The landlady of the Princess Alice had an hour to herself, at around tea-time. She was talking to one of her good friends, Edna, in the kitchen of the pub. They were having a mug of tea each.

"Letty, that's your nephew, isn't it?"

"Yes, he's just got out of prison, but it's never been easy for him. Did I tell you about my sister, his mother?"

"No, I don't think you did."

Letty settled into story mode, in her hybrid cockney and Kent accent. She would be difficult to stop.

"Well, she was four years younger than me and better looking, but she was thin, skinny. Never put any weight on, but she was a lazy bitch, never did any work. Anyhow, when she gets to sixteen, she finds she likes a drink. But being as thin as a rake, she didn't need much, so she was always Brahams and Liszt. Well, she gets a boyfriend of sorts, likes men she does, and in no time she is pregnant. Well, that doesn't stop her drinken' and shaggen'. So, she has the baby but has no interest in 'im. My mother and me bring him up for a while, till he's about seven. Then my mother dies, and my father is ill. So, she takes the lad in with her. She just lets him out of the room they rent every day. He has to fend for himself."

One of the bar staff enters the kitchen; "There's some trouble in the pub!"

Nothing annoyed Letty more than being interrupted while she was speaking.

"Hold on Edna; I'll sort this out," she said angrily and then entered the pub area. "What the fuck's goin' on 'ere?" she shouts from the bar in a more cockney accent.

The pub goes quiet.

"Nuffink, it's fine," one man with a group of prostitutes said. "We're sorted now," another man shouted.

"Well, just see there's no more fucken' trouble; otherwise, my fist will be finden' some Hampsteads."

The customers were looking relieved. "It was just a bit of fun," a woman said. The customers all knew that the six-foot landlady was not to be messed with.

"Sorry about that, Edna. It's like runnen' a farm in 'ere; only the cows and pigs that I used to look after have got more fucken' sense than this lot. Where was I? Oh yes, she is making money on the game and drinken'. The kid is watchen' all these strange men come and shag 'is mam. It's no way to bring a child up. She abuses 'im, knocks 'im around a lot. Tellen' 'im, he is useless and wished she had never 'ad 'im. He doesn't get any schoolen'. After a while, she is kicked out for non-payment of rent, and forced to go to the workhouse. One day she ups and leaves the workhouse and her son. So, he stays there a while, then sent to an orphanage. Again, he gets physical abuse there, and eventually he learns how to stick up for 'imself. By the time he is 13 years old, he's getten' into trouble for stealen'. It is the only way he has learned to survive. Anyhow, I took 'im in for a while.

"He's a real pain in the arse mind, but I put up with 'im. He knows how far he can go with me. Anyhow, he starts robben' and then gets banged up in prison. Something 'appened to 'im in prison. He came out different like he was in a trance or something. He doesn't talk about it, though. And that is 'ow it is with 'im; in and out of prison. Never done a proper day's work in his life, mid-twenties now. I don't know what will become of 'im. Anyhow, my sister died of TB soon after she left him, 27 years old she was, as fucken' useless as the year is long.

"And I tell you something else, some of her men that visited her, also liked the boy, if you know what I mean. She told him to earn his keep, by sucken' some of them off for money. She rented 'im out. She was an evil bastard. I hate prostitutes myself now, after what she did to 'im. They're no fucken' use, they are like 'er, spenden' all their money on drink. He fucken' 'ates 'em and all."

"Well, he was better off without her, and you helped him when you could," said Edna.

"He 'ain't right in the 'ead, Edna. Damaged by my sister mainly, and prison."

"It's a bad world we live in, Letty; it's hard, tough and unfair," Edna said, as she helped herself to more tea.

"You do what you 'ave to do, to survive. But there's no way I would sell myself, not that anyone would buy me," Letty said, laughing. "Back to work for me now."

There was a crowd of men and four or five prostitutes, laughing loudly and drinking merrily. The landlady glared at them from time to time but took their money, all the same. There were also a few families in the pub as it was preferable to the workhouse or the lodging house. It was even better than the one-room many families rent, as this was all they can afford. They all drank the cheap, weak ale, including the children. The Princess Alice, like many pubs, was in effect a second home for many families; it provided a sense of belonging for many people and where they could get warm, after spending a day out in the cold.

The nephew was sat on his own at a table in the Princess Alice. He had consumed several drinks, so he was quite relaxed, for once. A similarly aged man came over to him.

"Awright? I hear you have just got out. I did a stretch last year; I half-inched some lead."

"Yeah, and I'm not goin' back, neivver. I've been in prison, the workhouse, the orphanage and on the fuckin' streets and they're all shit."

"You're from round 'ere, ain'tcha?" the man said.

"Un-fuckin-fortunately, I was born 'ere. I fuckin' 'ate the place. Apart from a few years livin' with me Aunt on a farm, I 'ave been 'ere."

"You have done awright 'ere though, ain'tcha?"

"It'll do till I get sorted; if I can get sorted. I'm goin' to give it a go 'ere first and see what 'appens."

"That's a nice jacket you got there," said the man who's own clothing had seen better days.

"Was me Uncle's, but he's brown bread now. Me Aunt said I could use his old clothes. When you've been in rags in the workhouse and prison, it makes me feel better, to 'ave somefink decent to wear."

"Ave, you got a job, then?"

"Not yet, me Aunt says I can work 'ere a bit, till I'm sorted, like."

"Some lovely gals in 'ere ain't there?"

"I don't go wiv whores; I don't fuckin' like 'em."

"Ok, maybe I'll see you around sometime?"

All the nephews' replies were in the same low tone, with minimal facial expression and hardly any eye contact. He was not socially adept, nor could he start a conversation and keep one going. The other person usually ran out of things to say.

He went to the bar to get another pint of porter ale; he liked drinking more than anything else. As he sat down alone at a table, he got out a clasp knife and started carving his name into the side of the table. He had killed animals and cut one or two people when he had been involved in a fight. As he looked over at the group of prostitutes, anger started to build up inside him. He looked away, and squirmed, he then drank his beer, and the feelings of anger subsided for a while.

Quite close to the nephew were a family grouped around a table. A female member of the family came in and sat down at the table. Like many people in Spitalfields, their clothes had all seen much better days, and not one of them was clean.

"Where the fuck 'ave you been?" a man at the table said.

"Earning money, what do you fink?"

"What, sellin' yourself as a whore?"

"Well you won't want a drink wiv the money then, will ya?" she shouted.

"Well, I didn't say that, did I?"

"Well, shut the fuck up then, awright!"

"Yeh, leave her alone," another woman said.

Most of the people in the pub, and Spitalfields generally, were in the same desperate plight. Poverty was a way of life, and people had to survive as best as they could. Much of the unskilled work was poorly paid, for the hard graft and long hours. If one could not afford the rent of a room in a house, the only available accommodation was the common lodging house or the workhouse. This resulted in many people staying in a pub, particularly at night, until closing time.

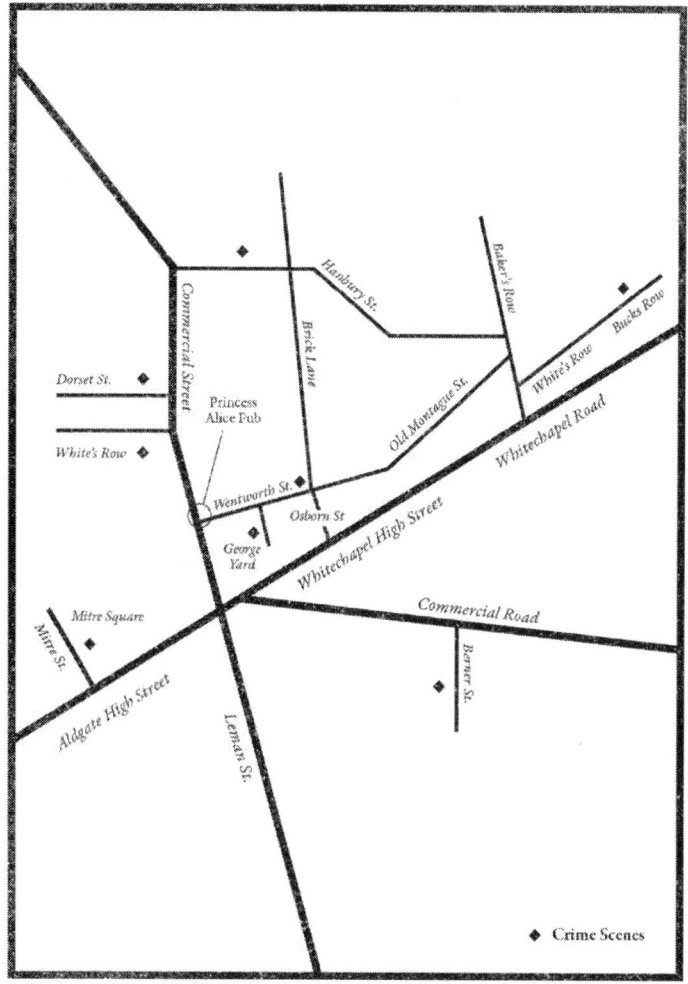

Map 1 – Location Map
The above map shows the main roads feeding Whitechapel and Spitalfields. The crime scene locations are noted with the small diamond. The scene of crime at Mile End, which was the stabbing of Ada Wilson, is not shown. Mile End is about one-mile further East from Bucks Row. The map is not to scale, but the distance from Mitre Square to Berner Street is approximately a half a mile, or about 12 minutes, walk.

REID AND THE RIPPER

February 25th
The attack on Annie Millwood

It was cold outside, yet there were barefooted children in rags, playing in the street of White's Row. They also begged people for money, as they had been taught to do. Begging was a way of life for many people in Spitalfields. On the corner of White's Row, a scruffily dressed old man was sat down begging with his upturned cap on the pavement. It seemed that the beggars of Spitalfields, each had their favourite spot.

"Could you please give me a couple of coppers, your reverendness?" a middle-aged man gently asked a passing priest.

"Come to church on Sunday, brother, and you can be fed on the Holy Spirit."

"I won't last till Sunday, sir."

"Then pray that you do last because there are greater rewards in heaven. Besides, I can smell drink on you."

"I 'ave no work, no 'ome, I have to beg for food and a bit to drink; what else can I do?"

"You need to lay yourself before Christ; he will nourish you."

"Your Christ doesn't care for me, sir; If he did, I wouldn't be beggin', would I?"

"You have no faith brother, trust in the Lord."

The priest then went into the Britannia pub, with a young male companion, apparently to preach to the poor.

"Sorry to 'ave troubled you, sir," the man replied as he moved on.

White's Row was a small, dark and dirty street that joined with Commercial Street, which in turn was one of the main streets in Spitalfields. It consisted of a mixture of three and four-storey brick-built terraced houses. Many of the properties were divided into separate rooms for rent. Spitalfields Chambers, at number eight, White's Row, was one such conversion. The common parts of the building were dark and musty and in need of cleaning. There was a small, basic, communal kitchen and two privies were in the yard.

Annie Millwood was a 38-year-old widow. She was a small, plump woman with dark hair. Annie was not in the best of health and walked with a limp on her left side. She worked long hours in a laundry which didn't help her health. In the late afternoon of the 25th of February, Annie heard someone knocking loudly at her door. She got up from her chair and hobbled towards the front door. She also put a shawl over her shoulders, as it was quite cold outside.

On opening the door, she simply said, "Hello, can I help you?" and looked up at the man in a dark overcoat and large hat with a broad peak. The man didn't answer at that point; instead, he pulled out a clasp knife and began to stab Annie.

"Help! Please help, please stop! I'm being attacked!" Annie shouted while trying to deflect the blade as best as she could as her shawl fell to the floor. The man started jeering as he stabbed her, he then ran out of the building laughing before any help arrived.

There was a severely handicapped boy on his own, outside one of the properties. He was making a groaning noise and rocking backwards and forwards with his upper body. He groaned, hoping that the other children would give him some attention, but they ignored him. Annie's attacker quickly walked past and kicked him; the boy moaned louder, and the man just laughed.

Annie staggered to a neighbours' door pleading for help. Many of Annie's neighbours were families, so help arrived quickly.

"Oh my Gawd, what's 'appened? You're bleeding luv. Stay here, and I'll go for 'elp," one of the neighbours said.

"Is everyfink awright?" another neighbour said, then went to Annie's aid.

A policeman arrived within minutes, and he asked Annie about her attacker. He later took statements from all of her neighbours.

"I never got a look at the man's face. I opened the door and saw him take the knife out of his pocket. It all 'appened so quickly. I started to scream, and then he ran off laughing," Annie said in tears, as she told the policeman and the other people around her. The doctor soon arrived and instructed some of the people to take her to the Whitechapel Workhouse Infirmary, on Baker's Row and Thomas Street, as it was possibly the closest. This very large infirmary was previously the workhouse until the new workhouse was completed in South Grove in 1872.

"I've never upset anyone. I fought he was going to rob me, but I 'aven't got much meself. Since me 'usband died, I've been scared to walk out onto the street at night, but I didn't fink that I would be attacked on me own doorstep," she recounted, in a state of shock.

Meanwhile, the attacker had quickly made his way back to the Princess Alice pub.

"That was amazin', that was fuckin' amazin'," the young attacker said to himself. "The look on her face, ha! Stupid woman. I'll do worse than her before I'm finished," he added. He had stabbed animals in the past, but the thrill of it had waned. This was the first person that he had stabbed, and he was elated with this next level of crime. It felt better than he could have ever imagined.

The attacker was approximately five-foot-seven-inches tall and a medium stocky build, with light brown hair and a small moustache. Facially he was not attractive; he had a crooked nose as it had previously been broken. His face was asymmetrical, and the right ear was sticking out more than the left. He was quite thin in the face and had several front teeth missing, due to decay. He always had a nervous or agitated disposition and was rarely relaxed.

He robbed and stole whenever he could, but he didn't do so today. He had intended to rob her, but for some reason, the urge to stab had overtaken him, so he gave in to his desires. He was on a high. He had seen Annie Millwood hobbling home and decided to follow her as he thought she would be an easy target for him. He liked stalking women and observing their habits.

After washing his hands, the attacker ordered a pint of porter ale and sat down to drink it.

"What are you looken' so pleased about?" Letty said.

"Nuffink Auntie, I'm just 'appy. Do you need any 'elp wiv fings?"

"Why is it my lucky day?" she said. "Go and check the barrels in the cellar and collect these glasses. Them over there needs washing," she added, nodding with her head towards a pile of used glasses, as she finished pulling a pint for a customer.

"I'll just finish this and get started. I can do the bar tonight if you want."

"It is my lucky day. It's about time you made yourself useful."

"If there's any trouble in 'ere I can sort it for you, Auntie."

"I don't need no 'elp from no-one. I'll sort anyone out."

"I can believe it, Auntie. I wouldn't mess wiv ya. Can I get a drink or two for this work?"

"Yes, when things are done, sunshine," she stated in a loud voice.

"Don't call me fuckin' sunshine," he said softly to himself. He finds people difficult to get on with, even his auntie at times. People tended to annoy him; even mild comments can anger him quite easily.

An old man came into the pub and ordered a pint of ale.

"Ere a women's been stabbed, round the corner on White's Row. There are a few coppers about," he said with a cigarette in his mouth at one side.

"Can't be too careful," the attacker said with a smile. "It will be one of those gangs; they're villains, they are."

"You're probably right son," the old man said as he went to sit down with his beer.

"Ere what's 'e been sayen?" Letty enquired.

"Oh, some woman's just been attacked, just now," he said.
"Attacked, how?"
"Why don't you go and ask 'im? Stabbed, I fink he said."

The aunt went over to the older man. She craved gossip and so put up with his reeking body odour, while he recounted the details. She spent a lot of time talking to the customers, even when others were waiting to be served. The attacker was now serving behind the bar.

A young police constable entered the pub and went to the bar. "You haven't seen anyone with a knife on them or with blood on them, coming in 'ere 'ave you, sir?" the constable enquired.

"No Officer, not in 'ere, it's been quite quiet all day, to be 'onest," the attacker said. "You can ask about if you want, Officer. Do you want a drink?"

"Thanks, no, I'm on duty. The sergeant'll bollock me if he finds out that I've had a drink on duty."

The policeman spoke to several people, who all said, that they hadn't seen or heard anything. The landlady collared him though and obtained the story for the second time in a matter of minutes. After a few minutes of the landlady's opinions, the PC was looking nervous, wanted to get on, but Letty was still talking in full flow.

"I think there is someone outside who needs me," he said, putting his hand and index finger up and quickly made his escape.

The landlady then started retelling the story to other regulars in the pub. She enjoyed such gossip.

The attacker was also enjoying this time, but much more covertly than his aunt. He was pleased with himself and the attention his act had brought. He felt powerful because he knew something that no-one else did. He laughed to himself, thinking of the woman screaming, as he stuck his knife into her. He happily drank another pint of porter ale. He had found a new release for his anger, so he drank merrily, and he was pleased with his days' work.

People were singing local East End songs in the pub, and others were enjoying some banter. But there was some sat down who looked thoroughly miserable; life could not offer these people anything other than hunger, cold and a beer now and again. Many had become beggars, and others had fallen on hard times because they could no longer work and relied on the support of their families.

At times when he was alone in the beer cellar altering the barrels, he sang happily in a low voice so that he couldn't be overheard. He was always contented with his own company.

"Oh, hewp me, I'm bein' stabbed, oh hewp, oh hewp.
Please hewp me; I'm bleedin'.
Oh, hewp me, please."

He was repeating these lines, in no order, laughing as he was singing, with his hands waving in the air at head height. Such acts are indicative of his callous and cruel nature; unfortunately, much worse was to come in the following months.

February 29th
Inspector Reid investigates

Inspector Reid visited Annie as she recovered at the large and poorly heated Workhouse Infirmary. She was sat up, on a bed, when Reid introduced himself.

"Can you tell me, anything madam, about the attacker?"

"I couldn't get a look at him, he had a large hat on, and he was taller than me. I think he was a younger man, by the way he sounded when laughing."

"Without a description of the man, it would be almost impossible to find him, madam."

Annie stayed silent.

"How old would you say he was? You said he was a younger man, madam."

"Probably mid-twenties, he seemed a medium height and build."

"Did he say anything or just start laughing, madam."

"He may have said something, but I couldn't make it out, but he laughed childishly."

"Did he rob you, or attempt to rob you?"

"No, not at all, he just started stabbing me," she said, crying as she remembered.

"Did anyone come to your aid immediately?"

"No, I had to knock on some doors, then people came out to help me."

"Would you be able to recognise this man again, madam?"

"No, Inspector, I wouldn't, sorry."

"Well, you just rest and get better. If you do recall anything else, please contact me."

Reid left the cold infirmary, pulling up the collar of his overcoat and putting his hat on. His breath was visible as he exhaled in the chilly air outside. Inspector Reid had a genuine, compassionate manner with people. He didn't judge others but tried to empathise and understand them.

Reid thought that the attack was the type that an immature man may do, as some sort of prank, rather than attempted murder. The doctor told him that the stab wounds were not very deep, and the major organs of the body were unharmed. Robbery and sexual assault were quickly ruled out. There was no evidence that she was a prostitute or that she knew the attacker.

The inspector then went over to White's Row, searching for witnesses and people who had been on the street at that time. He asked if there were any unusual characters, displaying signs of madness or acting strangely. Such people are usually easy to find, but, unfortunately, there were no leads. There was nothing significant on the street nor elsewhere in the vicinity. The information about the attack was kept on file. Reid thought to himself, why would a supposedly ordinary person, carry out an unprovoked attack for no apparent reason? Later in the year, he would find an answer to his question.

Reid turned to go back to Leman Street station and passed the corner of White's Row and Commercial Street, where a small group of people had assembled, having just come out of the Britannia pub. The warm air from their lungs was rising above them. One of them was a young Irish woman called Mary, with dark auburn hair, who he knew to be a prostitute. Further along, an older, drunken man was urinating next to a horse and cart. The horse seemed to be the healthiest living creature in the area. It would, one day, feed the surrounding people.

As Reid crossed over Commercial Street, close to the Queen's Head pub, a group of three women were talking when a man came out of one of the houses.

"Oi! Where the fuck's you goin' at this time, you lazy bastard?" a large woman of about 20 years old said.

"I'm just goin' for a quick 'arf, if that's awright wiv you; ya fat slag," a small middle-aged man replied

"Don't call me fat, you useless piece of shite."

"Wew, you are fat and a slag. No sorry, I take that back; you're not a fat slag. You're a useless, fat, ugly, slag," the man shouted in the street.

"What's up wiv 'im then? Why is 'e 'avin a go at ya?" her friend said.

"I've 'ad enough of 'im. I'm gonna tell the police that 'e's the one that stabbed that woman in White's Row. That'll piss 'im off."

"I would stick a knife into 'im, if I was you," the other woman said.

"I might just do that 'n' all. Still 'e is me dad, all said and done."

Reid ignored them and headed down Commercial Road, towards the police station. A constable on his beat said hello to him.

"Constable," Reid replied. "Have you a minute?" he added.

"Yes, sir."

"There was a stabbing a few days ago, on White's Row. Have you seen a man threatening anybody with a knife, or looking suspicious in any way?"

"I know the attack, sir; it was on my beat. I have also asked several residents at the time of the attack, but no-one noticed anything."

"Let me know if you hear anything, will you?"

"Yes, sir. Pub gossip is probably your best source of information if you know who to ask, sir."

"Thank you. I will bear that in mind. Abberline will know who to ask."

Just before Inspector Reid reached his office at Leman Street, an elderly man hobbled towards him with a walking stick in one hand.

"Spare us a few coppers, guv'na, I 'aven't eaten in free days; I can 'ardly walk," the old man begged.

"I have no spare money, sir, I cannot give you money," Reid said and the old man then fell to the floor.

"I'm too tired to stand anymore; just leave me 'ere to die, sir."

"Look, here is tuppence, go and get some food," Reid said to the man as he was helping him up off the pavement.

"Thank you, sir, you are so kind," he replied as he quickly hobbled away. A minute or so later the man was in the nearest pub, "a double rum if you please," he said, smiling to himself.

Later that evening, Inspector Reid was at home with his wife Emily, in their rented police house, at 124 Commercial Street, Shoreditch. After the children had gone to bed, they sat in the living room and began to talk.

"How has your day been, Emily?" Reid sincerely asked.

"Oh, well apart from my usual duties, I visited a poor woman who has been ill. She is a relation of my friend, Sarah, the schoolmistress. Her niece is suffering badly with a disease that is caused by working at the match factory. The phosphorous causes rotting of the skin, particularly around the jaw. Her lower left jaw has a big hole where the skin has gone, and her teeth on that side are exposed. She has been to the London Hospital, and the decay seems to have slowed down since she is no longer working there. I don't know how she will cope in the future, though, it must be challenging to eat. I believe it is a common illness at the match factory, yet no-one does anything about it. Anyway, how has your day been, Edmund?"

"Well, firstly this horrible disease, which I have seen for myself, is preventable if safer working practices were adopted. We could write to our MP if you wish. As for my day, well, it has been rather troubling. I visited a woman today at the Workhouse Infirmary. She had been stabbed several times as she came to her front door. She is recovering, but she cannot describe her attacker except that she thought he was a younger man."

"Who would do such a thing?"

"Well, that is what I have been puzzling over, and I don't know. There was no hint of a robbery or sexual assault; it is a mystery."

"Maybe she has upset someone, and it is some sort of a revenge attack."

"Yes, I have thought of that, but it isn't the case; she is a respectable, hard-working widow, with no enemies."

"Maybe it is just a madman with a knife."

"Yes, well I thought of that also. If it were, you would expect other similar attacks and being a madman; he would be easy to identify."

"Do you know that sometimes strange things happen, and when you just focus on them, there is no answer. However, when you look at a much bigger picture, you can see how each small detail fits. A friend of mine had an aunt who lived on her own. She was quite wealthy and a widow. She had many valuable trinkets and pieces of jewellery in various places in the house. One day she accused a younger male cousin of stealing a gold brooch when he visited. She had him arrested, and he denied ever seeing the brooch. She then became more security conscious and had a locksmith fit extra locks to the doors and windows. Even when she had not had visitors for days, she would wake up, and something else was missing. Again, she went to the police; but there was no sign of a break-in, and they scoured the house. Yet as she woke up each day, something was missing that was there the night before. As time went on, her trinkets and jewellery dwindled. A relative thought she was selling them to pawn shops, but no-one had seen her valuables at any pawn shop.

"Then the aunt went to live with my friend for a short time, and she noticed that her aunt would get up during the night, walk downstairs as if a trance, and take something, then hide it and then go back to sleep. She was sleepwalking. When my friend confronted her aunt, she denied everything. So, they both went back to her aunt's house and did a thorough search, and under a loose floorboard in the back bedroom, they found all the supposedly stolen items.

"Sometimes, the obvious answers do not fit, but that doesn't mean there is no answer; you have to look for it differently."

"You are a smart one, Emily; that's why I love you, as well as your beauty. You should be a detective. One day women will be, I am sure of it."

"And not before time. Never underestimate a woman, Edmund; you will be surprised at what we can do."

"I never underestimate you, dear; you are as smart as me and better looking."

"What? Even with that moustache of yours."

"Yes, even with my splendid moustache."

"So, getting back to my conundrum; you think there could be something else going on, that we haven't thought of?"

"Like you are always telling me, and anyone else that would listen, that there will always be new developments and progress. Maybe this act is part of something new, that you are not yet aware of. But keep looking Edmund, there are always signs if you look in the right places and ask the right questions."

"Are you sure you don't want my job, or Abberline's? You would probably solve a case before me."

"Maybe one day I will, Edmund. Maybe one day, I will," she said, smiling.

March 28th
The attack on Ada Wilson

It was dark and late into the evening, and all was quiet in a respectable part of Mile End. Ada Wilson resided at number 19 Maidman Street, Mile End. She used her ground floor rooms for prostitution, mainly in the evening. She made a comfortable living from her clients and from renting out the remainder of the house. Ada was very discrete and informed her neighbours that she was a seamstress by profession and worked from home.

Shortly after midnight Ada rose from her sitting room chair, she put a shawl over her shoulders and went to answer the front door.

"Not another one, at this fucking time," she said.

At the door was a relatively young man with fair hair and a moustache. She was about to say, no, not tonight, but the man spoke first.

"Give me some money, or I am goin' to kill you."

Ada reeled back into the hallway, and the man forced his way in.

"Get out; I am not giving you any fucking money, fuck off!"

"Well, you've asked for it, bitch. Take that," the attacker said as he plunged his clasp knife twice into her throat. Ada Wilson immediately started to scream, and another resident of the property, Rose Bierman, began to come down the stairs to see what the commotion was. She just had time to see the attacker open the door and make his escape into the street. Mrs Bierman came to Ada's rescue and held her.

"Stop that man," she coughed out. "He has just stabbed me in the fuckin' throat," she said, shaking and in fear for her life. Mrs Bierman managed to raise the alarm by running into the street and drawing the attention of two police officers. One of the officers went in search of a doctor, who subsequently treated Ada at the scene. He felt the injuries were life-threatening, so she was taken to the London Hospital in Whitechapel, where she made a full recovery.

It was just after 12.15am on the 28th of March, that the attacker headed down Mile End Road towards Spitalfields, and home. He had no money and didn't want to walk the distance to the Princess Alice pub.

"Fuckin' woman," he muttered to himself, "she should have given me money; she got what she deserved."

He hurried away quickly, as it was icy outside.

"I'm fuckin' freezin', and me plates are killin' me," he complained to himself.

This was not the first time he has acted on impulse. He needed some money and so decided to threaten someone, oblivious as to whether he would be caught by a policeman or men at the house of Ada Wilson. There was no clear thought or planning to the attack.

He began talking to himself. "If I see a fucking' whore, I will rob her." He then passed Whitechapel station and turned off the Whitechapel Road and walked down Old Montague Street. He was talking to himself, quite loudly, when a Jewish looking man, on the opposite side, looked over at him.

"What the fuck are you lookin' at, cunt? Do you want to see me fuckin' knife in your froat?"

The man stopped and turned his head away and hurried on, out of the way of danger.

"This place is fuckin' full of nosey four-by-fuckin-two's," he blurted out angrily. He had spent the evening, like many evenings, stalking and watching people, but he couldn't see the contradiction.

He then tripped up on the pavement and fell onto the ground.

"Twat, fuckin' twat," he said in a loud voice, as he got up and picked up his hat, then started walking with a slight limp, because of the fall.

"Fuckin' sick of this place."

There were several bins on the corner of an alleyway, he went up to them and kicked them over, strewing the contents on the footpath and road. He regularly vandalised property, he also lit fires and pushed people over in the street for no reason, other than that he was angry. Several times he had even urinated on people sleeping rough outside. He had also thought about setting them on fire while they are sleeping. Such things made him happy.

There were still quite a few prostitutes about on Old Montague Street, mainly as he got closer to Spitalfields. One of the women asked him kindly if he wanted any business.

"Fuck off," was the response.

"There's no need to be like that, sir."

"I'll be something fuckin' else, in a fuckin' minute. Fuck off!"

Another prostitute was about to speak to him, but before she could say anything, he had snapped, "Fuck off!"

Further down the road, there was a third prostitute in an alley just off the street; she was on her own. She also asked him regarding business. He went up to her and started hitting her with his fists in the face and abdomen.

"That's me fuckin' answer."

Prostitutes reminded him of his mother, and when he thought about her, the rage welled up inside him. As time went on, this was only to get worse.

Back in the warmth of the Princess Alice pub, Letty noticed he was agitated.

"What's up with you then?"

"Nuffink just 'ad a bit of an argument, that's all. Can I get a drink, Auntie? I have walked all the way from Poplar."

"What you doen' over there, then?"

"Lookin' for a job, I fought there might be jobs that way, as I 'eard some people say."

"Well, did you get one?"

"One what?"

"JOB!" Letty replied loudly.

"No, I didn't, but I keep tryin'."

"Go on, get yourself a drink, only one mind."

"Fanks Auntie."

When his aunt left the bar area, he helped himself to some more ale.

"That's anovver one done, fuckin' woman, fuckin' sick of 'em," he said out loud. "I was fuckin' lucky not to be caught. I'll be somewhere quieter next time. She could afford to give me money; it's all her fault," he said to himself, meaning his mother.

Once again, it amused him that he has caused injury and harm to someone. He enjoyed the fear the woman had shown; even though this was a completely senseless act, and it did not achieve the objective of obtaining money. He had a violent streak in him, and he lacked any sort of empathy for the victim. It did not occur to him that his two attacks were cowardly. He would be offended if someone had called him a coward, as this would lower his, already low, self-esteem. He was not a person that thought about the consequences of his actions; he was a reactive and impulsive person. He lived for the moment and not the future, and he lived only to meet his own needs.

Detective Inspectors Wildy and Dillworth, from A Division, were charged with making enquiries that would hopefully lead to the arrest of the culprit. They visited Ada in hospital later the same day. She was able to speak in a softer voice.

"Can you give us a description of the attacker madam?" Inspector Dillworth asked.

"Yes officer, the man was about 30 years old, with fair hair, a tanned face and a small fair moustache."

"Can you give us a description of what he was wearing madam?" Inspector Wildy asked.

"He was wearing, a dark coat, light trousers and a dark, Quaker style, wide-awake hat," Ada said with her eyes closed trying to remember the details.

"Do you know of anyone that has a grudge against you? Anyone who would do such a thing?" Inspector Dillworth probed.

"Not in the slightest, I have no enemies."

"What do you do for a living, madam?" Wildy asked calmly.

"I'm a seamstress, Inspector."

"You seem to make a very good living from making dresses madam, if you don't mind me saying," Wildy stated abruptly.

"I do mind Inspector. It is none of your fu... business."

"What my colleague here means madam, is that you have a lot of evening visitors, male visitors. We were wondering if it could be one of them?" Dillworth explained as tactfully as he could.

"I have not seen the man who attacked me before. Is that clear enough, Inspector?" Ada said firmly.

"Perfectly clear, madam. We are only doing our job," Dillworth stated calmly.

"Good day, madam, we will do all we can to apprehend the culprit," Inspector Wildy stated.

When the two detectives had walked far enough up the long hospital corridor to be sure they wouldn't be overheard, Dillworth said to his colleague, "she was a bit touchy, don't you think?"

"Well, she must think we are stupid if we don't know what she is up to. They all get a bit like that when we find out. Still, at least she is okay. Quite attractive too," Wildy said.

"Not bad, not bad, I've seen better, but worth a go," Dillworth replied, laughing with his colleague.

"I don't think there is much hope of catching him, as he might not be from this area. We will give the press the details to publish and wait to see if anything turns up."

"It's all we can do, fancy a pint?"

While the detectives were searching a pub, in vain, for the man; the attacker was back in Spitalfields, where no-one was looking for him.

April 3rd
The killing of Emma Smith
and a surprise attack

Emma Smith was a 45-year-old prostitute and like many prostitutes, spent most of her money on alcohol. She stood five-foot-two-inches tall, with a fair complexion and light brown hair. She was quite shabbily dressed and was known to drink to excess, according to the deputy lodging house manager. She had lived at the lodging house for about 18 months and paid the usual 4d per night for a bed.

At about 1.30am, Emma was returning to her lodgings at 15 George Street, Spitalfields. Her hands and face were so cold, that her breath was visible as she breathed out. Emma turned her head as a horse and carriage clattered by, while she walked down Whitechapel High Street, close to Whitechapel Church. She then noticed a gang of three men that were coming towards her. There were many gangs in Whitechapel that would rob prostitutes, so Emma was keen to avoid them, and get back to her warmer lodgings.

Consequently, she picked up her pace and walked faster. She crossed over the main road and started walking up Osborn Street, walking northwards to Brick Lane. Emma was now aware that the men were following her, and her heart was beating faster. She rushed over Wentworth Street and was attempting to walk up Brick Lane when the gang caught up with her and stopped her. She was outside the Cocoa factory at number 10 Brick Lane.

"Oi! Where do you think you're goin?" the older gang member said.

"Please leave me alone; I'm going home," Emma replied in a distressed tone.

"Ave, you got any money, deary?" the tall man said, as he cut her ear with some sort of blade.

"Leave me be, I 'aven't got any money," she said, almost crying.

The two older men got hold of her, one on each side and marched her into an alleyway. They proceeded to rob Emma and beat her up quite severely, tearing her ear.

"Give us your money, slag," the teenage gang member said as he punched her in the stomach. Emma started to cry in pain and the gang started laughing.

"You're a scruffy lookin' bitch aren't ya?" one thug said.

The tall man, who had previously ripped her ear, grabbed hold of the bleeding ear lobe and said' "'ere give us a kiss luv," to which the gang laughed.

Rather than scream out to alert attention, Emma just pleaded with them to leave her alone.

"Please let me go, you have my bit of money," Emma cried with pain and feared for her own life.

Unfortunately, the worst of her ordeal was yet to come. It was not known as to whether she was gang-raped, but one of the gang members, forced his walking stick into her vagina, causing excruciating pain from which Emma passed out.

As she came to, she attempted to walk to her lodgings. She used some of her clothing to try to stem the flow of blood. She could only move very slowly and was crying with the pain at every step. No-one came to her aid, not even a policeman on his beat. She sat down several times, hoping the pain would ease. She took about two hours to hobble the excruciating 300 yards to 15 George Street. As she got to her lodgings, at about 4.00am, Emma just wanted to lie down, but Mary Russell, the deputy manager, and Annie Lee, a lodger, decided that she needed some medical treatment.

"You're bleedin' badly, love; you need a doctor. We need to get you to the hospital," Mary said.

The London Hospital was half a mile away, making this an excruciating walk for poor Emma. The three women arrived at the hospital at about 5.00am, where she was attended to by Doctor George Hellier. He found that her peritoneum had been ruptured. The injury would soon prove to be a fatal one. She couldn't say much about the attack except that it was a gang of three men, one of whom was about 19 years of age and the attack happened near the Cocoa Factory on Brick Lane.

Doctor Hellier made Emma as comfortable as possible. She soon lost consciousness and so could not provide any further details than may have led to the apprehension of such callous thugs. It was, unfortunately, an all too common sight for the doctor. There was much violence in the society around Whitechapel and Spitalfields. It would be a while yet before it was to get any better. In the short term, it was to get much worse – much, much, worse. At this stage, no-one had informed the police of the attack on Emma.

During the attack on Emma Smith, another man was stalking the streets of Spitalfields. He was a lone predator looking for potential victims. He was not part of any gang, and he preferred his own company. He did not come across Emma Smith; otherwise, he may have stabbed her, like the one he stabbed last week, or the one in February. He liked to stalk women generally, and prostitutes in particular.

Running between Whitechapel High Street and Wentworth Street was an alleyway called George Yard. It was a dark and enclosed place at night-time, and as such, it was avoided by many people. About half-way down George Yard, he approached a prostitute. She was middle-aged and relatively attractive and quite slim. Her clothes had seen much better days.

"Awright love, you lookin' for business?"

"Yes," he answered, "lift up your skirts."

"You don't waste any time, do ya?" she said, as she lifted her dress, revealing her pubic hair. He moved towards her and started placing his fingers up inside her vagina.

"Careful, will ya!"

"Shut it," he replied. He took his fingers out of her vagina and put them in her mouth. "Here taste your own cunt, bitch."

"Leave me alone, someone is coming," she said to him and made her escape.

He looked around, and she ran down to Whitechapel High Street, where there were people. He grinned and muttered to himself, "there are plenty more slags like her about."

He strolled down to the High Street and then turned left into Angel Alley, which was parallel to George Yard. This alley was also a very narrow alleyway that was frequented by prostitutes. A man was urinating against a wall. The alley reeked of the foul stench of slaughter yards, urine and the privies. There was a prostitute further up the alley with a man having sex. He started watching them. She had her back against the wall and looked quite bored. They must be careful because most alleys were part of the beat of a policeman. As such, it was a short affair. The man walked off towards Wentworth Street, and she walked down the alley towards the High Street.

During his stalking and covert observation of her, he had noticed that the woman was younger than most of the other prostitutes, she was in her mid-twenties with what looked like dark hair. He thought he had seen her before in one of the pubs on Commercial Street. If she was the person he was thinking of, then she was known to be quite violent when drunk. He didn't know her name. He stepped out in front of her and remained silent.

"Are ye lookin' for business at all?" she said in an Irish accent. He could smell the alcohol on her breath as she slightly staggered towards him. He could see that she was reasonably well dressed and quite pretty, compared to most of the prostitutes in Spitalfields.

He pulled his hat down to obscure his face and pulled out his clasp knife. He wanted women to be afraid and shocked. He enjoyed the look of fear on their faces. He liked the power and control over them, as it made him feel manly. Unfortunately for him, he was to be disappointed. As he got closer, she pulled a hammer from her bag and struck him on the face and forehead. He hit the ground immediately, with blood gushing from his wounds and his knife was flung somewhere in the alley.

"Take that ye bastard!" she shouted at him and walked off, calmly down Angel Alley. Prostitutes were regularly attacked and some, therefore, took protection matters into their own hands.

Fortunately, a policeman arrived shortly and called for assistance by blowing his whistle. Other police officers were quickly on the scene; this could be the reason why no policemen saw Emma Smith struggling towards George Street. Still unconscious, he was taken to the London Hospital, via the ambulance cart from the workhouse infirmary. He arrived at the hospital by 2.30am and was seen immediately by a doctor. Doctor Hellier ascertained that he had suffered a depressed fracture to the skull on his forehead, a fracture to his eye socket below his right eye and a broken nose. The doctor said he was lucky not to lose the sight in his right eye. However, the doctor was not confident of a recovery, as he felt there was likely to be some brain damage. He informed the police that he would send for them if there were any change in the patients' condition. It would be several days before the patient regained consciousness and a few weeks before he was in a condition to leave the hospital.

April 7th
Inspector Reid's enquiries

Sadly, Emma Smith died in the hospital on the 4th of April, without regaining consciousness. The inquest into her death was opened by the coroner, Mr Wynne Baxter, on Saturday the 7th of April, at the London Hospital. It was only through the inquest date being set that the police became aware of her death. Doctor George Hellier described the victim's injuries to the inquest and explained that he had conducted a post-mortem.

"Death was caused by peritonitis as a result of a blunt object penetrating the peritoneum with great force. Otherwise, her other organs were normal."

Inspector Reid managed to interview the last people to see the victim alive. Margaret Hames, of 15 George Street, had also seen her.

"I saw Emma talking to a man near Farrant Street, off Burdett Road. The man was dressed in black with a white scarf; the time was about a quarter past twelve, Inspector," said Mrs Hames.

"Did she seem distressed in any way?" asked Reid.

"No Inspector, she was fine. I know her well."

"Did you know of anyone who might have wanted to harm her?"

"No Inspector, she was just not that sort, she never caused anyone trouble."

"Do you know of any gangs in the area, specifically targeting prostitutes?"

"No Inspector, I'm sorry I don't, none that would kill like this, that's for sure."

Inspector Reid was now taking on three cases, and once again, no-one ever saw or heard anything. The murder of Emma Smith, the attempted murder and robbery of a man in Angel Alley, and the stabbing in White's Row in February. He was recently informed that Annie Millwood died on the 31st of March, but not as a result of the stab injuries. The victim from Angel Alley had not yet been named or regained consciousness. On the face of the scant evidence, Inspector Reid felt that the two robberies, four days ago, may have been done by the same person.

Some of the gangs were from other areas. They went to a new area of the City and carried out a few robberies then moved to another area, where they wouldn't be recognised. This action made detection difficult. Fortunately, most gang assaults did not result in death, as robbery was usually the motive.

Inspector Reid spoke to Chief Inspector John West after the inquest.

"I have spoken to Mary Russell and Annie Lee from Emma's lodging house, and they confirmed her identity and that it was a gang that attacked her. We have no description of the attackers What I don't understand, sir, is that if this woman is taking two and a half hours to walk 300 yards to her lodgings, why have none of the beat policemen seen her?"

"They have all been questioned, and all say they didn't see her, The woman is dead now, so we can't question her. We have nothing to go on, Edmund. We only have her word that it was a gang. She may know who had assaulted her but was too scared to give a name."

"Then we have another assault in Angel Alley, sir, another apparent robbery, but a different method of assault. This one was some sort of blunt instrument used on the face and the head. I'll ask around and be on the lookout for gangs in the area. That's all we can do."

"There was also a stabbing in February of a woman, on White's Row. Do you think there is any link, Edmund?"

"I can't see it, sir. That was a one-person attack. We still don't know who he was, but there was a description in the press of a man who stabbed a woman in the throat in Mile End in March. Robbery was the motive, just like the Emma Smith attack. The two recent attacks may be gang-related robberies, but we can't be sure. The attacks on women, particularly prostitutes, like Emma Smith, seems to be increasing. They are an easy target, some just get beaten up, after the sexual act is completed. Some other men then run off without paying. It is a miserable and a hard life for them."

"We may need to put some of the beat coppers into plain clothes so that we can keep an eye on them," West stated.

"The two stabbings could have been done by a younger person, according to the descriptions, but they don't make any sense. If robbery was his motive, why stab someone before you have taken their money?" Reid asked, hoping some sense could be made of these attacks.

Inspector Reid then decided to walk to Spitalfields, hoping to find out further information on the attacks. He spoke to the publicans of several pubs in the area. Reid was trying to trace the routes of the two attack victims. He stood on the corner of Church Street after visiting the Ten Bells pub, to talk to the landlord there. While he was there, a beggar approached two very well-dressed middle-aged ladies coming out of Christ Church.

"Excuse me, madam," the old man said with his hat in his hand, "could you please 'elp me to get some food? A few coppers will 'elp madam if you please."

"Go away, you filthy creature, and don't touch me," the large and overly dressed woman said. "You are disgusting, do you ever wash?" she added.

"I can't afford a wash or a bed to sleep in; I am 'omeless."

"That den of iniquity, the public house is your home no doubt; leave us alone, or we will call the police."

"Sorry madam, if I offended you," the man said gently.

"Come, Cicely, we have to make arrangements with the vicar, for feeding the poor this evening. I am sure our vicar will have a good sermon for them also."

"Yes, Andromeda, only the deserving one's mind; not the drunkards or those disgusting, *ladies of the night*," the thin Cicely said to her friend.

"Quite right, Cicely, but we need a good lunch first. We need the strength to help God's poor brethren."

"We do what we can Andromeda; the Lord knows all."

"Yes, the Lord gives us our daily needs. Come, Cicely, I have a nice bottle of sherry at home, waiting to be opened," the large and soon to be drunk, Andromeda said.

Reid was not surprised by the attitudes of the two women; the more he got to know Whitechapel and Spitalfields, the less surprised or shocked he became. There was, however, a look of dismay on his face, and he commenced his journey towards the station; passing the miserable homeless masses as he went by.

April 10th
The patient and the policeman

The London Hospital had been on its present site since 1753. It started in 1740 as a medical charity to care for poor people who could not afford medical care. It developed over time to cater for an increasing population and was funded by benefactors, including Jewish businessmen, as it provided care for the large Jewish community in the East End of London. It catered for wealthy patients too. Joseph Merrick had also lived at the hospital since 1886, under the care of Doctor Frederick Treves. The structure was, therefore, of a Georgian style, built from London brick with brick pediments and Georgian style windows. It was an imposing structure and directly opposite Whitechapel Station.

On one of the wards, a patient had awoken after being unconscious for a week. He was lying in a bed with his head and face bandaged up. Doctor Hellier sent a message to Inspector Reid to inform him of the patient's progress. Inspector Reid was keen to question him.

"Inspector, you can't talk to him for too long, he will have difficulty speaking, due to his facial injuries. I must also warn you that because of the head injury, he may not remember anything or be completely confused. He has not said anything so far except to question where he is and how he got here."

"Very well, Doctor, I just have a couple of questions for him," Reid replied. He went to the patient's bedside and calmly introduced himself.

"You were injured a week ago, in a place called Angel Alley. Do you remember that?"

The patient moved his head slowly from side to side.

"Did you see who attacked you? Was it a gang or a single person?" Reid asked in a concerned manner.

"It could have been a gang," the patient said very softly. "I'm quite handy meself; I can put up quite a fight. Me 'ead hurts, and I can't remember everyfink that 'appened," the patient whispered.

"Have you any relatives that we can contact?"

"She's 'ere now."

Reid turned around, and a large woman towered over him. "Who are you? What do you want?" she asked aggressively.

"I am a policeman madam, Detective Inspector Reid," he said proudly, looking up at her, "and you are?"

"I'm Letty, his Aunt. I want you to find who done this," she said formally and confidently, looking down at Reid.

"That is why I am here, madam. A woman was murdered by a gang around about the time of the attack on your nephew. I wondered if the two attacks were linked in any way. We are treating this as attempted murder and robbery. We are dealing with some vicious people in these two cases."

"Oh, I see," Letty said in a more conciliatory tone. "I am sure you are doen all you can to catch whoever did this. Whereabouts in Kent, are you from? I recognise your accent, Inspector."

"Canterbury, madam. I also note the similarity between our voices. If he recovers and gets some of his memory back, or has any other information, I want you to contact me immediately. We need help if we are to catch whoever did this to your nephew."

He then excused himself and left the ward. These recent two attacks left Inspector Reid puzzled. He would spend some time thinking about who could have carried out such attacks. The problem was that to deduce who the perpetrators of these two crimes were, without any evidence. One victim was dead and the other without any memory.

On the ward, Letty was talking. "I didn't know where you were? I know that you wander off places for a while. It was when you woke up this morning that the doctor got in contact. I've brought you some food and something to drink." She thought for a moment, then added, "what really happened? Was it a gang?"

"I don't know, it was dark, maybe a gang. When you are 'it in the 'ead, you don't tend to see much. 'sides I 'ave bad 'eadaches and can't remember everyfink. I do know one fing; if I gets better and I find whodunnit, I'll fuckin' kill 'em; I will," he said in an angry tone, then winced in pain.

"Well, you can stay with me for a while, till you get right, then you'll 'ave to find work and pay your way. 'ow long are you in 'ere for then?" she enquired.

"Two or free weeks, the doctor said, depends on the damage it done to me brain and fings."

"There was a woman murdered, the same night you were attacked. Do you know what they did to that poor gal?"

"Well it wasn't me, and I've me own problems to bovver about, wivout finkin' of someone else."

"I never said it was you. Stop feelen' sorry for yourself. If I ever caught the bastards that did it, I'd break their fucken' necks for 'em I would," she snarled.

"Well no-one's gonna mess wiv you, Auntie. Not unless they 'ave a fuckin' army behind 'em. I needs to get right and get out of 'ere."

"You've been asleep a week; it takes time, that's all."

"Well don't overdo the sympafy, will ya?"

"I'll be back tomorrow, sometime. You just rest, do ya 'ear?"

Inspector Reid was waiting to speak to the aunt alone at the main entrance of the hospital. The unmistakable frame of the landlady appeared in the corridor, and the diminutive Inspector approached her.

"Excuse me, madam, could you please spare me a few moments to aid me in my enquiries?"

"Alright, Inspector, but I have to get back to the pub soon."

"What do you think your nephew was doing late at night in Angel Alley, is he normally a nocturnal sort of person?"

"Well I haven't always been with 'im, but he is out late quite a bit, but what 'e gets up to, God only knows."

"He is staying at your public house, the Princess Alice, is he not?"

"Yes, that's right."

"How long has he been staying with you, madam?"

"Since about January, why?"

"Well, I wondered if he had any enemies, due to the nature of the injuries? Where was he before then?"

"In the nick, Inspector, for theft and violence if you must know."

"He doesn't say much, does he?"

"Well, when someone hits you in the head, and you are out of it for a week, maybe you wouldn't be sayen' much either!"

"Forgive me if I have offended you in any way, madam. Does he work at all?"

"He does some work in the pub, that's all as far as I know."

"He's not married then, or has a girl?"

"I don't think he has ever 'ad a girl," she said politely.

"He's not, er, well, you know?"

"Know what?"

"Well, er, inverted."

"Inverted!" she shouted. "How the fucken' 'ell do I know! Why don't you ask 'im next time you see 'im? What fucken' business is it of yours, anyway?" she said, angrily.

"Madam, you don't need to keep swearing, I am a policeman."

"You don't need to ask such personal questions as to whether 'e's, a Mary-Ann," she shouted. "Do you like it by the back door, Inspector?"

"Madam, any more of that and I will arrest you," Reid said with a red face.

She lifted her hands way above the Inspector's head. "Go on then, cuff me," Letty shouted in her Kentish accent.

Reid turned away and left in a hurry, without speaking to her.

May 7th
The London Hospital resident

The patient that was attacked in Angel Alley early last month left the hospital after two weeks. He went back to see Doctor Hellier for a check-up on his progress. Although he had been released, he had rarely ventured outside. This was partly because of the facial injuries and because standing up brought on severe head pain. He had been lying down most of the time to ease the pain, but, by walking to the London Hospital, he now had a headache. It felt like a tight band was fixed around his head, and his face was throbbing.

"Doctor, me 'ead hurts when I stand. It is a sharp pain behind me eyes. Bright light also makes me 'ead hurt," the patient said, in a slow monotone voice.

"Well, I can see the swelling is going down, and as it does, the pain will subside. I can give you some medication for the pain, but the best medicine is complete rest," the doctor said.

"Fortunately, you can see out of your right eye now; there is no damage there. Your memory should return in time," the doctor added. "By the way have you had any seizures or dizzy spells? Anything like that?"

"No Doctor, but I can't always fink what to say, me mind is a blank at times. I can't fink of the right words to say. So, I keeps meself to meself," the patient said slowly.

"It takes time; you will feel better when your body heals. If you get worse in any way, you must contact me at once," the doctor said in a supportive manner. The patient nodded without saying a word.

"You have been lucky to survive this injury. I am pleased with the relatively quick process of recovery with you. Standing up will bring the headaches on. Lying down will ease any pressure in your head."

The patient nodded again and left the doctor's room with some medication. He then glumly wandered around the hospital, moving slowly. Today was the first time he had been out in a month, and he didn't have much energy. He saw the hospital garden and decided to sit in it for a while before heading back. He was sat on a bench with his head in his hands, just resting, when someone spoke to him in a strange voice.

"Hello, are you alright?" the man said.

He didn't look up, he just said. "I don't feel well, I've been injured. I get bad 'eadaches."

"I do too, I've had a lot of pain, not just physical pain, but I try not to think about that."

The patient raised his head from his hands and looked at the man who was speaking to him. He reeled back, shocked.

"Do not be afraid, I mean you no harm," the man said.

"What's wrong with your face?" the patient said calmly.

"What's wrong with yours?" the man said with a smile. He then added, "I have an illness, don't worry, you can't catch it. Parts of my body have swollen up. Mr Treves looks after me. My name is Joseph Merrick."

"Does it hurt? Your boat, does it hurt?"

"I don't have a boat; I have never had a boat."

"No, boat means face. Boat race, rhymes wiv face, boat for short."

"Oh, I see. That's a strange way of speaking. No, my face doesn't hurt as such," Joseph replied.

"What about your face? Your boat, does that hurt?" Joseph asked with a smile.

"Yes, someone attacked me wiv an 'ammer, one night."

"Oh, dear, I am so sorry. You must be in great pain."

"My life's been one of great pain."

"Mine too, but I don't think of the bad times, just the good things in life."

"There are no good times. Life is shit. I fuckin' 'ate it."

"Oh, I don't like that sort of language," Joseph said.

"Well, it's how I feel. I've 'ad a bad life."

"Bad things do happen. But good things happen too. Look at me. I live here in the hospital, and I have my own room. I also have the company of Mr Treves and the staff. I think I am fortunate. I visit this lovely garden every day. I love to hear the birds sing and look at the beautiful flowers; these are good things," Joseph said encouragingly.

"I've never fought about them fings. I've never noticed the flowers or birds. There are no flowers where I live."

He saw the world differently than Joseph. It was as if the patient and Joseph were looking at different things.

"You have to change things, change the way you feel. Make life better for yourself. You need to take control of your life and do the best you can. Feeling sorry for yourself won't change things. I should know, I used to feel sorry for myself all the time until Mr Treves, found me," Joseph said, positively.

"I'm goin' to make fings, better for me, but not in the way you mean. I am gonna get who did this to me."

"That won't make you feel better."

"I can't 'elp bein' angry. It's 'ow, I feel. I don't know any uvver way."

"There is no point blaming anyone else, or God even, for your situation. You have to try to do good things while you can and enjoy life," Joseph stated clearly.

"There's no fuckin' God. Why would God make you like you are? Why would he give me an alcoholic whore for a movver? Why would he make Spitalfields, where everyone is poor and 'ungry?" the patient growled, "I do what I do to survive. That is all."

"I can feel your pain and anger. But don't let it rule your life."

"I have to go now. Back to Spitalfields," the patient said as he rose from the bench.

"It has been nice talking to you, friend," Joseph said.

The patient left the hospital and walked back slowly towards Spitalfields. He was thinking about what Joseph Merrick had said. "It's alright for 'im. If 'e lived where I live, 'e wouldn't be so fuckin' 'appy. Spitalfields. Shitalfields, more like."

As he arrived home, he led on his bed due to the severe headache pounding in his head. Eventually, he fell asleep, but he got no rest. His dreams were vivid and traumatic due to the pain. The images recur from night to night: His mother was there abusing him, beating him, laughing at him while drunk. He could hear her high-pitched voice screaming at him inside his head. His head exploded, at which point he woke up sweating with his heart pumping rapidly. It took a minute for him to start to breathe normally again.

"Why can't you just fuck off and leave me alone," he said out loud to his mother, "it's all your fault, everyfink. If I could fuckin' kill you, I would."

'You are a useless piece of shite' she told him in his head. *'Why don't you do everyone a favour and kill yourself,'* he heard.

"Fuck off, fuck off, fuck off!" he shouted and rushed out of the room and down the stairs to the pub to get a drink. His mother faded away from his mind as he drank. He knew that she would be back again.

July 15th
The stalking begins again

Inspectors Reid and Abberline were in Reid's office at Leman Street Police Station. It wasn't the tidiest of small offices, but it made sense to Reid. He knew where things were, even if no-one else did. It was almost a contradiction in that Edmund had a very logical mind and was always tidily dressed, but he could never manage to keep his office tidy. It was a gloomy office, but Reid didn't mind because he didn't spend a lot of time in it. It was a place where he could just sit and think about the case now and then, while having a mug of tea.

"We have been getting more reports of violence towards prostitutes, Fred. Some involve theft, others refusing to pay afterwards but nothing as bad as the Emma Smith case. Pimps and gangs of thugs control some of them and give them a good hiding if they haven't earned enough. They pick up vulnerable young women, feed and clothe them, possibly give them a place to stay, then force them to earn money as prostitutes in order to make money from them. These men are scum Fred, and I want them off the streets. These women don't deserve violence. Their life is hard enough as it is. There are also gangs of young men operating in the area who go about mugging lone people, both men and women. We have some plain-clothed police dressed up like wealthy men, and we will get them soon enough."

"Did you get any further with the Emma Smith case, Edmund? Or the stabbing?"

"Neither. At least we haven't had any more stabbings, but the Emma Smith murder was bad. We have been on the lookout for gangs, but I think I have said before that they would have moved on to another area. I don't think they meant to kill her, but they are sick savage bastards."

"I did get a report from A Division, about a stabbing in Mile End, Bow, in March. A woman was stabbed in the throat, during an attempted robbery. A younger man, maybe around 30 years old, fair hair and moustache, with a large hat on and a dark coat. Do you think there are any links with the stabbing in White's Row?"

"It's possible, Fred. The younger man element fits with the type of crime. Neither crime is what a more mature criminal would do. I think some of the attacks on prostitutes could also be by younger men. I will have a word with A Division and keep it on file. We had two bad attacks in April, but fortunately nothing as bad since."

"Keep asking around in the pubs and build up some good contacts, get to know what the locals are talking about. Pub landlords are a good contact for knowing what is going on. Keep checking the lodging houses also, for any reports of violent men about. Make it known that we will make it worth their while if they come forward with information on who may be responsible. It is local knowledge policing that always gets them in the end. Someone will always give a criminal up, eventually."

"Yes, Fred, I know what you mean. A man of violence on the streets is also likely to beat his wife. When she has had enough, she grasses him up to us for the crimes he has done, and then she is rid of him."

It was mid-July before the attacker had sufficiently physically recovered from his injuries for him to commence his nightly stalking activities. He had seizures that caused him distress and pain, as well as the psychological damage that he carried with him all the time.

He did not venture too far at first. The areas close to the Princess Alice pub were his primary hunting and stalking ground. These included Wentworth Street, George Yard, Angel Alley, George Street, Thrawl Street, Old Castle Street/Castle Alley, Frostic Place, Finch Street, Osborn Place, Osborn Street and Brick Lane.

He hated Spitalfields. He hated the people, the buildings, the smell, the horses, the horseshit, the vomit, the prostitutes, the gangs, the pickpockets and the police. He hated them all. However, Spitalfields provided a stage for him to fulfil his fantasies of stalking, attacking and killing. He had recently fantasised about stabbing a prostitute to death, but he didn't want to be caught by someone hearing her screams. He waited for the right moment and the right place.

By stalking, he got to know the prostitutes' habits, their favourite locations to do business and the proximity of police that were on their beat. He needed a secluded spot where he wouldn't be disturbed. He knew he would find it soon. Many prostitutes did not venture too far from a pub; a few of them, though, went to secluded residential areas.

Early in the evening, he spied a prostitute that he had previously seen in the Frying Pan public house. She was a middle-aged woman called Polly Nichols, and she was in Frostic Place with a client. Frostic Place was between Finch Street and Old Montague Street. When the brief liaison ended, she started walking towards Finch Street in the general direction of the Frying Pan pub. He stood in her way. Straight away, she said, "four pennies for you, sir."

He grabbed her and pushed her against the wall. "Okay, let me see what you have got."

She lifted her skirts, and he grabbed her vulva, hard. She brought her right knee up swiftly and made hard contact with his testicles and spat in his face, then ran off.

"Fuckin' slag. I'll have you; you bitch!"

He continued stalking and watching, but, he didn't want to get caught. He moved down Frostic Place, along Old Montague Street and into Wentworth Street, where a gang of three youths, maybe 18-20 years old, stood in his way. One of them threw his head back and said to the attacker, "and who are you?"

"Fuck off!" was the response.

"You what?" was the reply.

He pulled out his knife and repeated in a low, menacing tone, "fuck off."

"Okay," one of the gang members said, and they moved off. You had to stand up for yourself in Spitalfields, or you would be robbed and beaten. Most gangs didn't want to get into a fight, so they picked on people that would give in without any trouble.

Over the next few weeks, he continued stalking and abusing prostitutes. He was not well, though. He still suffered from nasty headaches and had difficulty controlling his anger at times. He was furious at being attacked, but he had very little recollection of that evening.

Back in the relative comfort of the Princess Alice pub, the nephew went to work behind the bar and began pulling a pint for a customer.

"Where 'ave you been? I thought you would be back an hour ago," complained the landlady.

"I got held up, didn't I, but I'm 'ere now," he replied, hoping she wouldn't ask any more questions.

"I need some crates of beer from the cellar bringen' up when you 'ave a minute."

"Right I will do that next, Auntie."

A customer came to the bar; he was a costermonger selling fruit and vegetables. "'ere what's 'append to your boat?" he asked the barman.

"An accident, what do you want?" came the sharp reply. He didn't like people commenting on his scars.

"I didn't mean anyfink by it son, just curious like, know what I mean? porter please, two."

"Anyfink else?"

"I'll 'ave a mur, I mean, rum, for me chest."

"You're one of these costermongers, that talk backwards wiv other street sellers, what's all that about?"

"Keeps other people guessing, it does, especially when you add in cockney slang, as well."

A fight broke out in the pub between some dock workers; then suddenly, a loud noise echoed around the pub.

"What the fuck's goen' on 'ere?" the landlady bellowed, storming through the pub to the action, and everyone backed up, out of her way. She punched one man straight in the face, knocking him and another docker to the floor. She picked up another worker and threw him through the front doorway of the pub. The two remaining, standing dockers stopped fighting.

"He started it, 'im that you just frew out," one of them said.

"And I am fucken' finishing it. You can drink proper, or you can fuck off!" The two dockers on the floor got up and apologised, and they all decided that they had better leave.

"That's the second one in 'ere tonight!" the landlady said to a friend of hers. "Get some singen' going, get that piano playen' and just try to enjoy yourselves for fuck's sake."

Abberline and Reid entered the pub and saw people putting the furniture back in place.

"Having trouble in here?" Abberline asked the landlady.

"Nothing I can't handle, Inspector," Letty said while breathing heavier.

"We will have two porters if you don't mind, please."

"How's your nephew doing madam?" Reid said, looking up to the landlady.

"Down the cellar maken' himself useful. Have you found whodunnit yet?"

"No, unfortunately not, but if he remembers anything, he can let me know. There have not been any further such attacks madam; it may be a one-off attack," Reid said.

"Let's sit down over here, Edmund," said Abberline as he walked to an empty table. "There are a few rough types in here, they work, they drink, and they fight; that is what many of them like to do. There are always quite a few bangtails in here, and they are all over Commercial Street as well. Still, we just keep order, Edmund."

"No-one knows anything about the murder of Emma Smith. How is that possible, Fred? What bothers me, as I have said before, is that none of the beat policemen saw her."

"Maybe she didn't tell the true story. No-one will ever know now. If she is taking two hours to walk to George Street, then she must have been spotted by our men."

"I have nothing on the attack on the bloke that is now behind the bar. It was on the same night as the Emma Smith attack."

Abberline took a good look at the young barman with the injured face. "He looks like he's a wrong un, been in the nick, I suppose."

"He got out in January, robbery. He is trying to mend his ways."

"They don't change; he's a wrong un. Keep an eye on him and who he is with. If there are robberies around here, come in here and ask him to account for himself. Let him know we are onto him."

"Smith was a robbery, but he is ruled out of that. There are many men of violence here, Fred."

"Hang the fucking lot of them; they don't change."

Reid looked around the pub quickly to see if anyone overheard Fred's comments. He breathed a sigh of relief when he realised no-one was taking any notice.

"Fred, we can't hang people for theft and robbery. Even many murderers get off with manslaughter," Reid responded in a firm voice.

"I know, I am tired, I am not sleeping well lately. I am going to take some leave in September."

"Quite right, too, you work too hard. I am off ballooning in late August, taking Emily and the kids, before they are back at school. Just keep a focus on your job; we can't cure the world."

Later in the evening, the attacker had a seizure and was lying on the cellar floor. He heard his mother's voice in his head, *'you're a useless bastard, why were you born, you little piece of shite? – Sucking off, that's all you are fit for – lick my cunt, you useless bastard.'* He sat up, but there was no-one there. He placed his hands over his ears.

"Fuck off, leave me alone!" he shouted. He banged his forehead against the wall, the voices lessened, but the pain increased. He opened several bottles of beer and gulped them down. He sat alone in the cellar, shaking and sweating. His psychological pain was with him when he was awake and asleep; there was no escape; life was just a living torture for him.

After a few more drinks, he ventured outside; he will take his anger out on someone. If he is in pain, why not inflict pain on someone else? He always felt the same about the attacks, that they are not his fault, but his mother's fault, she made him like this.

He walked the streets in the early hours of the next morning. There were people about walking because they had nowhere to sleep. The police always moved people on if they saw anyone asleep. Prostitutes were working to earn their doss money or money for a drink when the pubs open again at 5.00am. People had to sleep away from the streets; in stable yards, under bridges, near railway embankments or anywhere that is remote enough from the main patrolled streets. Such people also slept together in small groups against a wall; it was much safer and warmer huddled together in a factory doorway than sleeping alone somewhere. Prostitutes could usually earn enough money for a bed, so they rarely had to sleep outside. It was mainly men that slept rough. These men were unfit for work, even if there was some. They had no energy and were very undernourished. It was a slow death for such men.

A prostitute curtly propositioned the attacker, and he followed her to a side street. She lifted her dress, and he felt in his right pocket for his clasp knife, but it was not there. He had left it somewhere in the pub. He started to walk away, but she called him back and insulted him. "What's the matter, 'ave you, not got a dick?"

He moved towards her and started beating her, with his fists. She cried in pain, "I'm sorry, mister, please leave me alone; I am sorry." She fell to the floor, crying in pain. If only she could realise that she had been extremely fortunate tonight, not to be repeatedly stabbed and probably killed. He only hit her a few times and found he didn't have the strength to hit her hard. He knows he is still weak, and the quick movements had set off his headache again.

The attacker felt some relief through his actions and returned home. "She was a lucky bitch tonight. If I see that slag again, she will get more than a beatin'," he said to himself.

As he drank, he calmed down. He was tired and now had a banging headache. He held his head in his hands.

"Just as well I didn't take me knife, I 'avent got the fuckin' strenff," he muttered to himself.

"You've been out a while, what's the matter with you?" his aunt asked.

"Tryin' to clear me 'ead wiv a walk and that. I don't feel well."

"Come on up these apples, as you cockney's call 'em," she helped him up the stairs and into his room. "You're pushing yourself too much; you've been told to rest, so rest," she added.

August 6th
The predator stalks his prey

On the evening of Monday the 6th of August, Martha Tabram and Mary Ann Connolly had been spending their time drinking ale and rum in various pubs, with two soldiers. Martha was an unattractive 39-year-old prostitute and was wearing a green skirt with the frayed hem of a brown petticoat showing beneath and a long black jacket. She also had a black bonnet on her head, and black side spring boots. Martha had been separated from her husband for 13 years, due to her heavy drinking. She had lived with Henry Turner for the last nine years, but he had recently left her due to her excessive drinking habits. For the last few weeks, according only to Connolly, Martha had been going by the name of Emma, for some reason. Most of her immoral earnings went on drink. Mary Ann Connolly, who was also known as Pearly Poll, was aged 50 and a prostitute with a drinking problem. She was like Martha – a large woman, but with a much deeper voice and masculine features.

The last few hours of Martha Tabram's life are mostly unknown except for Mary Ann Connolly's version of events. According to Connolly, she and Martha had met the two soldiers earlier in the evening and were in the Two Brewers pub at about 10.00pm. The Two Brewers was re-built in 1860 and stood on the corner of Brick Lane and Buxton Street. It was a three-storey brick building with stonework around the windows frames that were of a Victorian sash type.

If someone was buying Martha a drink, she was happy. "Ta deary, you are such a gentleman," Martha said to the soldier, with a smile on her face, as he passed her a pint of brown ale.

"Get that down ya," he said, "it'll put hairs on your chest."

"It would need a lot of hairs on me chest to cover these two," she said with a laugh, pushing her two, half-covered breasts out in front of her. Her round, fat, red face had a friendly smile, that was spoilt a little by two missing front teeth.

Mary Anne was less attractive than Martha but was as loud and as brash. The other soldier asked her, "Do you come in 'ere often?"

Mary Anne replied, laughing, "I come all over the place dear if ye get me meaning."

The group had one drink in the Two Brewers and then exited onto Brick Lane. The street was dominated by the massive Truman Brewery, which is opposite the pub and has been there since 1701. They then called in at the Frying Pan pub further down Brick Lane, on the corner with Osborn Street. They had one round of drinks there and then moved on to the White Swan at around 11.00pm. Unbeknown to the four friends, they had been observed and followed since entering the Frying Pan pub.

At 11.45pm the quartet leave the White Swan public house and Mary and her soldier head towards Angel Alley. Martha and her companion walk towards George Yard Buildings, where she leads him up one of the part-open concrete and brick staircases. George Yard Buildings are a group of tenement flats, each with access onto an outside concrete deck that leads to several common stone and concrete internal staircases. The buildings are four storeys high and contain 48 flats. The buildings are accessed from George Yard, via a sizeable Gothic brick arch, close to the junction with Wentworth Street.

The soldier and Martha had oral sex on a landing, which, apart from them, was quiet and the time was almost midnight. The soldier left quite quickly, saying he had to get back to the barracks.

"You go, I'll be there in a minute, luv," Martha replied breathlessly. She thought she heard someone coming up the stairs, but there was no-one there. Martha then heard some people talking on the ground floor.

She left George Yard Buildings and walked the streets for a while and got friendly with two other soldiers on Wentworth Street. These were the last hours of Martha Tabram's desperate life. Once more, she was being observed.

While Martha Tabram was with the two soldiers and Pearly Poll, the attacker of Millwood and Wilson was frequenting various pubs himself. He was not typically out on a Monday evening as he has had quite a bit of casual labouring work, or working in his aunt's pub. However, he had no job today or tomorrow. He carried a new clasp knife that replaced the one he lost in April. Over the weekend he had also acquired a much larger knife, a dagger. It needed a bit of cleaning and sharpening, but it had a long stiff blade of about eight inches. He fantasised about the idea of stabbing his clasp knife into people, listening to their screams, as he ran away. The two women he attacked in February and March, had excited him, and he had wanted to do it again since. The anger swelled up inside him with the voices of his mother in his head; and the desire to take revenge for the attack on him. He could switch to being very angry in an instant, especially when someone reminded him of his mother.

He went into the Frying Pan public house as there were some people in there he didn't mind drinking with. He had been looking for a man called Bill, who may be able to get him a job at the slaughter yard. His luck was in, and he found Bill in the pub.

"Bill, any news on that job you mentioned at your place?" he asked.

"Yeh there's a couple of jobs, I don't know how long for though. I'll have to show you the ropes; then you'll know what you need to do, like. It's quite easy when you get the 'ang of it," Bill replied.

"I'll get you a drink then."

The attacker was medium build and slightly stocky. His mate, Bill, was a bit overweight and taller. They both looked unclean and unshaven; neither seemed friendly nor happy. Bill had large, filthy hands, with blood and dirt ingrained around his fingernails and his speech was slow. A lone woman called Polly Nichols, bumped into the attacker at the bar, she was looking for someone, and he seemed to recognise her. "Over 'ere Polly," someone shouted. The attacker and his companion both drank a few ales and conversed about how miserable their respective lives were. Then after about one hour or so, they parted ways.

Two prostitutes and two soldiers then entered the Frying Pan pub at around 10.30pm. They were drinking with each other and being friendly with other drinkers. He kept hearing the larger of the two women laughing at the bar with her friends.

'What the fuck has she got to be so 'appy about?' he thought to himself. "Fucking whore," he muttered to himself. She continued laughing loudly along with her female companion. Images of his mother now started coming into his mind.

The joyful quartet at the bar, then exited the pub, at about 10.50pm, so he followed them to their next destination. He kept a watch over them from a distance in the pub. The fat woman was as loud as ever; he wished he could just shut her up. He was feeling agitated and downed a few more pints of ale. Even though he was irritated by the group, he felt compelled to observe them and follow them. He moved outside the pub and waited for them to come out. He urinated up against a wall while keeping a vigil on the pub entrance.

At about 11.45pm, the four of them came out of the White Swan pub and onto the High Street. One pair went down Angel Alley. Martha Tabram with a loud laugh and her soldier went down George Yard. He followed them at a distance; he knew what they were going to do. They went into George Yard Buildings, and he could hear her giving oral sex to the private on the landing above. Suddenly, some people started to enter the building, and he quickly exited.

August 7th
The killing of Martha Tabram

As midnight passed, he continued his stalk of the streets into the early hours of the new day, lurking quietly in the dark alleyways of Spitalfields. He saw the woman that bumped into him in the pub, the one they called Polly Nichols; she was a prostitute. He remembered that she was the one that spat at him last month in Frostic Place. She had just gone off with a man, but there were quite a few people about on Brick Lane, so he didn't consider attacking her at this point. He followed her for a while, but she went back to her lodgings with someone. He walked for the best part of another hour, stopping only to watch prostitutes have sex, from a distance where he can't be seen. He moved up towards Dorset Street and onto Brushfield Street, where the market was. He watched there for a while, then started to move back to his lair. The time is around 2.00am.

He then saw the same fat woman that he had stalked earlier, talking to two different soldiers on Wentworth Street, on the opposite pavement. They must have been drinking after hours somewhere. He anticipated that she was going back to George Yard Buildings again. He arrived there before them, watching their movements and waiting for them.

Only one soldier entered the dwellings, the other waiting outside somewhere. He listened and could hear her giving oral sex again. He kept in the shadows until the soldier left, then moved down the flight of stairs, she was on the landing rearranging herself with her back to him. She was not getting away this time. He felt powerful; his heart was racing with excitement at what he was about to do.

As she turned around, he was standing in front of her. Before she could scream, he grabbed her by the throat with his right hand, and his left hand was over her mouth. She was a strong woman, but he forced her onto the floor, with his left hand still over her mouth. She started to struggle and fight back with her fists, and he was having difficulty holding her still, while also preventing her from screaming. Now, with his left hand tight against Martha's throat, with his thumb pressing on her windpipe, he reached into his right-hand pocket and started plunging the clasp knife, that was already opened, into her chest and neck. Martha was fighting for her breath, and the blood in her throat produced a gurgling sound. He repeatedly stabbed her in the chest and abdomen; he was now in a rage.

"I am goin' to shut you up for fuckin' good," he said to Martha as if it was his mother. She was stabbed many times, but she kept fighting for her life. He struggled to hold onto her throat, but he continued to stab her as she scratched at his face.

"Why don't you leave me alone, bitch?" he said to her as he looked at the body before him. For a moment or two, he only saw his mother's face, not Martha's. The adrenaline that rushed through his veins gave him the extra strength he needed to overpower her. She started to weaken rapidly due to blood loss and shock. He then remembered the dagger. He dropped his clasp knife, and with his right hand, reached for it on his left hip and plunged is straight into her heart.

"Fucking bitch; leave me alone," he said as she died. The killer was sweating and out of breath and the place now smelled of blood and urine. It was a messy and uncontrolled kill; his hands and his jacket were covered in blood. It was lucky no-one heard him or came up the stairs, he thought to himself. He got up and got out of there quickly. It was just 2.15am by the sound of the church bells. He travelled the short distance back to the Princess Alice pub. On his return home, he went to the toilet twice, took off his bloodied clothing and washed the blood from his hands. He then had a few drinks and spent the rest of the morning asleep.

At approximately 4.45am on the 7th of August, John Reeves, a waterside labourer who resided at George Yard Buildings, was on his way to work. He discovered the body of a woman on the first-floor landing of the stairs. He immediately went in search of a policeman and recounted his find to PC 226H Thomas Barrett. In turn, PC Barrett called for Doctor Timothy Killeen from Brick Lane to examine the body. Doctor Killeen arrived quickly and pronounced that she was beyond all help. He made a note of the body and placed her skirt down to cover her. He then ordered her to be moved to the Whitechapel Mortuary at Eagle Place.

Soon after the discovery of the body, Inspector Reid arrived on the scene and began talking to the eyewitnesses and residents of George Yard Buildings.

"Now, you are John Reeves; you found the body?"

"That's right, sir. I live at number 37. I left home at a quarter to five this mornin', to look for work. I am a dockside labourer, see. When I come down to the first-floor landin', I sees the woman lyin' on her back in a pool of blood. It shocked me, sir."

"Did you see anything else?"

"Well, it looked like she had been in a struggle as all her clothes were disarranged, like. There were footprints on the stairs, but I didn't see any weapon. I was too frightened to touch the body, but she was clearly dead, sir."

"Did you hear any disturbance during the night, a scream, maybe."

"Nothin', sir, I would have said if I had."

A while later, the inspector then spoke to Alfred Crow, who had just got up and volunteered himself to the police.

"Now, you also saw the body, am I right?"

"That's right sir. I live at number 35. I drive cabs and came back home at 3.30am this mornin'. I saw a body there, but I

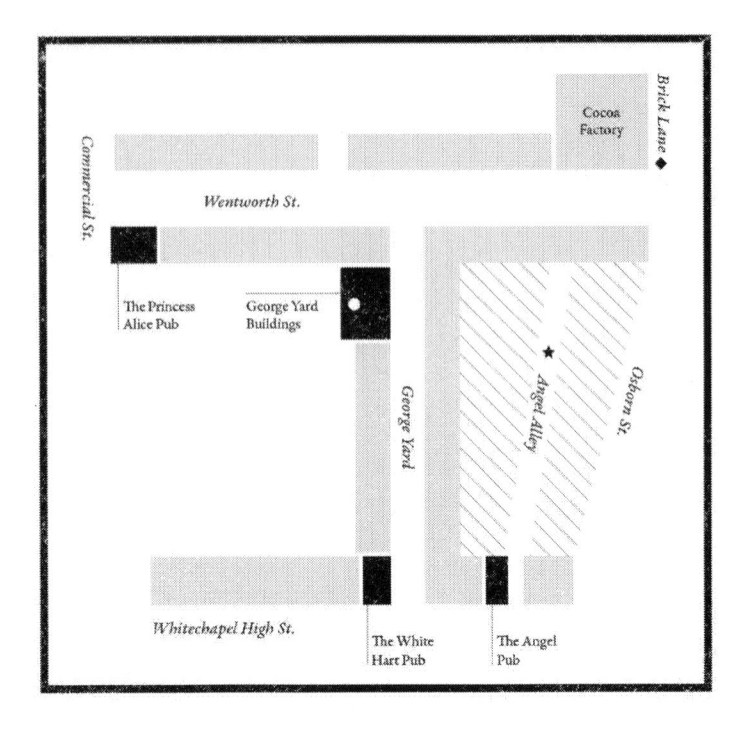

Map 2 – George Yard Buildings

At about 11.45pm, on the 6th August, Martha Tabram and Mary Ann Connolly left The White Swan on Whitechapel High Street with two soldiers. Tabram then went into George Yard Buildings and Connolly went into Angel Alley.

Martha Tabram's body was found on a first-floor landing of George Yard Buildings at 4.45am. ●

It is assumed that Martha went with a soldier to George Yard Buildings, just after 2am. His mate was seen by a PC on Wentworth Street at the same time. Her killer must have followed her.

Emma Smith was attacked by a gang, possibly here, outside the Cocoa Factory on the 3rd April 1888. ♦

The star in Angel Alley denotes the position of the attack, in this novel, on the man that would become known as Jack the Ripper. ★

The Princess Alice pub is where the Ripper lodges with his Aunt Letitia.

thought she was asleep or drunk. I took no notice. It isn't uncommon to find people sleepin' on the landings, sir."

"Did you see or hear anything else?"

"No, sir. When I went down the stairs just now, the body had gone. But I heard nothin' at all."

"Thank you. You have been most helpful."

Ried then turned to a woman standing a little way off. "Hello madam, I believe you have some information for me. I'm Reid."

"Hello, Inspector. I'm Mrs Elizabeth Mahoney; we live over there at 47 George Yard. Me and me husband came back just before 2.00am this mornin' and there was no body on the landin' that's for sure. I then went out to get some provisions, and when I came back a few minutes later, there was still no dead body. I never heard no screams or anyfink, Inspector."

Inspector Reid tried to gather information from other residents of George Yard Buildings, but no-one else had seen or heard anything. PC Barrett came up to Reid. "Inspector, I saw a Grenadier guard at 2.00am on the corner of George Yard and Wentworth Street. I asked him what he was doing. He replied that he was waiting for his mate that had gone with a woman."

"What did the soldier look like Constable?"

"22-26 years old, five-foot-nine or ten-inches tall, dark hair and a small brown moustache turned up at the ends. Do you think his mate was with the victim, sir?" PC Barrett enquired.

"It's possible; we will have to make further enquiries. Would you recognise the man if you saw him again?"

"Yes, sir," PC Barrett replied very confidently.

"We'll, go over to the Tower of London later and see if you can pick him out, Constable," Reid stated abruptly. "Oh, Constable, thank you," he added to soften his tone.

The inspector was thinking about the statements from three residents, Mahoney, Reeves and Crow, that placed the time of death between 2.00am to 3.30am, then he gathered the policemen that were at the scene.

"We need to find out who the victim was and then trace her whereabouts. You will need to ask in the pubs and lodging houses in this area first. You have a description of the woman and her clothes. We need to bring any witnesses in for questioning and make a statement as necessary. Is that clear?" The policemen replied, 'yes sir', almost in unison.

"I am going to the mortuary to get more details and talk to Doctor, er, Killeen," he added, looking at his notebook.

During the period of Reid's investigations, Dr Killeen had carried out the post-mortem. He ascertained that the unidentified woman had been brutally stabbed 39 times. She had sustained stab wounds to her neck, chest, abdomen and genitals.

Inspector Reid made an appointment to visit Dr Killeen in his surgery at 68 Brick Lane. Doctor Timothy Killeen was a very young doctor of 24 years. He was from County Clare in Ireland.

"Thank you for seeing me, Doctor," Reid said, smiling. "I wanted to ask you a few questions following the post-mortem."

"Yes, that's fine Inspector," the doctor replied in a strong Irish accent, shaking Reid's hand at the same time.

"What sort of weapon was used in the killing of this poor woman, Doctor?"

"Most of her vital organs have been stabbed, including her heart, liver lungs and the spleen. Most of the wounds, 38, were made with a small clasp knife. The fatal injury to the heart, through the chest bone, was by a longer blade."

"Have you seen such ferocity before Doctor, on a woman?"

"No Inspector, I have not. It was a brutal attack carried out with much rage. I don't know why two weapons were used, unless there were two killers."

"It's possible, but I don't think so, Doctor. Prostitutes usually only take one client at a time; it is a bit safer. Besides, I have evidence that she took one client at around 2.00am, while his mate waited elsewhere."

"She seemed to have fought back; she was moving when the smaller knife was inside her, which enlarged some of the cuts. She wouldn't have struggled after the heart wound, though. That was a fatal wound."

"So, he used his clasp knife, but he is struggling to kill her, so he then stabs her with a… dagger?" Reid deduced and asked at the same time.

"It's possible, yes, that fits with the injuries."

"Why didn't he just use the dagger then?" Reid said out loud, asking himself more than the doctor.

"Maybe he likes stabbing, Inspector; this is overkilling."

"Yes. The killer likes to stab," Reid said thoughtfully and as he paced around. "But the woman is strong and struggles on the ground with the killer. Maybe she knocks the blade out of his hand, or he drops it in the struggle. So, he uses his other knife to kill." As he spoke, Reid was almost acting out his theory.

"It could well be Inspector, that would explain the injuries."

"He will have learned something with this attack; the next one will involve less struggle."

"Are you so sure there will be a next one Inspector?" the doctor said, looking worried.

"Yes, there is a pattern here, it is still vague, but there is some clarity. The violence is escalating. There have been at least two clasp knife attacks against lone women recently, but this could be his first killing. Thank you, Doctor, you have been most helpful."

"You are welcome, Inspector."

After obtaining the post-mortem information from Doctor Killeen, Inspector Reid arranged to meet PC Barrett, to visit the Tower of London, as previously mentioned. Although the Inspector's hopes were up at seeing the guard in question, they were soon diminished when PC Barrett failed to identify the man he saw at 2.00am.

No-one had initially come forward to identify the body formally. The police had circulated the woman's photograph and description to aid identification from that afternoon.

The killer woke up excited at what he had done a few hours earlier, but at the same time, he felt fear - he may have been seen. The paranoia started: *'What if the police question him? What does he do now?'* he thought to himself.

He had a lot to drink last night, he couldn't remember everything clearly, and his head was hurting as usual. He knew what he had done, though, he could remember that. This was his first kill of a person. He masturbated twice before he got up and got dressed. His memory was improving with time; he knew all along that it had not been a gang that attacked him. He knew he had been hit with a hammer, but he couldn't remember who. It may come back eventually.

"I made fuckin' sure that this one didn't have time to pull out anything on me, but she put up a good fight. It was hard goin'," he said out loud. "I got her to the ground, alright, but she took some killing. If I find the woman who attacked me, I'll do 'er, once and for all."

He was still furious at being attacked with a hammer and desperately wanted retaliation. He dreamed about revenge and planned his response in his head. He still had awful headaches and couldn't remember everything too well. He was prone to having fits since his injury, especially when stressed.

He remembered that someone had a job for him. *That's what I'll do. Carry on as if nothing has happened,'* he thought to himself. Then went outside in search of the new occupation. He knew Spitalfields well and acted above suspicion. He then made his way to the slaughterhouse.

"Is Bill in?" he asked, "he said there is a job goin,' I'd want."

"He's over there. Go and tell 'im," a worker said.

"Bill," he shouts. His mate acknowledges him with a head movement, meaning come over here.

"You can start. A couple of the old geezers have snuffed it. Like their 'orses," his mate said, laughing. "It's a dirty job, this. And it stinks, but you get used to it."

The smell must have been bad because Whitechapel and Spitalfields reeked of dirt and disease, rotting waste, boiled bones, fish, urine, horse dung and human waste. Then there was the overcrowding of people who rarely washed, and their clothes were washed even less.

"It's easy when you get the 'ang of it," Bill shouted. "You'll need these," Bill passed him a long leather apron and a knife, "the way they are killed is by cutting the neck art'ries. It's quick and painless as it can be. Know what I mean?"

"I'll give it a go. I may be better at it than you fink," the killer said with a smirk on his face that twisted up the right side of his mouth.

"You need to stand away from where you are cutting, or you will get sprayed with blood. So, if you are cutting the right side first, stand to the left side."

Over the next few weeks, the killer would become quite adept at slaughtering animals. He also discovered that he got a great deal of sexual excitement from the disembowelling of horses. He felt alive and powerful. He then started fantasising about using his newly acquired skill on prostitutes. The killer had found a new sexual outlet.

After spending some time at the slaughter yard, he returned to the Princess Alice Pub.

"I've got some news, Auntie. I've got anovver job," he said proudly.

"Well, are you goen' to tell me about it?" Letty asked eagerly.

"I've got a job at a slaughter yard. A mate of mine, Bill, he sorted it out like. That's where I've been most of the day."

"And where were you last night and this mornen'?" Letty asked sharply.

"I got in a bit late, about two o'clockish and then slept in a bit. It was the best sleep I've 'ad since I was attacked. I didn't wake up in pain."

"Oh, well at least that is somethen'; you are supposed to be worken' here tonight."

"Yeh, I know, that's why I am back now. But I can now start payin' you back proper, like."

"Did you hear about the murder in the early hours of this mornen'?" Letty said with her hands on her hips.

"No. I slept in, then went to see Bill, about the job. Why are you askin me?"

"Well, everyone is talken' about it. Don't you want to hear about it?" Letty said excitedly.

"Well you can't wait to tell me, and I get most of the news from you, like everyone else does."

August 9th
Questioning Pearly Poll

The Inquest into the death of the woman murdered in George Yard Buildings was opened on the 9th of August 1888 at the Working Lads Institute, Whitechapel Road. It is located next to Whitechapel Station and opposite the London Hospital. This tall five-storey red brick building, with decorative stonework around the doors and windows, was built in 1885. The institute provided a place for education and leisure activities to prevent young boys from entering a life of crime. It also provided accommodation and education for homeless boys.

On the same day, at the Commercial Street Police Station, Mary Ann Connolly came to identify the victim only as Emma, as she didn't know her surname. Inspector Reid was sent for, and she then recounted the story of Emma and herself meeting the two soldiers.

"We picked up two soldiers, me and Emma. We went into several pubs on Monday evenin' of the bank 'oliday. About a quarter to twelve, we split up. Me and the corporal went up Angel Alley, while Emma and the private went into George Yard, I fink. That was the last time I saw her."

"What did the two soldiers look like? What were they wearing?"

"I don't know what regiment they belonged to, but they wore red tunics and 'ad white bands on their caps."

"Could you recognise them again?"

"Yea, possibly, but I am not too sure. We 'ad a lot of drink, so me mind isn't that clear if you gets me meanin'."

"How long have you known the deceased?"

"About four or five monfs and she is called Emma as I've already said."

"What is her surname?"

"I don't know, I only know her as Emma. Don't you listen?" she said, giving the policeman a sharp look. The mild-mannered Inspector Reid was getting annoyed with Connolly, but he managed to hold in his temper and remain professional.

"You and Emma had been drinking, were you both drunk?"

"No, we 'ad 'ad a few drinks, but we weren't elephants."

"You have just said you can't remember because you had a lot to drink, which is it?"

"Well I don't know, do I. We 'ad some drinks, that's all I know."

"Which pubs did you go in?" Reid asked, getting more and more frustrated with her.

"Well, I don't know, pubs!" she shouted.

"Now look, this is a murder investigation. You have told me you were with the victim, so which pubs were you in?"

"We left the White Swan at a quarter to twelve, as I have said."

"You never mentioned the pub before. Where were you before that?"

"We met the two soldiers in the Two Brewers, I fink, then we may 'ave gone into the Fryin' Pan, but I don't know what times. I 'avent got a watch, see," she said very cockily.

Reid took a few breaths and lowered his voice before asking, "where did Emma live?"

"She was lodging at 19 George Street, a doss house."

"Are you willing to take part in an identification parade to pick out these two soldiers?"

"Yes, I can do that. How much money do I get?"

"You don't get any money. It is your duty to help find out who murdered your friend."

"Well, awright then, if I must," she said begrudgingly.

Inspector Reid felt that the evidence of this fifty-year-old prostitute, who was behaving like a spoilt child, was unreliable. Since being at H Division, he cannot remember a more obnoxious individual that he has had the displeasure to meet. Reid thought that the killer he was now looking for, would be hard pushed to be more offensive than Connolly.

He had arranged to meet Connolly the following day for an identification parade. However, she didn't turn up. Reid made a point of informing officers to keep a lookout for her and bring her in if they find her.

August 16th
Further police investigations

Mary Ann Connolly went missing for a few days but was eventually found by Inspector Eli Caunter. She then attended the barracks with Inspector Reid on the 13th and 15th of August to identify the two soldiers. Unfortunately, an identification could not be made.

Henry Tabram, her estranged husband, came to the police station and identified Martha on the 16th of August. "I haven't seen her for 18 months, and we have been separated for thirteen years. Her name is Martha Tabram, and she is 39 years old."

Later the same day, Henry Turner, also identified her to the police.

"I have lived with Martha for nine years, but we split up three weeks ago because of her drinking habits, but we got back together on the 4th of August. I gave her some money, and she spent it on drink."

Mrs Bousfield of number 4 Star Place, Commercial Road also identified Martha, "I knew her as Martha Turner. She and her husband Henry used to lodge with me until about three weeks ago. They owe me two weeks of rent. She liked a drink, did Martha. She would rather have a glass of ale than a cup of tea."

Martha's sister-in-law, Ann Morris, identified Martha from the police photograph.

"I last saw Martha at 11.00pm on the Bank Holiday, outside the White Swan, on her own. This was the last time I saw her; she was alone and appeared sober," she formally stated to the police.

There were no other leads for Edmund Reid to follow up and he was sceptical of Mary Ann Connolly's story. It seemed to the inspector that it was a random killing of a prostitute. There was no apparent motive, and robbery was ruled out. He thought back to the early attacks on Annie Millwood and Ada Wilson, but this attack was different, as murder was clearly the intention here. The two assaults with a blunt object, in April, were also different from each other, and to this latest killing of Tabram. As much as he thought about the cases, he could not see any links yet.

Before the end of the day, Inspector Reid caught up with Inspector Abberline at Leman Street Police Station.

"We have managed to identify the woman killed in George Yard Buildings, Fred. She was a prostitute called Martha Tabram. I have four identifications of her now. What we are still not clear on, are her last known movements. I think her so-called friend, Mary Anne Connolly, has been making some of her story up, as it cannot be corroborated."

"I know Connolly, Pearly Poll, I told you about her in the pub in January. Her brain has been pickled with alcohol, she is a totally unreliable witness," Abberline responded.

"She claims to have known Tabram for months but does not know her real name. All the people that knew Tabram recently, know that she was called Martha. Yet Connolly says she was called Emma!"

"Connolly is mixed up, Edmund. She probably can't remember her own name at times. She is a liar and a wrong un. We have only her word that they were with two soldiers, but her story doesn't check out."

"The thing is Fred, apart from Connolly, the only other sighting we have of Tabram is by her sister-in-law, who saw her outside the White Swan at 11.00pm, on her own; with neither soldiers nor Connolly in sight. I have been in the pubs that Connolly said they were in, but no-one saw Tabram with Connolly."

"We now know who she was; a drunken whore called Tabram. There is a possibility that she was with a soldier at about 2.00am because one of our men saw a soldier waiting for his mate. We don't know if this soldier was with Tabram, but she turned up dead about 90 minutes later. No-one will admit to being with her, even if they are totally innocent."

"I think that I am going to have to look at these recent crimes differently, Fred. Rather than trying to find who may have done it, we may have to look at why the crimes are being done; this then could lead us to the killer. On their own, these crimes of stabbings, assaults and killings don't make any sense. There was much more anger with the Tabram killing; but why, Fred, why all this anger? Is this a man who hates prostitutes, or women in general?"

"Well if the three stabbings are related then one person is going around stabbing prostitutes. He will soon get caught. Local knowledge is the key here, Edmund. We need to get men around to talk to the women; they may have seen an unusual character. Someone will know something. He will be one of their punters. You mark my words."

"We can do that Fred, but it will take a lot of manpower. You will need to get Swanson to second officers from other divisions, to here. There is something else bothering me about this Martha Tabram killing, but I don't know what. It seems strange, somehow, and I can't see any motive."

"We keep working away, asking questions, until something turns up."

"What like another dead body, Fred?"

"These are just local, individual incidents. There is no need to suspect there will be any more, Edmund."

August 23rd
Inspector Reid's discussions

Martha Tabram's killer was now working happily at the slaughter yard. The animals provided him with plenty of practice. He remembered the fight that the woman in George Yard put up; he didn't want to go through that again, and he didn't want to be attacked by a prostitute carrying a weapon.

"The next one is going to get her froat cut on the ground," he said to himself. "I'm not gonna fuckin' mess about wiv 'em. Quick and clean, that's how it's done."

He now knew how to sharpen a blade correctly, so that it could slice through flesh in one stroke. It was long enough and sharp enough to cut someone's throat from ear to ear deeply. He felt confident in his newly acquired skills and smiled to himself when he fantasised about how he was going to use them. His method of attack was to overpower his prey, strangulation stopped them screaming, and a deep neck incision stopped them fighting back. It was only a matter of time now before he struck again.

He was still having bad headaches, and sometimes he felt dizzy, other times he would fall and start shaking. Every time this happened, it was a reminder of what had happened to him, and every reminder increased his anger and self-pity. If only he could remember something about who attacked him, but he couldn't. He sometimes remembered certain things, and then he would forget them again. Due to his facial appearance, which was still swollen and disfigured, he was very conscious of people looking at him. He, therefore, wore a hat with a peak to conceal his face, and he walked with his head down. He preferred going out alone at night, as usual, but now he was angrier than ever because of the hammer attack. There was a lot of rage inside him, and there was only one way for him to release his anger.

In Leman Street Police Station, Inspectors Reid and Abberline were discussing the case after attending the final day of the inquest earlier that day. The inquest jury returned a verdict of wilful murder by person or persons unknown.

"I want to put this case by you, Fred, because there is something about it that bothers me. Martha Tabram was stabbed 39 times on the 7th of August in George Yard Buildings."

"Yes, Edmund, I am aware of the case, I get all the murder reports. What is it that is bothering you?"

"Well, stabbing someone 39 times with two different weapons is overkill. The killer must be furious, but who would do such a thing?"

"A lunatic Edmund, some crazy bastard."

"Okay Fred, but this lunatic is calm enough to follow her and wait until she has finished duties with someone. She was a prostitute and used to go to that place for sex. Can a lunatic remain unseen and calm? Would he not be wandering the street with blood on his hands, probably carrying a knife?"

"It is probably one of her clients."

"But why do this? This is someone that wants to stab and to kill. How do we find such a person?"

"We ask about until we find something."

"I don't think that will work in this case. Her clients are not going to come forward, and no-one has seen anything. It took over a week just to identify her."

"We just have to hope that something turns up; you have done all you can."

"I went over to 19 George Street where Martha Tabram had been living recently. No-one had a bad word to say about her. She liked a drink but was quiet and good-natured. Some of the people living in the lodging houses are there through no fault of their own; some have had tough and unlucky lives," Reid said thoughtfully.

"There are a lot of people who have tough lives, but they don't go around murdering people," Abberline responded.

"That's not what I am getting at Fred, listen to this: I met a man in there and started talking to him. He said he worked on the docks when he could get work. When he could get work, most of his earnings went on food and board. He was on his own and couldn't afford to rent a room on a regular basis as he has no regular income. He said that when he has no work, he must walk the streets at night and find somewhere to sleep outside, like many others. He told me that sleeping outside and walking through the night with no food; you don't have the energy to work the following day. He said that many people just give up; they lay down and die from cold and hunger. Some others throw themselves into the Thames. This last bit really shocked me; he had a wife who killed herself because she was slowly starving to death. The verdict is always the same, suicide whilst temporarily insane. He said it should be suicide whilst cold and hungry. Nobody cares about these people Fred; society wants to pretend that they don't exist."

"You've a good heart Edmund, and a good head," Abberline said to his friend.

"Thanks Fred, but back to the murders, I may not be able to help the poor, but I can catch villains. This is the second murder and the fourth attack in Spitalfields, since February. I think they are all linked somehow."

"How? The first murder of Emma Smith was a gang attack. The stabbing in White's Row was one man. The attack in Angel Alley was a gang apparently, and this Tabram murder could be one man or two, as two weapons were used. Of the four attacks, only two were stabbings, and of them, only one was fatal."

Reid thought for a moment, "I know what you mean when you put it like that, but I don't think several different people are going around Spitalfields attacking people at the same time. I am missing something, Fred, the two stabbings could be the same person. His attacks have escalated from an attack to a kill. There are not many murderers who start with a kill; there will be some violent behaviour before that."

"Well it doesn't get us anywhere Edmund, does it? According to you, there's one gang and one killer out there, that's not unusual, is it?"

"Yes, Fred. I just like to speak out my thoughts to someone. It helps to clear my mind and put things in a logical order. I also wanted to ensure you were up-to-date with my enquiries as I am going on holiday shortly, just in case something turns up. I am sure it won't, but you never know. Maybe things will be more apparent after my holiday."

"Well, you have a good holiday. I am not expecting anything to happen either."

"Let's go for a drink first, I wanted to check on someone in the Princess Alice," said Reid.

The killer of Martha Tabram was in the Princess Alice pub early in the evening. He was about to get a drink at the bar when someone tapped him on the shoulder.

"Hello, I thought it was you. Are you feeling any better now? following the attack on you, in April."

"What? Who are you? How do you know?" he responded totally surprised at someone talking to him, that he can't recognise. He feels his heart rate quicken and starts to look nervous.

"I'm Inspector Reid; I met you in the hospital after the attack."

"Oh, yea, I remember now. Sorry Inspector, I didn't recognise you," the killer said, and he breathed a sigh of relief.

"Well?" Reid enquired.

"Well, what?"

"Are you feeling any better?"

"Oh sorry, yes, Inspector. I still get confused and have 'eadaches."

"Have you found the man that did this to me?"

"No, sorry we haven't. I was hoping that you may get your memory back, but you think it was a man?"

"I still know nuffink. I assumed a bloke, but I just don't know."

"Are you working at all?" Reid enquired, quickly changing the subject.

"Yea, I've got a job as an 'orse slaughterer. It pays well, you know."

"You were in prison a while ago, for stealing, weren't you?"

"Yes, but I am straight now." A worried look comes over the killer's face, not knowing what to expect next.

"Glad to hear it, and if you have any idea who may have attacked you, just let me know."

"Will do, Inspector," the killer replied, nodding his head and very relieved.

"Nosey, fuckin' mutton shunter," the killer said to himself, as Reid sat down with Abberline, who had ordered the drinks already.

The killer then went upstairs in the pub to have a lie-down, as he now had another headache. As he got into his room, he started to shake and fell to the floor. He was making a sort of groaning sound; sweat was pouring off his face. After about 30 seconds, the seizure subsided. He lay there for a while, unable to move. When he came to, he was in a state of shock at having a fit. It made him even angrier. He wanted to get his own back, but he still couldn't remember about the attack on him.

'You're a waste of space, you little bastard' he heard in his head. He looks in the mirror, and for a moment, he can see his mother's face, sneering at him. He turned around, but no-one is there.

He held his head in his hands while sitting on the floor, and then started hitting his head with his fists. He felt the anger building up inside him once again. His life was a living hell; he cannot escape from his demented mother. He could hear some commotion in the pub, so he decided he would go back down shortly.

Suddenly, a woman staggered into the pub with her face bleeding; she was shaken up but not seriously hurt. The landlady saw her straight away and came over to her.

"What's happened, love?" she asked.

"I was wiv a punter, and he just started hittin' me until I gave him the money that I 'ad. It wasn't much, only a few coppers. He had a knife wiv 'im, so I just gave 'im the money like, I fought 'e could be the one that killed that woman in George Yard," the young prostitute said.

"Well you know it was no-one in 'ere that attacked you, so you are safe now. Here have a drink of gin to calm yourself down," the landlady said.

"I've no money to pay for it now."

"It's on the house love, just rest a while."

"Fanks a lot, Letty," she replied.

A man at the bar said to the landlady, "I might be attacked, can I 'ave a free drink?"

The landlady replied, "Yes, but it will be me that will be attacking you."

"No, you're awright; a drink isn't worf that," the customers in the pub started laughing.

Reid and Abberline moved over to the woman.

"What did the man look like?" Abberline asked.

"Wew, he was foreign lookin' like. He was about fortyish and might have been a sailor or somefink."

"Would you be able to recognise him again?" asked Reid.

"Yeh, prob'ly, I fink."

"Well if you see him in 'ere let me know love, I'll sort the bastard out," said the angry Letty.

"Madam, you can't go around hitting people. You send for the police," said Reid, and Abberline smiled. She just looked disparagingly at Reid and said nothing.

The killer then came back into the pub and sat down on his own to drink his ale, but still feeling unwell. Reid and Abberline sat down again to drink their ale.

"Do you think this attacker is the same person that killed Tabram, Fred?"

"I don't know Edmund. If it was, she was lucky to escape."

"Yes, I agree. This man only threatened her with a knife, but he didn't use it. Many women are threatened and beaten up by men and gangs."

"Still, we have a description, so we will just keep it on file for now," Abberline said before finishing his pint.

"By the way, who did you want to see in here?"

"The young man who lives here. The one who was injured in Angel Alley. I wanted to know if he remembered anything about the attack. As it happens, he doesn't. But he told me that he had got a job at a horse slaughterers. I have a feeling that it may be relevant somehow.

Polly Nichols and one of her friends, Ellen Holland, then entered the Princess Alice pub to have a drink and a chat. Polly and Ellen were no longer as attractive as they were when they were younger, and it was increasingly more difficult to make money on the streets unless the punters were quite drunk. Polly began to look around the pub to see if she recognised anyone. In the corner near the bar, she spotted someone that she thought had assaulted her recently.

"Do ya see 'im over there; sat on 'is own wiv the big 'at on; wew, 'e gives me the creeps, 'e does," Polly said to her friend.

"Why is that then, luv; has 'e done somefink to you?"

"He was a bit rough, that was all, but I don't like 'im."

The man was the killer of Martha Tabram, and he looked over towards Polly and her friend.

"Oh, Gawd, 'e's lookin' over 'ere now; I hope 'e doesn't come over to us," Polly said.

"'e's not gonna bovver ya; stop worryin'; you're in the pub now. There are loads of rough men in 'ere. Just keep out of his way," Ellen said.

Suddenly a large bellow rang out through the pub. "Right you, get your arse behind this bar and get some of these served."

The landlady shouted to her nephew. He got up and went behind the bar; he looked over towards Polly again.

"See 'e can't be too bad if 'e works 'ere. She won't 'ave any nutters workin' for her," Ellen said, confidently.

"Suppose you're right; 'e's still creepy though."

After their drink, Reid and Abberline left the pub, to walk home. On Brick Lane, an old lady, in clothes that were more like rags, approached Inspector Abberline.

"'ave you got a few pennies for some food, sir? I 'ave free children and they're all 'ungry, sir."

"Come with me, I will buy you some bread and cheese for your children," Abberline said kindly.

"I didn't say I wanted food. I asked for money!" she shouted at Abberline.

"Good evening, madam," Abberline said and slightly lifting his hat.

"Miserable cheapskate," she replied.

Later in the evening, Edmund and his wife Emily were having a fresh cup of tea after dinner, and once again he discussed the case with her, following the death of a prostitute in George Yard buildings.

"I am certainly ready for a holiday dear, but I am going with a major murder case hanging over me. I just hope that there are no more attacks or murders while we are away."

"Well, you can't do anything to prevent them on your own. I am sure your colleagues can cope without you, Edmund."

"The inquest of Martha Tabram, who was murdered on the 7th of this month, closed today and we are no nearer catching her killer. I am still nowhere with the stabbing in February or the two attacks in April, one of which proved fatal. There was also a stabbing of a woman at Mile End at her front door; this is very similar to the Annie Millwood stabbing in White's Row in February. Somehow, I think they are all linked, but Fred doesn't. He is treating each case separately, but I believe there is a pattern here."

"Well, it is possible that the three stabbings are by the same person; and the two assaults with a blunt weapon are by another different person. Fred, I think, is focussing on who could be the offender of each separate crime, but you are best suited to focus on why the crimes are being committed."

"Yes, that is what I have been trying to do. However, I don't have any clue or evidence as to why the crimes have been committed. The two early stabbings seem to be done by a younger person with a clasp knife, and Martha Tabram was stabbed 38 times with a clasp knife, and once with a dagger. But I can't see the motive for these stabbings."

"Maybe the stabbings *are* the motive, and there doesn't need to be a logical reason. Do you remember last year on holiday, the old man in the village? He struggled to walk even with a walking stick, yet every day he would hobble out of his cottage, whatever the weather, and walk about. He then came home in the late afternoon. We asked ourselves, why does he do it? Why doesn't he sit and rest? Although his actions are strange to us; the reason he walked all day was that he enjoyed it. He liked being outside, even if it is cold and wet. People are different and have different reasons for doing things. If you find out why these crimes are being committed, you are more likely to find who is committing them."

"Maybe you should take over the case when we get back; I am sure you will figure it out."

"So, will you. I have never met a more positive person who wants to be involved in everything than you. You have a logical mind and are as determined as anyone I have ever met. You need some more pieces to the puzzle to start to see the picture clearly. What you sometimes lack is patience; you are so alive with ideas that you want everything at once. Give yourself time; this holiday will do you good, Edmund."

"You are right, Emily; I have been working too much and neglecting you and the children. I have so many things going on in my head, that I just need to sit and relax. My brain will work it out eventually."

Emily walked across the room to a small cabinet and poured a little amber liquid into a small glass.

"Here take this glass of brandy and relax, think calm thoughts like a slow-moving river or birds singing in the trees. Your brain needs to rest, just like your body does."

Reid sipped his brandy and closed his eyes; in a short while, he was asleep in his chair. Emily continued reading her book until it was time for them both to go to bed.

August 31st
The killing of Mary Ann Nichols

It was late into the evening of the 30th of August that 43-year-old Mary Ann Nichols, who was also known as Polly, was seen plying her trade along the Whitechapel Road at about 11.00pm. She was wearing a brown ulster overcoat, with a brown linsey frock underneath. Her only other possessions were the men's boots and a bonnet. Polly, at five-foot-two-inches tall, was a common prostitute who sold herself for a few pennies at a time. The bulk of her meagre earnings went on alcohol to feed her addiction. After completing her duties leant against some wall in a dark alley, she headed back towards the Frying Pan pub on the corner of Brick Lane and Thrawl Street, to spend her earnings. She also met up with fellow prostitutes and further potential clients. The pub itself was a large three-storey brick building with stone cornerstones and stone facings around the windows. It was a popular public house with a lot of the traders and their customers on Brick Lane.

"Ave, you 'ad any luck, dear?" Ellen Holland asks Polly, meaning, have you got any money?

"Nah, not much Ell. I was staying to the main road where it's safer, but not many punters there."

"Don't blame you luv, that nasty business with that woman stabbed in George Yard, gives me the creeps."

"It wiw be some sort of crazy madman or a foreigner, you mark me words," Polly confidently stated. "I'm stayin' wew clear of any lunatics and fugs."

"Well you're in the wrong place then, 'cos Spitalfields is full of 'em," Ellen sarcastically added.

"Ow about you? 'Ave you any money?"

"Enough for a drink or two and me doss money."

"Good," Polly said. "I've enough for a couple of drinks. Usual, is it?" she asked with a grin that showed several of her front teeth were missing.

Polly got up and obtained two gins, making conversation with whoever was at the bar and then sat back down, next to Ellen. Ellen was one of the housekeepers at 18 Thrawl Street and shared a room with Polly for the last six weeks. Ellen was about 50 years old and was married.

"There are some in 'ere I don't like the looks of now, they get drunk, then get violent. If they're too drunk, I steer clear of 'em, unless I think I can nick their money and they're a bit of a pushover." Polly was already slurring her words a bit.

"You wanna be careful gal; you don't wanna make any enemies here. They'll cut ya froat as soon as look at ya if you cross 'em," Ellen stated angrily with a sneer on her face.

"There's been a few attacks on women lately."

"It's our lot in life, we don't mean nuffink to no-one," Ellen said while coughing at the same time.

During the late hours of the 30th of August and the early hours of the following day, a man was out stalking. Shortly he would strike, his target was once again, a lone prostitute.

The killer spent many an evening, going from pub to pub, watching prostitutes, observing the beats of the police, seeking opportunities to strike unnoticed. He was a very streetwise stalker who knew the area intimately. The streets of Spitalfields and Whitechapel were busy, even at night. One must always be on the alert. There were many dark and poorly lit alleyways where people could lurk unseen. If you looked like you had money, then one of the many gangs of street robbers and thugs would find you. It was best to be wary and on your guard. What better way to defend yourself than by carrying a knife?

He had spent part of the evening in his aunts' pub. He sometimes thought of his mother with rage and anger. *'She was no movva, she was a drunken whore, who cared for no-one but 'erself,'* he regularly said inside of his head.

"What you up to tonight then?" the landlady asked him.

"Er, dunno," he said while looking down at the table, "er, just out, you know."

He seemed fidgety, nervous, on-edge. He couldn't keep his left leg still. It shook a little when he was agitated. The drink calmed him to an extent and took away some of the headache pain.

"Is work alright then?"

"Er, yeh, good fanks, I like me job. I don't know why, but I do," he said with a smirky grin on his face.

He doesn't like much conversation, so he bid farewell to his aunt and left the pub. Since he obtained his latest job, he had been working much less for his aunt in the pub.

A woman called Lizzie came over to his aunt and asked, "ere, Letty, isn't that your sister's son?"

"Yeh, he's my nephew."

"How is he, since his accident?"

"It was no accident. He was attacked by a gang and one of them 'ad a hammer. It was the same night that woman was killed, by a gang. 3rd of April."

"He was just getten' 'imself sorted, wasn't he?"

"He's always 'ad his problems, Liz."

"He doesn't look very 'appy, does he?"

"Well, that's just 'im ain't it. I suppose if I'd 'ad his life, I wouldn't be too 'appy as well," Letty stated jokingly.

"He's definitely got worse since being attacked. You know he nearly died, fractured skull and all. Lost his memory, he did, for a while. He has terrible 'eadaches and is bad-tempered a lot of the time. He has been in and out of the shovel, as you know, thieving mainly. Still, he seems a bit 'appier now he has a job."

"What does he do?"

"Horse slaughterer," Letty said, loud and confidently, "at the knackers' yard, he's been there two or three weeks now. He doesn't mean no 'arm, not the brightest penny if you know what I mean. Keeps himself to himself," she whispered in her ear.

"Best way, if you ask me, especially around 'ere." Then Lizzie nodded and responded with a wink.

Ellen went to the bar to get two gins. The Frying Pan was quite busy as it was the weekend. While most people were engaged in local banter or just singing; there were a few lone men who were quiet and watching what was going on. One of these was a young, slightly stocky looking man with a hat on; he kept his head down a lot and lifted his eyes upwards to look around. He was sat next to an old man with a terrible stammer who was rambling on about something. A taller, well built, man with a large moustache was at the bar talking to another customer. He was quite well dressed compared to most of the pub regulars, so he looked out of place.

"We need to watch out for one anovva," Polly stated, finishing off her gin.

"The woman that was killed used to come in 'ere, Tarbum I fink she was," Polly said, nodding her head at the same time.

"Tabram, Martha Tabram," Ellen replied, "at the inquest, they said she was stabbed 39 times."

"I wonder if the killer comes in 'ere?" Polly asked. "It might be 'im over there at the bar, or 'im in the corner there looking as miserable as sin. Makes you wonder, doesn't it?"

"You fink too much; you do, get that down ya."

"Where you goin' next."

"I might go and see the dock fire, are you comin' too?"

"I'm gonna try me luck round 'ere a bit more yet."

Polly and Ellen left the Frying Pan pub at about midnight when the pubs closed. Polly sauntered towards Whitechapel Road, with the regular noise of horse's hooves trotting on the road. She hung around looking for business, while Ellen crossed Whitechapel Road and headed south to the docks. Polly didn't attract any business, and after an hour or so of walking the streets, she was now cold and tired. As Polly walked back up Osborn Street to Brick Lane, she started to feel a little nervous for some reason, looking back over her shoulder.

"It's just me stupid head," Polly said to herself. At 1.20am she was back in the lodging house. Polly had stayed on and off at 18 Thrawl Street over the last six weeks; sometimes, she would stay at 55 Flower and Dean Street. She hadn't always been a prostitute, but started out well, got married and had five children, but then she succumbed to alcohol. Her husband left her nine years ago, taking the children with him. He continued to support her with five shillings a week until he found out that she was a prostitute, which was six years ago. She had lived in various workhouses over the years. Polly did get a lucky break earlier in the year, taking up the position of a housekeeper on the 12th of May. However, she absconded on the 12th of July with stolen clothes, to move back to her old ways of drinking and prostitution. The pull of alcohol was too strong for Polly, and prostitution was her only means of paying for it.

"You got me bed then?" Polly asked the deputy manager.

"You got any money then?"

"No, but I will 'ave soon, I've just come in for a warm," Polly replied as she sat in the kitchen.

"Well, you'd better get out then until you can pay."

"I'll get me money, see what a jolly bonnet I've got!" Polly said proudly, as she got up and walked out of the lodgings for the very last time at 1.40am, with her velvet trimmed black straw bonnet and on her head. All her clothes had seen much better days, but Polly was still proud of her worn, second-hand bonnet.

Polly made several more unsuccessful attempts to get her doss money. She rested a few times in doorways until she was moved on by policemen. She staggered down Osborne Street towards Whitechapel Road at 2.30am, where she met Ellen again at the junction of the two roads.

"What you up to, Ellen?"

"I've seen the fire, and now I'm going back to me doss 'ouse, are you coming back with me?"

"No, I've 'ad me doss money free times tonight, but spent it," Polly said. "I am going up here to try me luck," Polly said, pointing up Whitechapel Road.

Whitechapel High Street with Whitechapel Road was the main thoroughfare through Whitechapel. It had been in existence since the 1750s and consisted of buildings from the late Georgian period through to the early and middle Victorian Period. By 1870, it was entirely built up on both sides. There were many significant buildings along this road including The London Hospital, The Whitechapel Church, Saint Mary Matfelon, Whitechapel Station and many commercial premises, as well as public houses. Many of the buildings had ornate brickwork and stonework and were of four storeys or more in height.

Polly then slowly proceeded Eastwards up Whitechapel Road, which was now much quieter. She was tired, cold and hungry. Polly walked past Whitechapel railway station and turned left into Brady Street which was quite dark. She passed a watchman snoring in his watch hut. Within an hour, Polly would be dead. She passed the Roebuck public house on the corner of Brady Street and Bucks Row, which was now closed for the night. Then she moved down Brady Street and walked around where there were a few night workers in the slaughter yards. Eventually, she got lucky and left with a somewhat well-dressed man and headed up Bucks Row to the dark and secluded factory gates, opposite the terraced houses.

Someone was behind them, and Polly turned around.

"Oh, it's okay, I thought he was a copper," she said.

A couple of minutes later, her client walked back to work, and Polly crossed over the street and headed Westwards towards Thrawl Street.

Suddenly, a man stepped out of the gateway to the stable yard.

"All right luv? You gave me a real fright then," Polly blurted out, "are you looking for business then?" she asked.

"Yes," he said then quickly took Polly by the throat, threw her to the ground holding onto her neck...

Meanwhile, Martha Tabram's killer, who left the Princess Alice pub a while ago, had spent an hour or two in the Frying Pan pub and started stalking the streets between Old Montague Street and Whitechapel Road. He knew most of the public houses around these two roads and so casually frequented them, looking for potential prey until closing time at midnight. He knew the police beats around his home, but he became less confident as he travelled further afield.

He watched prostitutes pick up their punters in the pubs and on the streets. He liked to follow them cautiously, watching them having intercourse against a wall or fence. What was more enjoyable for him was when he witnessed acts of domination and violence.

He saw one woman with a man walking up Whitechapel Road. He waited until they got off the main road; he then followed and watched them from a distance. He paused and could feel himself becoming more agitated; his heart was beating faster. He heard a policeman's boots on the pavement and moved off quickly.

He then saw Polly Nichols on Whitechapel Road. He remembered that she had spat in his face a while back, and he followed her. She turned into Brady Street, and he followed closely. He stood in the corner doorway of the Roebuck pub, which was now closed until 5.00am, watching her as she made her way along Brady Street.

Bucks Row runs at right angles to Brady Street and looking from Brady Street, there are 24 brick terraced houses on the left-hand side in a row, with the Roebuck pub at the Brady Street end. After the last terrace, called New Cottage, there was a small stable yard, then a gap for the railway line that passed under the street. At the other side of the railway embankment was the Board School. Backing onto Bucks Row was Winthrop Street, where Barber's slaughter yard was situated.

He saw the woman walk towards Bucks Row with a man. They went across the road to the gateway of the factory on Bucks Row, opposite the houses. He followed close by, and the woman turned around. He kept his head down and walked past them. He waited on the opposite side of the road by the gates of the stable yard. There was no-one else about. He watched as the man left and headed towards Brady Street. He was about to go over to the woman when she appeared and crossed the road towards him. As she got onto the pavement, he stepped out, his heart pounding in his chest and he was breathing nervously. She looked at him, concerned.

"All right luv? You gave me a real fright then," she blurted out.

She said something else, but he couldn't make it out. Then he grabbed her by the throat and forced her to the ground.

Before she could scream or fight back, he had taken his knife out and cut her neck and throat from left to right, while kneeling at the right-hand side of his victim, to avoid getting blood on his clothes. Within a second, he had cut her throat again from ear to ear, almost decapitating her.

He lifted her skirts and wild with excitement, slashed at her abdomen. He heard something; someone was coming. He repeatedly stabbed her in her genitals and then made his escape quickly and silently. It was about 3.40am. He could smell the urine as her bladder had emptied onto the pavement.

He found himself in Thomas Street and near to the Whitechapel Workhouse Infirmary, he defecated with excitement. He composed himself and carefully made his way back to the heart of Spitalfields. In the distance, he could hear a policeman running towards Bucks Row.

Back in the security of his home, the killer was still excited. He commenced to masturbate and uttered the words, "that's for you, bitch, fuck you, fuck you all."

His rage started to subside when he ejaculated. He was now grinning and very pleased with himself.

"There's no time to scream or fight back when the froat is cut. It is quick and clean. That Tabram whore struggled too much. Why didn't I cut her froat first?" he said to himself.

The killer was expressing his satisfaction as if people were listening. His face was beaming with a smile.

"It's more fun cutting a woman's froat than it is cutting a horse. I'll fuckin' show them. I'll fuckin' show them all." The killer drank the remainder of a gin bottle and slept soundly. He had a feeling of elation, and it took a while for the feeling to subside.

At approximately 3.40am Charles Cross entered Bucks Row from Brady Street on his way to work. As he came towards New Cottage, he saw a bundle in the stable yard doorway. As he got nearer, he could make out that it was a woman. At first, he thought she was asleep or drunk. He then heard someone else walking towards him.

"Ere come and look at this, it's a woman," Cross blurted out. The other man, Robert Paul, also on his way to work, was a bit wary. He didn't know Cross or his intentions. He slowly made his way over to the body while keeping an eye on Cross. He saw the body and touched it, he could feel it was still warm, and there may have been a slight breath.

"The body is warm, I'm not sure if she's dead," Paul said quietly.

"We had better tell someone," Cross said. "We'll flag down a copper, come on!"

Robert Paul agreed. He didn't want to stay alone with the body. They made their way westwards and drew the attention of PC 55H Jonas Mizen, at about 3.45am.

"Officer we have just found a body in Bucks Row, a woman has been attacked," Robert Paul stated. They gave their names to the constable and carried on with their journey to work.

Almost immediately after Cross and Paul left Bucks Row, PC 97J, John Neil came across the body while walking his regular beat Eastwards in the direction of Brady Street. He knew the body was not there when he last walked the spot 30 minutes earlier. The time was about 3.45am. He started shining his lamp towards Brady Street to attract the attention of PC 96J John (Jack) Thain.

"Jack, go and fetch the doctor, quick!" he said and waited at the scene until PC Thain, and the doctor returned. PC Neil was

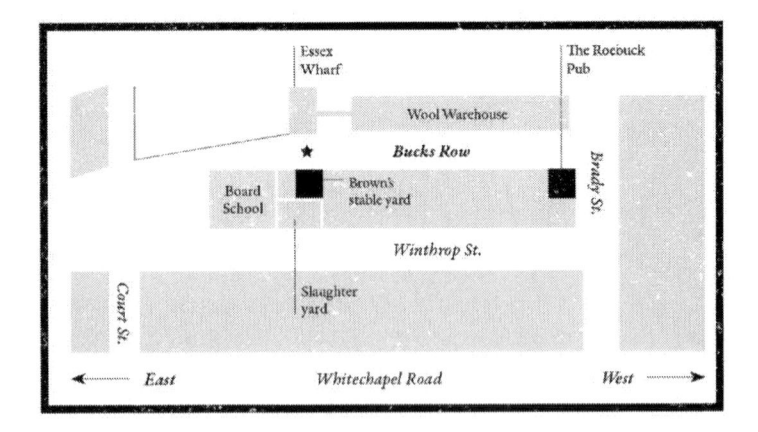

Map 3 – Bucks Row

Polly Nichols walked up Whitechapel Road and eventually into Brady Street. She solicited any night workers, and eventually picked a man up. They walked into Bucks Row and had intercourse in the gateway that was set slightly back between the Wool Warehouse and Essex Wharf.

Her killer had followed her, and watched her from the corner of the Roebuck pub. When Nichols and her punter go to the gateway, as mentioned above, he waited for her outside Brown's stable yard. This is the shaded area next to the murder spot.

Route of PC Neil 97J at Bucks Row 31st August 1888

3.15 am He started his beat from Brown's stable yard on Bucks Row, he walked Eastwards on the pavement next to the houses. He turned right into Brady Street then turned right again in Winthrop Street and he headed West. He then turned left into Court Street and headed towards Whitechapel Road, where he then turned left and walked Eastwards and turned left into Brady Street. He passed Winthrop Street, on his left, and then turned left into Bucks Row, and walked Westwards on the pavement next to the Wool Warehouse.

3.30 am He passed the murder site on the opposite pavement (he believed there was no body opposite at this point) and walked towards the Board School. He turned left here and walked Eastwards down Winthrop Street. (He may have stopped here at the slaughter yard for a chat and a cup of tea.) He then continued towards Brady Street and turned right, then right again to Whitechapel Road. He walked Westwards and turned right into Court Street and headed Eastwards down Bucks Row.

3.45 am He arrived at the murder spot outside the stable yard, from where he would normally recommence his route. A star indicates the murder spot.

The route forms a double figure of eight and takes 30 minutes in total. The murder was probably at 3.40am or just after.

Note: The Roebuck pub is shaded on the corner of Bucks Row and Brady Street.

shocked as he stared down at the lifeless body of Polly Nichols and could see blood oozing from her throat wound. PC Neil felt the victim's arm, which was quite warm and noted that her eyes were wide open. He was looking down at the work of a brutal murder that had been committed moments earlier. PC Neil rang the bell of the Essex Wharf, to see if anyone heard a disturbance, but the occupants told the constable that they heard nothing.

PC Mizen arrived at the scene from Whites Row at about 3.47am and was told by PC Neil to fetch the ambulance. About the same time, PC Thain was knocking on the door of Doctor Rees Ralph Llewellyn, at 152 Whitechapel Road, just around the corner from Brady Street.

"Doctor come quickly, Bucks Row, a woman is injured!" PC Thain said slightly breathlessly.

The doctor quickly dressed and took his bag, following the constable to the crime scene. Doctor Llewellyn was 38 years of age and had lived all his life in Whitechapel. He displayed a full-face beard and moustache and was a very respected doctor.

At the crime scene, at 4.00am, the doctor and PC Thain saw the body, as PC Mizen arrived with the handheld cart from the workhouse infirmary. The wooden wheels, of the ambulance cart, clattered on the cobbled road. PS 10J Henry Kirby soon came and started knocking on doors and asking if the residents heard anything. Doctor Llewellyn immediately pronounced that the woman was dead. He felt the woman's chest and heart and determined that she had been dead less than 30 minutes. The doctor could see that there was no evidence that she had been moved to this spot. He then said that she was to be transferred to the mortuary via the ambulance cart. The doctor noted, for his records, that Polly Nichols was lying on her back, lengthways across the entrance, with her left arm almost touching the stable yard door.

People were starting to turn up to the scene, including several workmen; the police, therefore, wanted to remove the body quickly. Both PC Thain and PS Kirby attempted to lift her body, one at each side of her. Immediately her head fell downwards towards her back, opening the neck wound.

"Shit, her head is coming off!" Kirby shouted.

PC Thain held the head up with his left hand and then placed her on the cart with Kirby's help.

The police constables knocked on the doors of the surrounding buildings, at about 4.00am. Both Emma Green of New Cottage (number 6), Bucks Row and Walter Purkiss of Essex Wharf, which was opposite the body, were questioned, but both heard nothing at all.

At about 4.20am, three men from the slaughter yard on Winthrop Street (Tomkins, Mumford and Brittan) visited the scene; again, they had heard nothing. It was as if the killer came from nowhere and vanished into thin air.

Inspector John Spratling, who is the divisional inspector of J Division, arrived at the scene at 4.30am, the body had already been taken to the mortuary. He talked to the remaining officers at the scene and then went to the mortuary.

Detective Inspector Fred Abberline of Central CID, Scotland Yard, was appointed to the case, in the absence of Reid, who had just commenced his annual leave. However, much of the police work was dealt with by J Division detectives.

The mortuary was in effect a very basic single-storey shed that was part of the Whitechapel Workhouse Infirmary in Eagle Place, just off Old Montague Street. It was in a poor state of repair, with little natural light and elementary facilities. Inspector Spratling saw the body was still on the ambulance cart and asked for the body to be moved inside. Robert Mann, one of the pauper inmates, then opened the mortuary at 5.00am. Robert suffered from fits and was known to be unreliable. He and another inmate called James Hatfield, an elderly man with a poor memory, placed the body on the table in the small mortuary room. Sergeant Enright, of J Division, told the two inmates that they must not touch the body. He stayed with the corpse while the two inmates took breakfast.

Inspector John Spratling entered the dark and dismal mortuary, just after 5.00am. He looked at the body and made notes of the victim's clothes, her height and appearance etc. He lifted her skirts and saw the deep wounds to the abdomen, which shocked him. The inspector could see that the back of her skirt was soaked in blood and urine. He held his nose as the smell was quite bad. Spratling knew the doctor would be unaware of the abdominal wounds; he, therefore, returned to Bucks Row and sent a message to Doctor Llewellyn, that there were further injuries on the victim. Inspector Spratling then continued to investigate the crime and looked for evidence on the railway lines. Sometime later, both Mann and Hatfield returned from breakfast and began stripping the body for the post-mortem.

The two inmates couldn't remember Sergeant Enright, who was now outside of the mortuary building, telling them not to touch the body. Doctor Llewellyn arrived at about 6.30am, to look at the wounds and later conducted the post-mortem. Several police officers, including Spratling and Helsen, turned up a short time after the doctor. Detective Inspector Joseph Helsen was 43 years old, and he was the local CID officer for J Division, the equivalent of Detective Inspector Reid at H Division.

"How do people expect me to work in these conditions? This is no place for a post-mortem," Doctor Llewellyn complained.

"I noticed these other wounds, Doctor, to her abdomen, I have never seen anything like it before," Inspector Spratling stated, trying his best to placate the doctor.

"These are severe wounds; they would have also caused instant death. None of them was self-inflicted."

"Are you suggesting they were carried out first and these wounds killed her?" Spratling asked in a surprised manner.

"It is difficult to tell. The throat wound would also cause a quick death. There are two deep cuts to the neck which severed all the neck arteries."

"What type of weapon would make those cuts, Doctor?" Inspector Helsen asked.

"A long-bladed, moderately sharp knife would make all the injuries, Inspector. The abdominal injuries appear to be running from left to right, which may indicate a left-handed person," the doctor stated.

Afterwards, in the slightly fresher air of the yard, Inspector Spratling starts a discussion with Detective Inspector Helsen.

"What do you make of that, Joe? What sort of person would do that?"

"I don't know John, but we do know that it's not suicide, thanks to the doctor."

"So, we are looking for a left-handed person Joe?"

"Not necessarily, those were rough cuts carried out very quickly, a sharp knife in either hand could make those cuts. Her neck was cut open when she was on the ground, so if the killer knelt on the right-hand side, he could cut her neck from left to right to avoid getting sprayed with blood. The killer could then move to a position between her legs for the abdominal cuts. He could do that with either hand."

"Oh! I see what you mean! Do you think the abdominal wounds were inflicted first, as the doctor thought?"

"No, John, it was clearly the neck wound. Why else would you cut the neck? Besides, if he attacked her abdomen first, she may have screamed or put up a fight. We know this did not happen," Helsen concluded.

The killer got up at about 11.00am and went downstairs to the pub. He heard some people talking about the murder he had committed, and this gave him a sense of satisfaction, that he knew something no-one else did.

"Ere, you are missen' all the gossip! Have you 'eard what 'appened last night?" his aunt asked.

"I've just 'eard someone talkin' about it. Where and when did it 'appen?"

"Near the workhouse, last night in Bucks Row. A woman was killed, it's bad, dreadful. I'm not goen' anywhere near there," Letty, said, clutching at her chest.

"Do they know who it was?" he asked.

"They 'avent found 'im yet, it's only been a few 'ours."

"Not 'im, 'er, 'er, that was killed, do the police know who she was?" he stated angrily.

"Well, I don't know that either. I'm sure we'll find out soon," she roared. "Anyway, where were you last night?"

"Out."

"Out where?"

"Out, out."

"It's like getting blood out of a stone, talken' to you! Never mind, I've got better things to do than talken' to the likes of you. Are you gonna make yourself useful for a change?"

"Fuck off."

"Don't you 'fuck off' me or I'll knock that fucken' head of yours, clean off your fucken' shoulders, ya cunt," she responded, very angrily.

"Sorry, Auntie, you know what I mean," he said apologetically.

She was the only person he deferred to, and this was as much out of fear as it was out of respect. She was too big and strong to get on the wrong side of.

He left his aunt's establishment and ventured out, heading towards Bucks Row. He liked to see the reaction that he had caused. Visiting the murder sites gave him a feeling of power and satisfaction, where he could relive his experience. He walked up Old Montague Street, passing people on his way. There were plenty of people begging for any change – barefooted kids playing in the street, looking for something to steal or eat. Shops and businesses were open, for those with money, but there was a lot of hardship and hunger amongst the non-working poor. He regularly saw people standing in the cold, early in the morning, for two or three hours to get into one of the Salvation Army churches. This was followed by two hours of a sermon on how God loves them, followed by a small cup of soup and a piece of bread. *'Mugs,'* he thought to himself, with no pity for them.

The Whitechapel Workhouse Mortuary was in Eagle Place, near the end of Old Montague Street, where it meets Bakers Row. He stopped there and waited to see if anyone was speaking about the murder. He couldn't get close to the mortuary as there was a PC guarding the entrance; he would go back later. He moved towards Bucks Row, where there was still a crowd and slowly walked directly to the spot where he had killed Polly Nichols.

"What's been goin' on 'ere then?" he asks a woman at the door nearest to the murder spot.

She was happy to oblige him in recounting the events of the early morning. He listened intently, enjoying every word, but said nothing. He then headed towards Whitechapel Road.

Whitechapel Road was one of the main roads in the area. It was a wide road with shops and pubs on either side. He turned left onto Union Street, just before St. Mary Matfelon's Church. The previous church on this site was painted white, hence the name Whitechapel. He didn't visit any of the churches; he had no religion. He looked after himself and didn't need anyone.

He came to the junction with Commercial Road, the other main road of the area, then crossed over this road and walked around the area, looking in the shop windows. Already he was surveying the area for another kill, checking to see if there were plenty of potential places for killing and the means of escape. He wanted to build up his knowledge of the immediate surroundings where a murder may take place.

It was a bit quieter here than in Spitalfields and consisted mostly of terraced houses, but there were still pubs, prostitutes, children in rags, and old people sat outside the houses. Many Jews in this area, were trying their best to make a decent living, but they were subject to a lot of abuse. He then sauntered onto Fairclough Street and up Berner Street, looking for pubs that he could observe from, then he went back onto Commercial Road.

Fred Abberline was the ideal man to have in charge, because he knew the area as good as anyone. He had been the local CID Inspector at H Division for nine years, until his promotion.

Inspectors Abberline and Helsen discussed the events of the day following Abberline's visit to the mortuary to see the body. They were in Helsen's office at the Ainsley Street Police Station. They were both calm and were relaxing with a mug of tea each.

"We have been able to identify the victim, Fred. She was Mary Ann Nichols, also known as Polly, and had been, at some point, an inmate of the Lambeth Workhouse, from the identification marks on her clothing. We were then able to contact her next of kin from the workhouse records. Her father, Edward Walker of 15 Maidwell Street Camberwell, has formally identified her. She had been lodging at both 55 Flower and Dean Street and 18 Thrawl Street. The father also said that she was married to William Nichols, who is a printer's machinist. We are looking for him as we speak. The father hasn't seen her for over two years. He confirmed that she drank, which led to the marriage break up. She was the mother of five children. She left her husband and children about seven years ago," Helsen added.

"Good work on the early identification of the victim. I have never seen anything like it, Joe, it's hard to believe. I went to the mortuary yesterday to see the body for myself, and then I talked to Doctor Llewellyn. There was a killing earlier this month in George Yard. Do you think there is any connection?"

"Well, both victims were prostitutes, Fred, and both were stabbed. But the injuries are different. This victim today has had her throat cut, very deep down to the spine. A large knife would be needed. The murdered woman in George Yard was stabbed mainly with a clasp knife and no neck cutting. If they are by different persons, then we have two maniacs on the loose."

"I wish Edmund were here for this; he has a nose for this sort of thing. We will treat both enquiries separately for now. We will see what leads each enquiry picks up. I will take an overview of both enquiries to share information where necessary. We don't want to start chasing shadows that don't exist. We need to find people that can verify the whereabouts of Polly Nichols, such as other prostitutes and her clients. Where did she normally go? Had she any enemies, etc?"

"I think you're right, Fred. Edmund was well into the Tabram Case. We asked some the residents of 18 Thrawl Street, who knew the victim, to formally identify her also. I am sure something will turn up soon."

Helsen studied Abberline for a moment, then adds "What is it? You look worried."

"Well Joe, as you have just said, we either have two men at large that have each stabbed a prostitute to death recently, or we have one man who has killed twice."

"It would be difficult to imagine two separate killers operating in the same area at the same time."

"I agree. So, there must be some link, but we don't know what."

"But why would one man separately kill two prostitutes?"

"I don't know Joe; I just have a weird feeling that we are dealing with some sort of maniac. The woman was nearly decapitated and then almost disembowelled. Was it personal? Was it an estranged husband, or was it something else? How could anyone be that angry? What the fuck is going on? Put the detective sergeants and constables that you have, on the case. Divide the work up between everyone. We will then meet up to see what we have got. Is that clear Joe?"

"Yes, Fred. I will get on with that now."

"I will go and see if there is anything in the Tabram case notes."

Inspector Abberline started to head back to Whitechapel, to Leman Street. He wanted to see what progress has been made on the Tabram case, in Reid's absence. He had to work his way through the crowds of people. Whitechapel and Spitalfields were very busy with people during the day. The place was teeming with all those who stay in the common lodging houses as well as the homeless. There was also a significant influx of people coming into the area to work, and this also helped to swell the streets and the pubs.

September 3rd
Abberline's investigations

Inspectors Abberline and Helsen attended the inquest into the death of Polly Nichols, which was opened on the Saturday morning of the 1st of September and again on Monday the 3rd of September. It was held at the Working Lads Institute, Whitechapel Road by the coroner Mr Wynne Baxter.

Abberline and Helsen discussed the inquest that they have just attended:

"We haven't been able to find which streets she normally worked, Fred. There are not that many people about from 2.30am to 3.40am when the body was found. There are some slaughter yards around Bucks Row, but no-one saw the victim."

"Two prostitutes have been murdered in August. One behind us in Bucks Row and one in Spitalfields at George Yard. There are a lot of prostitutes working Spitalfields, but less of them working around Bucks Row. Why would the killer also kill one here? Does he live or work around here?" Abberline added, "If he wanted to kill prostitutes, wouldn't he have a better chance in Spitalfields?"

"Maybe he got lucky, Fred. Maybe he was out on the streets and came across her. It does seem strange, as you say. What type of person walks the streets looking for prostitutes to kill?"

"I don't know, Joe. My first suspect is always the husband, and I am normally right. We don't know if the two stabbings are related, because the wounds were different; they were from different weapons. We have too many questions and not enough answers. Get men to ask about if they have seen either woman, in pubs, lodging houses, other women working the streets. Someone must have seen something."

"Do you think that there are two killers, Fred?"

"It could be a gang who have a gripe with some prostitutes, but I can't see that either. We just have to keep looking until something turns up."

Helsen was struggling to understand the case and Abberline was not much wiser.

"There's nothing at the inquest as well, Fred. We have interviewed all those witnesses from both inquest days. So, the murderer may be a stranger to the victims. There has to be some motive, but it wasn't a robbery."

"Let's go over the witnesses, again Joe."

Helsen took out his notebook and flicked through a few pages, then started talking.

"William Nichols, the estranged husband, confirmed the father's story of the victim. He has formally identified her, as did Ellen Holland of the same lodging house as the victim, 18 Thrawl Street. She was the last person to see the victim alive at 2.30am, on Whitechapel High Street, near Osborn Street. She also confirmed that the victim also lodged in Flower and Dean Street."

Abberline interrupts Helsen's recap of the witnesses. He was getting more and more frustrated. His 'local knowledge policing' was not working in this case.

"What I don't understand, Joe, is where the victim had been from 2.30am. Why had no-one seen her? Not even the police on their beats. Where had she been? She didn't have any enemies."

Helsen gave a blank look to Abberline and turned his hands palms up, as if to say, 'your guess is as good as mine'. He carried on with his overview of the case.

"From the crime scene, we have statements from Charles Cross and Robert Paul, who found the victim in Bucks Row at about 3.40am. There are some discrepancies as to the exact time.

Cross was there with the victim when Paul arrived. They briefly checked the victim and went in search of a policeman and found PC 56H Mizen in Baker's Row. He confirmed the time was about 3.45am. Both men were on their way to work and have been checked out."

"So, it is in all probability, the murder occurred sometime between 3.30am, and 3.40am," Abberline stated and Helson nodded.

"PC Neil found her body at 3.45am and called immediately to PC Thain, to fetch the doctor. She was killed, and no-one has seen or heard anything. The three horse-slaughterers, in Winthrop Street, heard nothing. Neither did Patrick Mulshaw a night watchman also in Winthrop Street. Emma Green and Walter Purkiss who live next to the murder scene, both heard nothing also."

"We have nothing, have we? No one has seen or heard the victim or the killer. We are chasing ghosts," Abberline said dejectedly.

"A ghost with a big bloody knife, Fred. We do know the doctor said it was a long sharp knife and she was killed on the spot. He thinks the killer could be left-handed, but I am much less confident. The killer is taking a chance, not to be seen though."

"Reid is back next week, and maybe he will have some ideas. Until then, we need to get men to ask in the pubs and her lodgings if they have seen her last Friday. We need to know if she argued, with anyone. Put her photograph in the press and ask for anyone who had seen her, to come forward, in confidence."

"There may be another murder by then, Fred, if he is killing strangers."

"Don't say that Joe, don't say that. We can't cope with another one."

The killer walked into the Frying Pan pub on Brick Lane, ordered a pint of porter then sat down and listened to the gossip and banter. One of his workmates at the slaughterhouse came up to him and sat down.

"What you doin' in 'ere? Haven't I seen you in 'ere before?"

"I come in 'ere now and again, saw Bill in 'ere before 'e got me the job."

"Did you 'ear about the murders?"

"Course I did, everyone knows."

"Who do ya fink it is, what dunnit?"

"Might be you, you're good wiv a knife." It gave the killer pleasure to accuse someone else of his crime.

"Nah, don't be daft. It's some lunatic, a nutter. That's what the police fink."

"There's lots of nutters in 'ere. The police don't even know if it is one killer or two different killers. It is someone who goes with prostitutes, I fink."

"Well, there's a lot that does that," the workmate said.

"I don't. Do you?"

"Nah, I've got me a girl. You're bound to catch somefink from 'em anyway. Why do you fink he is killin' whores then?"

"You ask too many stupid questions. How the fuck do I know?"

"Sorry mate, I was only makin' conversation and that," his colleague said apologetically.

"There may be more yet when fings 'ave quietened down a bit," the killer stated confidently.

"I take me knife wiv me in case he attacks me."

"You dumb cunt. This killer attacks whores, not men. Anyways you wouldn't stand a fuckin' chance, knife or no knife."

"I'm fuckin' glad I'm not a woman."

Abruptly the killer stood up, "right, I'm goin' now, see you later." He didn't like conversation much and people in general annoyed him.

"Fuckin' had to get away from his rabbitin,' does me fuckin 'ead in 'e does." the killer said quietly to himself.

He went back to the Princess Alice pub to do some bar work. This way he got to know what was going on, without suspicion and he got paid in beer, which he liked.

The murder of Polly Nichols had certainly shaken people up. Prostitutes were going around in two's or three's, and people were avoiding the streets after midnight. The newspapers were playing on people's fears, and so were the churches. Their sermons claimed that the poor prostitutes were killed by the wrath of God for their immoral lifestyles. Prostitutes and the poor alike were told to repent of their sins or suffer eternal damnation in Hell. Spitalfields was already a living hell for many people, whose only sin was to be born poor. The Salvation Army continually preached about the evils of alcohol but were prepared to continuously enter public houses to take donations mainly from poor people. Hypocrisy was rife in Spitalfields, many men and well-to-do gentlemen, who used and abused prostitutes, happily filled church pews on a Sunday.

Following the murder of Polly Nichols, policemen on their beats were looking out for any trouble between men and prostitutes. At Leman Street Station, a police officer had brought in a man and a woman who were being charged with assault. The man was about fifty years old, with a limp and was quite fat. He wore a shabby suit and had large sideburns and a beard. The woman was well known to the police as a common prostitute.

"It's not what you think, officer, she tried to steal my wallet. I hit her to get it back, that is all," the man explained.

"Take them both down there," the desk sergeant, said to the young constable who had arrested them. He then sat them down and removed their handcuffs.

Detective Inspector Walter Beck sat them down in his small office.

"Now I don't want any nonsense or lies from you two; we're too busy with these murders. Is that clear?" Beck said forcefully.

"Alice, this man stated to the officer that you tried to steal his wallet, is that true?"

"Wew, I can't 'elp it can I? I needs the money, don't I?" she replied.

"Were you two having sex in the street?"

"No, certainly not, officer; she came up to me from behind and tried to grab my wallet. I tried to pull it off her, but she wouldn't let go, so I hit her, that's when the police officer came."

"Is that true, Alice?"

"Wew, sort of, but he hit me," she replied, putting her hand up to her cheek as if it was still sore.

"The likes of you deserve all you get; you are a thief and a drunken whore. You will be arrested, for theft, drunkenness and prostitution, is that clear?"

"You are free to go, sir. We will need your details and a statement as evidence, sir."

"I am not in trouble for hitting her?" the man asked.

"There is no evidence of that, sir. You were just protecting your property. The drunken woman fell and injured herself if you take my meaning, sir."

"Thank you, officer," the man said as he left the station.

There were several of these incidents involving prostitutes, and after the killing of Polly Nichols the police started to take such claims more seriously.

September 8th
The killing of Annie Chapman

Annie Chapman was not in the best of health; she had breathing difficulties and was also hungry. She was 45 years old and five-foot-tall, with a fair complexion, a large, thick nose, blue eyes and dark brown wavy hair. Annie was a woman of a medium frame. She was not a beauty, much like most women in Whitechapel and elsewhere. On this day, as with most days, she was wearing the same worn-out, old clothes, comprising of a black jacket, brown bodice, black skirt and lace-up boots. She resided at Crossingham's Lodging House, at 35 Dorset Street, Spitalfields.

Early in the evening of the 7th of September, Annie was taking a drink of rum in the Ten Bells pub and was sat with a friend from the lodging house. They could not help overhearing the loud voice of Mary Kelly, who was stood at the bar with three Irish men. The quartet were all drinking Guinness and telling Irish jokes.

"Oh, I feel like shit to be 'onest," said Annie while coughing.

"You don't look too well; you need to go back to the 'ospital," her friend said.

She was a prostitute and like Annie, spent most of her earnings on drink.

"I fink I will; I 'avent got the strenf to go on. Me chest hurts and I can't breave, prop'ly," Annie wheezed her words out slowly.

"We'll go back to the doss 'ouse after, and you can get your 'ed down and see 'ow you are in the mornin."

"I need anovver drink or two yet to get me to sleep; I'll then get me doss money," Annie mournfully said as if all life and energy was draining away from her.

At about 7.00pm she staggered back to the doss house and stayed in the kitchen, where it was warm. Unfortunately for Annie, she had spent her doss money and didn't feel like going out again as it was now around 1.45am to 2.00am.

"Can you let me 'ave a bed for the night?" she asked Timothy Donovan, the deputy manager of the house.

"Not unless you have the money, Annie," he replied.

"I'll soon 'ave it," she said, as she coughed, and left the doss house.

Earlier in the week, Annie was given a black eye by Eliza Cooper at Crossingham's, over a piece of soap. The bruise had now faded into yellow, making her more unattractive. There had also been disagreements between the pair due to Annie accusing Eliza of theft. The row later broke out again in the Britannia pub. This popular pub was situated on the Eastern end of Dorset Street, where it met Commercial Road. The pub was commonly known as 'Ringers' after the name of the landlord.

Annie had no luck in making her doss money, and she was tired. She found a place at the back of Spitalfields market to rest unseen. Annie fell asleep for a while but was awakened by a noise in the market; stallholders were getting ready, so she got to her feet and hoped to be able to get a client and get some money.

It was early on Saturday morning that Annie found herself walking down Hanbury Street looking for business that could provide her with somewhere to sleep or something to eat. Usually, it would be something to drink, but she didn't have the energy now.

Annie carried her meagre possessions with her; a few pills, a small comb, two brass rings on her fingers, a small tablet of soap and a couple of farthings. Not enough for a bed for the night. Her suffering, as a frail, alcoholic prostitute, would soon be over.

Hanbury Street joined Commercial Street at its Western End, and here it was near to Spitalfields market. The Eastern End terminated at Bakers Row, very close to Bucks Row, where the murder of Polly Nichols took place a week before. Just to the North of Hanbury Street and stretching Eastwards to Brick Lane, was the massive Truman's brewery.

Hanbury Street consisted of three-storey Georgian terraced houses on either side, at the Western end. Initially built for one family each, they were now home to several families, each one rented a room to live and sleep in. At number 29, six different tenants occupied the house, totalling 17 people.

A cold and hungry Annie staggered slowly down Hanbury Street and stopped outside number 29. A man was coming towards her from the opposite direction. She said something to the man, and the man replied, "Will you?" Just at that moment, a woman walked past them and looked at Annie, the time was 5.30am. Annie's date with death was almost upon her...

A week had passed since his second successful kill, and now he craved more. The experience as a slaughterman had helped him to hone his killing talent. He was up early, it was about 4.00am, but he was not working today. He'd had another nightmare about his mother. She is lying there on a bed, and he takes his knife and disembowels her. But she is not dead, and she attacks him with a knife, calling him a *'useless cock-sucker'*. He woke and then started shaking uncontrollably for a minute or two; he was having another fit. As he recovered and slowly came to, he began to feel rage again.

"She is there when I'm asleep; she is there when I'm awake. Why can't she leave me alone?" He said out loud to himself.

Sometime after 5.00am, he left the pub and walked North-Eastwards from his home. Due to his recent fit, he was just walking carefully and slowly and hoping to come to. He was more paranoid now and felt that other people were now watching him. He wore dark clothes, like many men, and always has a hat on to help hide his face.

As he was walking up Hanbury Street, he heard the chimes of Christ Church, indicating that it was 5.30am. As he continued towards Spitalfields market, he saw a woman stood on the pavement outside one of the houses. She had said something to a man, but he moved off. Hanbury Street was quite busy with people on their way to work. The killer walked in her direction.

"Hello sir, are you wanting any business?" she asked.

"What?" he replied, slightly taken aback, as he was still in pain.

"I'll do whatever you need," she added.

"Right, then," he said, as he became more alert.

"Come on through 'ere," she stated, as she put her hand on his chest, and then led him down the dark corridor of doom, towards the back door. She entered the back yard first.

"Which way do you want to do it?" she asked.

He turned towards her and unleashed his anger and pain by grabbing her throat with both hands. He threw her to the yard floor, banging her against the fence on the way down. Her meagre essential possessions fell from her pockets. With his left hand on her throat, he took his knife in his right hand and cut her throat deeply from left to right, from ear to ear. Blood spurted low down onto the fence. A moment later, a second even deeper cut to her neck. By cutting her throat away from him, he avoided getting splattered and sprayed with the victims' arterial blood. All life had gone in an instant, but he was not finished with her yet.

He took his knife and cut through her clothes from her chest and through the length of her skirt. He pulled the clothing apart to reveal her naked body. He stabbed his knife into her abdomen and cut downwards to her vulva. He cut her again, opening the gut and exposing the intestines. He cut into them and lifted some of them out of the body cavity and threw them across her right shoulder. Further skin and intestines were draped over the left shoulder. The killer cut out her uterus, with two rapid cuts of his blade, taking with it a large part of the bladder and some skin. He took this organ because it was an intimate feminine part of his victim. He stood up panting for breath, banging the fence in the process. His eyes were wide with excitement; his anger subsided with each second. He noticed two rings on her fingers, and took them as souvenirs, by wrenching them off. He wrapped the uterus and the bladder parts, in some wax paper that he had brought with him. He used her clothes to wipe his hands and his blade. He put his blade away and left the scene of carnage, through the door where he entered a mere five minutes ago.

As he stepped onto the pavement outside number 29, he bumped into a woman and almost knocked her over. She grabbed hold of him to stop herself falling, and they both looked at each other.

"You are in hurry?" she said in a foreign accent.

He immediately pulled away and ran off. The woman who was about five-foot-two-inches tall and in her forties was shocked at the look of fear upon his damaged face.

He moved onto Spitalfields market where he bought some meat from a butcher's and then made his way back home, carrying his two parcels, as if nothing has happened. He realised that he had reached a new level of crime. He had gutted a woman like other people gut an animal; he washed his hands and cleaned the knife, then went into the pub to drink.

He had no hate for the woman herself; he was butchering his mother by releasing his anger on the woman. His mother was still there though, in his head, making him angry. He drank ale, more ale and more ale until she was no longer there. The butchering and disembowelling bought sexual excitement to him; he enjoyed the act with a feeling of euphoria and achievement.

He kept the body parts in a glass jar, filled with water and salt, hidden in the cellar. He saw the organs as a token of his work and felt a sense of power as a result. If it hadn't been for his job as a slaughterman, he would have never thought of taking the body parts. But it seemed quite natural now, as he had got used to cutting animals open and holding their insides in his bloodstained hands. To him, Annie Chapman's uterus was just another piece of flesh.

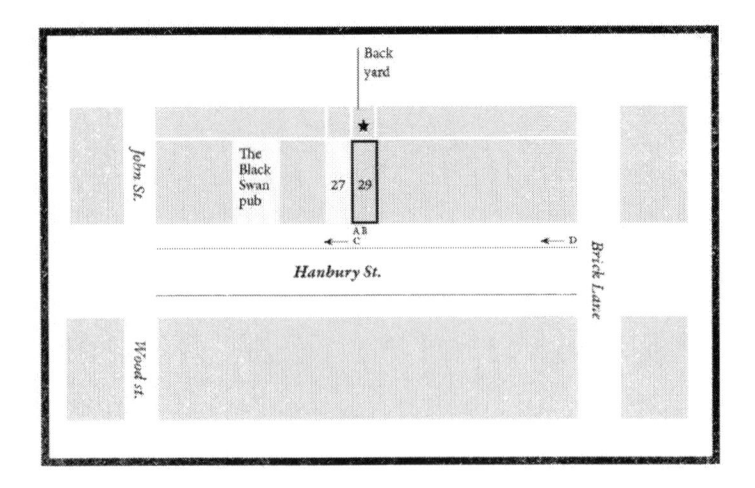

Map 4 – Hanbury Street

The star denotes the position of Annie Chapman's body, when found just before 6am, at number 29 Hanbury Street. It was lying between the fence and the steps leading into the yard. ★

On the same pavement, at 5.30am Elizabeth Long (C) passed Annie Chapman (A) standing still and talking to a man (B). Mrs Long had just walked down Brick Lane and turned right into Hanbury Street on her way to the market. The man was facing Annie so he had his back to Mrs Long, who could clearly see Annie's face. As she passed the couple, she managed to see the man's face as he looked at her.

The killer of Annie Chapman was at position (D) and walked slowly towards her. He had walked up Brick Lane and turned left into Hanbury Street. As the man talking to Annie walked off, she was then approached by her killer.

At number 27, Albert Cadosh heard noises coming from the yard of number 29 at approximately 5.20-5.25am. This therefore cannot be Annie and the killer.

John Davis was a resident of 29 Hanbury Street. He occupied the front room with his wife and three adult sons. Just before 6.00am, he visited the backyard, and he immediately saw the dead, mutilated body of Annie Chapman lying on her back with her head between the steps and the fence. He was instantly shocked and nauseated, and he steadied himself against the wall for a few moments to catch his breath. He then rushed out into the street to find a policeman. He saw two men in Hanbury Street.

"There's been a murder, come and see!" Davis pants out to the two men, who worked for a packing crate maker.

Davis and the two men rushed back to number 29 and viewed the body. They then rushed out of the house and went in different directions to tell a policeman and anyone else that they could find.

The first police officer on the scene was Detective Inspector Joseph Chandler, of H Division, who was on early duty at the Commercial Street Police Station. He saw men running up Hanbury Street, and he followed them and arrived at the house at approximately 6.10am. He secured the scene as best he could and removed people from the corridor at 29 Hanbury Street. John Davis and the two men returned to the house and identified themselves to Inspector Chandler, as James Kent and James Green, who worked at 23a Hanbury Street for Mr Bailey. He also covered the body, with some sacking material that was in the yard, he then sent a constable to fetch a doctor. By this time a mob had congregated outside the house.

Doctor George Bagster Phillips arrived at 29 Hanbury Street at approximately 6.30am. He coldly stated the obvious, that she was dead and pronounced that she had been dead at least two hours, by a mere touch of the body. He then said that she should be moved to the Whitechapel mortuary. Doctor Phillips made notes about the body in-situ, and mentioned aspects of it to Inspector Chandler,

"The victim looks as though she has been posed, Inspector, with her legs drawn up and her knees pointing outwards."

"Yes, Doctor, her tongue is also swollen. Would you say that is a result of strangulation?" Chandler asked.

"It is likely, Inspector; the post-mortem will confirm it."

"I've never seen such mutilations before Doctor, have you?"

"Never Inspector," Doctor Phillips said in a shocked tone.

Sergeant 31H Edmund Barry conveyed the body to the mortuary on the hand cart ambulance. Inspector Chandler arrived at the mortuary just after 7.00am, and the body was still on the ambulance and was undisturbed. PC 376H Barnes was left in charge of the body.

Later in the day, as Inspector Chandler submitted his initial report into the case, he was entrusted with the enquiries because Detective Inspector Reid was still on annual leave. Detective Inspector Fred Abberline took overall charge of this case as well as the murder of Polly Nichols.

Detectives Chandler and Abberline were discussing the enquiries to date, in the afternoon of the 8th of September, at the Commercial Street Police Station. Abberline was now perplexed, he knew that it was improbable that there were three separate knife killers targeting prostitutes at the same time.

"The dead woman has been identified as Annie Chapman or Siffey," Inspector Chandler stated while looking at his notebook. "She has already been identified at the mortuary by Timothy Donovan, who is the deputy manager at Crossingham's lodging house, 35 Dorset Street, where she has lived for the past few months. Donovan had known her for 16 months and knew that she was a prostitute. She was in the kitchen of the lodging house from 7.00pm till about 2.00am when she was asked to leave," Chandler added without taking a breath. "Amelia Farmer also from a lodging house at 30 Dorset Street, identified her and added that the victim had been complaining of being unwell all week. John Evans, the night watchman at Crossingham's, stated that he saw the victim leave the house at about 1.45am and head towards Brushfield Street."

Inspector Chandler went on, reading from his notebook. "The victim was seen by Elizabeth Long outside 29 Hanbury Street at 5.30am this morning, talking to a man. The witness couldn't see the man's face, but heard him say *'will you,'* and said he looked foreign and was in his forties. She recognised the woman as being the same as the one in the mortuary. This woman, Long, was on her way to Spitalfields market via Hanbury Street."

"We may have to ask her again if she can remember anything else about this man that Chapman was with," said Abberline in a supporting manner.

Inspector Chandler continued his narrative. "There was another witness, a Mr Albert Cadosh of 27 Hanbury Street. Now, this is interesting, Fred. He says he got up at 5.15am to go to the toilet, before leaving for work. Cadosh states that after having a tomtit, he makes his way back to the house and hears a *'no'* from next door."

Abberline was about to speak, but Chandler continued.

"After a few minutes, he needs to go again." Abberline opens his mouth. Chandler continues unabated. "When Cadosh comes back out, he hears something fall against the fence. He goes through the house and leaves for work at 5.30am. Just when Long is supposed to have seen the victim outside."

Abberline put his hand on Chandler's shoulder.

"Joe, let me just stop you there. If Cadosh is right about the time, then she was killed somewhere between 5.20am, and 5.30am, say. Then Long can't have seen Chapman outside at 5.30am because she is already dead."

"Yes Fred, but that's not all. At about 4.40am to 4.45am this morning, a John Richardson of number 2 John Street, went into the backyard and stated that there was definitely no dead body. He is the son of Amelia Richardson, who rents most of the ground floor and the yard making packing crates. He went round to see if the place was still secure. He says he sat on the backyard steps to cut some leather from his boot, so we know she was still alive at 4.45am this morning."

"Didn't the doctor say that she had been dead two hours, when he saw the body at 6.30am this morning?"

"Yes Fred, so if the doctor is right, then Long, Cadosh and Richardson are mistaken, all three being wrong is a bit of a coincidence, Fred, don't you think?"

"The doctor could be wrong, Joe," Abberline stated, getting a word in quickly. "It is cold in the early hours, she would have lost a lot of heat, after being ripped open. She could have been cold when the doctor got there, one hour later."

"I think you are right, Fred. This Cadosh geezer is certain of his timings because the Christ Church clock was at 5.32am when he passed it, which is just around the corner."

"So, this woman, Elizabeth Long, she must be mistaken with the time."

"That's what I thought Fred, but she is also adamant of her times. She says she knew it was 5.30am because of the Brewery clock."

"Where are we Joe, on the woman's movements this morning?"

"Well Fred, we have asked about at lodging houses, alehouses, the market etc. and nothing after 2.00am this morning. She left Crossingham's about 1.45am walking towards the market or Brushfield Street. No-one has clocked her since, but enquiries are still being made though, and something may turn up."

"Check all the witnesses again and ask all the street if they have seen anything, anything. Don't leave a stone unturned. For example, did someone else see Long at the market, to corroborate her story? Or was anyone else walking up that street about 5.30am that saw Long, Chapman or a man? Know what I mean, Joe?"

"Yes, Fred, absolutely crystal."

"Oh, and Joe."

"Yes, Fred."

"Check the story of the man who found the body. What was he called?"

"Davis, John Davis"

"See if he can give you an exact time when he found the body."

"Will do Fred, leave it to me."

"I am going over to see Joe Helsen at J Division. I want his opinion. I think this murder and the one at Bucks Row are done by the same person. I want him to see the body, and, I want the doctor's view on whether they are related."

"Of all the bloody weeks to take a holiday! Edmund, what were you bloody thinking?" Abberline muttered to himself. He was not happy.

Robert Mann placed the body into the mortuary at around 7.00am and remained with the body until the post-mortem. Just after 2.00pm on Saturday the 8th of September, Doctor Phillips arrived at the workhouse mortuary in Eagle Place for the post-mortem of Annie Chapman. As with Doctor Llewellyn, he raised objections about the unsatisfactory working conditions of the building and the fact that the body had already been stripped and washed by Elizabeth Simmonds and Francis Wright.

Doctor Phillips made a more detailed examination of the body. Later that day he recounted his findings and opinions to Inspector Abberline.

"Inspector Abberline, I have completed the post-mortem on the body found at Hanbury Street. I will give you the particulars and answer any of your questions."

"Thank you, Doctor, and by the way, her name was Annie Chapman. She has been identified."

"Thank you, Inspector. The woman was strangled and forced onto the ground. There is bruising around the face and chest, and her tongue was swollen. There were abrasions on the ring finger where two rings have been forcibly removed. Death would have been instantaneous due to the throat and neck being deeply severed. The uterus was removed and also part of the bladder."

"What sort of weapon was used, Doctor?"

"A knife six-to-eight inches long, a thin narrow blade, but not a sword or bayonet. A surgical post-mortem knife may have been responsible, as would a well ground down slaughterman's knife. Smaller knives used by the leather trade would not be long enough."

"Who might have done this Doctor? What sort of person would do this?"

"There were indications of anatomical knowledge, but the work was carried out in haste. My opinion of the time of death still stands. I would say she had been dead two hours, possibly more, from when I saw the deceased at approximately 6.30am this morning. However, Inspector, it was a cool morning, and the body would cool down quickly following the loss of a great quantity of blood."

"So, it is possible that it could be less than two hours?"

"It is possible."

"Did she put up a fight?"

"No, there was no evidence of a struggle. The woman was killed quickly, as she lay on the ground. He took hold of her by the chin and cut her throat from left to right. There are several blood marks low down on the fence. The post-mortem also revealed that she had brain and lung disease, but these did not cause death. The stomach was empty and did not contain alcohol. She was very badly fed."

"You said someone with anatomical knowledge might have done this, Doctor. Are you saying he could be a surgeon or medical man?"

"I don't think a surgeon. If I were to do this work, it would take me at least 15 minutes and maybe up to one hour, if it was done deliberately. Someone with a more basic knowledge of anatomy may be more likely, Inspector."

Abberline was keen to get Phillips' opinion on both murders. "Could you say if this killing and the one in Bucks Row are similar and done by the same hand?"

"The injuries are similar, but the injuries here are more severe," the Doctor said unconvincingly.

"Thank you, Doctor," Abberline stated as he left the surgery.

"I will, of course, make my full report to the inquest available to you as soon as practicable, Inspector. Good evening."

Later, Inspector Abberline caught up with Inspector Helsen, who had just seen the body of Annie Chapman in the mortuary.

"Well, Joe, what do you think, the same hand?"

"Definitely Fred. Both had their throats deeply cut left to right, and then the abdomen was mutilated. He was probably disturbed with the Bucks Row one and couldn't finish the mutilations."

"Thanks, Joe, those are my views also, but Doctor Phillips seems hesitant in confirming that. He is very vague about the time of death. The doctor also seems to feel that the killer would have taken from 15 minutes to possibly one hour to carry out the mutilations, but I can't see it taking anywhere near 15 minutes."

"The doctor doesn't want to commit to anything Fred, he is erring on the side of caution, possibly because he is unsure, but won't admit it."

"I agree, Joe, a surgeon would give us a more accurate time."

"This one is a real mess, Fred. He has killed twice in just over a week. Who do you think did this?"

"It is getting beyond me. I was speaking to Edmund before he left; we were talking about two other stabbings and the two murders. I would like his opinion if he thinks all these attacks are related. I don't think so myself."

"It is possible Fred; otherwise, there are two killers loose."

"What I don't understand Joe, is why nobody has seen him or has some inkling as to whom it may be. I rely on local knowledge for my policing and nothing is coming up."

"Maybe Edmund can shed new light on it, Fred, when he gets back on Monday."

"I hope so, I have everyone from above on my back now, including the press. I need a drink."

"I'll second that Fred, come on."

They carried on their conversations as they walked to a pub.

"There have been three murders in a month, Joe and none of the beat coppers have seen anything. No-one has heard a scream or seen a struggle, nothing. What's going on here? I am lost with this."

"I agree Fred, It is strange, not only three deaths, but no-one has seen or heard anything."

They then both carried on walking silently, with worried looks upon their faces.

September 9th
The killer is arrested

The killer did not take his large knife to work with him; a slaughter knife is different from a dagger. He was on his way home when he saw a prostitute in Angel Alley. As he got close to her, she said something to him, and he favourably responded. He got hold of the prostitute around her neck, and she screamed a little as she was surprised. He then lifted her skirt and felt a hand on his shoulder. As he turned around, he saw a policeman standing next to him.

"Right, you two are coming with me for questioning," he said as he handcuffed them together.

"We were only talkin' officer, I know her," the killer said.

"That's right, we know each ovver," the woman concurred.

"This is all your fault for screamin'. You, stupid whore," he said to the woman. He did not accept responsibility for anything.

"You got me round the neck; what do ya expect me to do?"

"Well, you can tell us all about it when you get to the station. Move!" the constable said.

At the station, the constable brought them up to the desk sergeant.

"Hello, Alice, not you again!" the desk sergeant said.

"I 'avent done nuffink," she replied.

"Take them down there, one of the detectives will see them," the desk sergeant ordered.

"Both of you wait here," the constable said as he sat them both down on a bench and took the handcuffs off them.

Sergeant Stephen White was familiar with the recent murders, as he had questioned witnesses and residents in both Bucks Row and Hanbury Street.

"Alright, Alice, you first," the sergeant said as he ushered her into his office.

"We are only looking after you, Alice; there is a killer about. Have you seen this man before?"

"No sir, I was bein' careful like. It's not dark proper, yet," she replied.

"Well, take someone with you in future; it is too dangerous at the moment being in Angel Alley and the like," Sergeant White stated firmly. "Go on; you can go," he added.

"Right your turn," Sergeant White said to the man.

"Name," the sergeant asked, and the man gave his name although part of it was false.

"Where do you live?" White asked quickly. He had been doing this all day.

"Princess Alice pub," he replied abruptly.

"Are you working?" White enquired.

The killer replied that he worked at a slaughterhouse and he had just finished work. He gave Sergeant White the address for him to check out.

"Have you been arrested previously?" the sergeant asked.

"Yeh, for feft and fings. I've not done nuffink to no prostitutes if that's what you're gettin' at," he replied.

"Alright, empty your pockets," Sergeant White asked and then checked his clothing for a knife. He could see that there was some staining on his boots that was most probably blood from the slaughteryard. As there was no other incriminating evidence on his person, he was allowed to leave.

"We have your details now, so just watch yourself," White stated.

As the killer looked young and was clearly not a foreigner; he didn't match the description given by Elizabeth Long. The sergeant, therefore thought no more about him. This would not be the only mistake the police would make concerning these crimes.

Outside the police station, the killer said to himself; "I was fuckin' lucky there; it's a good job I don't take the knife to work wiv me."

As he walked the short distance home, he started muttering to himself; "stupid woman getting me into trouble, fuckin' sick ov 'em. There will be no fuckin' screamin' next time."

In the Princess Alice pub, which was quite busy, his Aunt Letty came to him while he was at the bar.

"You've been a long time. I thought you would be home a while ago?"

"I was doin' some extra work," he said calmly. "Can I get a drink then?"

"There's some food in the kitchen if you're hungry," Letty replied, as she poured him a pint of beer.

"I'll get some after this, fanks," he replied.

Elizabeth Stride was out with her partner Michael Kidney. They had visited a couple of pubs and were about to make their way home.

"It's cold tonight, outside," Kidney said to Long Liz.

"It not cold; In Sveden, it cold; this not cold," Liz replied in a deep voice.

"Let's get anovver drink. I have been earning money this week," Kidney said.

"Okay, we have drink. I have beer, not gin."

"Two pints of ale it is. I will get them."

"First give me cigarette, I want cigarette."

"Ere take the packet." Liz lit a cigarette and blew the smoke into the air of the pub. She looked around and saw that several men were looking at her. She smoked the cigarette with an air of confidence, holding it up at head height. Michael Kidney came back from the bar and handed Liz a pint of ale.

"Cheers, as you English say. "Beer is better in Sveden and food too."

"If it was so good in Sweden, what did you come 'ere for? There can't be anywhere in Sweden as bad as Whitechapel."

"Is complicated; I have been unlucky, as you know. I had business once, coffee shop; is difficult to make living. You need money to make business; only Jews have money. I am not Jew." Liz said, then drank some of her beer and smoked her cigarette.

"We are born to this life; we will always struggle. People are poor here," Kidney said despondently.

"You born to this life, not me; I better than this. We need to move."

"Where to?" Kidney asked.

"Somewhere that's not this shithole; but not Sveden."

"It is the same wherever you go."

"What about United State?"

"America? How are we going to afford to go to America?" he asked in a puzzled manner.

"We find way. Soon, we find way. Drink beer, I want to go."

September 10th
The return of Inspector Reid

At 8.00am, Inspector Reid walked into Leman Street Police Station with less than the normal spring in his step, even after his two weeks summer holiday. He had seen the press and knew of the latest two murders; they were of grave concern to him.

"Good morning everybody, have you all missed me? I hope you've not been too busy," Reid said, trying to lighten the naturally tense atmosphere.

"Not too busy, he says!" the desk sergeant says to the two constables. "We've only 'ad two more murders, whilst you've been on your jollies, sir."

"I know, I've been following the events in the press. I believe Abberline is involved?" Reid said, in a more serious tone.

"Yes sir, there is a meeting at 9.00am with the Super, Inspector Abberline of central, and Inspectors Helsen from J Division and Chandler from here, and you, of course, sir. It's a briefing for you," the desk sergeant says politely.

"Well, I will go and look at some of the evidence then," Reid said as he went up to his office.

His small office was next to a larger room separated by a glass panel and door. On his desk was a file with two post-mortem reports in it and some of the internal correspondence. He had previously read some of the press reports and made some notes himself. He then added to his notes while perusing the evidence. He was interrupted by Abberline at about 8.45am.

"Well, Edmund, back at last. Trust you to go on leave at the busiest possible time. It's never stopped since you left."

"Yes, I have read accounts in the press, I believe you have overall control, so to speak, Fred."

"Well you're in charge here, in H Division, and Joseph Helsen, who has your old job, oversees J Division. Joe Chandler has been taking charge here at H whilst you were enjoying yourself, I have been coordinating things from the centre, and that's the way it'll stay."

"We have a meeting at nine with the Super; we will get you up to speed. Well, I'm just going to get some tea, and I will be with you shortly," Abberline said as he left the office.

Inspector Reid said to himself sarcastically. "Well, welcome back, Edmund, I hope you have had a nice, well-earned rest."

At 9.00am, they all met as planned in Superintendent Arnold's office for Reid's briefing and to discuss the next steps in the investigation. The formal introductions were done, and Arnold outlined the roles, much as Abberline has done with Edmund. Superintendent Thomas Arnold started the briefing.

"We will take each murder in turn, then consider the similarities together, and then our next steps. Inspector Helsen from J Division will start with the Bucks Row murder, then Inspector Chandler from H Division with the Hanbury Street one. Fred, you come in where necessary. Hopefully, together we can get you up-to-date and answer any questions you have Inspector," the Superintendent said, looking at Reid who nodded his head accordingly.

Inspector Helsen started his explanation by stating Polly's last known sighting, which was at 2.30am on Osborn Street by Ellen Holland. He explained that Nichols was identified as a result of the clothing she had on from Lambeth workhouse, from which her relatives were traced. There was no further information until her body was found at about 3.40am by Charles Cross and Robert Paul.

"Have the movements of these two men been checked out? Are they reliable? What were they doing at that time in Bucks Row? For example," Inspector Reid asked.

Inspector Helsen responded. "They have been checked; both were on their way to work. Cross lives at 22 Doveton Street, and Paul lives at 30 Foster Street, both Whitechapel. Cross left his house at 3.20am, and he arrived at his work at 4.00am. He discovered the body just before 3.45am, he thinks. And Paul left his house about 3.45am and saw Cross in the street near the body. They both left to find a policeman. PC Neil discovered the body at 3.45am and called for help."

"So, they discovered the body just before PC Neil did at 3.45am. Correct?" Reid asked, to which Helsen nodded. "Well, it doesn't take 25 minutes to walk from Doveton Street to Bucks Row. So, where did Cross go before he went into Bucks Row if he left his house at 3.20am?"

"This is Edmund," Abberline says, smiling, "a stickler for detail."

"Paul must have left his home before 3.45am to discover the body before PC Neil," Reid said. "Cross and Paul must have seen the body at about 3.42am, so Paul must have left his house at about 3.40am," Reid added. "We need to double-check Cross," he then stated forcefully. Everyone nodded.

Helsen carried on his narration of the enquiries. "PC Neil and PS Kirby both state there was no dead body there at 3.15am when they passed the murder spot together. Neil states that she was warm and blood coming out of the neck wound, but she was dead."

"Hold on a minute, Joe. The beat takes about 12 to 14 minutes, so where was PC Neil at 3.30am?" Reid enquired.

"He will have walked on the opposite pavement, so he could have missed the body then, but he doesn't think one was there then. He was definitely on the exact murder spot at 3.15am, of that he is certain," Helsen replied.

"So, she was killed at about 3.40am by her throat being cut. Also, she had stab wounds and cuts to her abdomen and genitals. It that correct Joe?" Reid enquired.

"That is correct, Edmund. We have talked to the residents of Bucks Row and the people living on Whitechapel Road, and no-one has seen her or heard anything. The post-mortem was conducted the same day by Doctor Llewellyn, 152 Whitechapel Road. The inquest was adjourned until the 17th of this month," Helsen stated.

"I need to speak to the doctor. I believe she has been buried?" Reid enquired.

"That's right, on the 6th at Little Ilford Cemetery," Helsen replied.

Helsen went through the other statements obtained to date, including details of her life and her family that were given at the two adjourned inquests on the 1st and 3rd of September.

The superintendent thanked Inspector Helsen and invited Inspector Chandler to explain the Hanbury Street enquiries.

"Could I just go back a minute, sir, to the Bucks Row case, I have some questions," Reid asked.

Everyone agreed.

"Well, first of all, has anyone thought why she was killed where she was?"

"I'm not following you, Inspector," Arnold said.

"Sorry sir, what I am thinking is this. If I was the killer and I wanted to kill this woman, why would I do it on this spot, in the open? Why not take her to somewhere more secluded? Usually, prostitutes take clients to more secluded places, so why not let Nichols lead him to somewhere that is safer for him to kill. He could have easily been seen, with a little luck, by a policeman."

"I see what you mean, Inspector, maybe the urge to kill was too strong," Arnold replied.

"Also, what is the killer doing hanging around Bucks Row? Does he stand in Bucks Row and just wait for a woman to come along? It doesn't make sense. If he wanted to kill, he would have chosen somewhere in Spitalfields where there are more women and more secluded places than Bucks Row. So, what was the killer doing there?"

Everyone looked puzzled, and no-one wanted to say anything foolish in front of everyone else.

"What I think, and it fits the circumstances, is that the killer didn't specifically *choose* Bucks Row or that spot. He was following her; he has seen her somewhere and decided to follow her.

He may know her, but I think not. Maybe their paths have crossed briefly before. He likes to follow women and possibly likes watching prostitutes having sex. He has followed the victim, and he took his chance when no-one else is on the street. The attack may have been less than a minute."

"You may be correct, Inspector," Arnold said.

"You mentioned sir that the urge was possibly too strong, and I think you are correct. I think the person has no real plan here, he follows his prey and gets excited, and when the chance is there, he strikes on impulse. A more thoughtful or cautious person would have been able to control his urges until he was somewhere secluded. So, it is a more irrational and immature person that we are looking for," Reid stated.

"Amazing Inspector!" said Arnold.

"And how does that help us catch him? If we ask around for irrational and younger men, well there's loads of them Edmund," Abberline said in a raised voice.

"I know Fred; I am just trying to understand the killer. Everything in crime happens for a reason," he replied.

"Very well, can we move onto the next crime, Joe, this is your turn," Arnold said to Chandler.

Inspector Chandler recounted the crime and the discussions that he had with Inspector Abberline, regarding the time of the attack and the conflicting witness statements of Mrs Long and Albert Cadosh.

Abberline interjected. "We both think that Long was mixed up somehow and Cadosh was correct, with the murder happening just before 5.30am."

"Well, I've read the witness statements, and they both can be correct," Reid said, and everyone looked puzzled.

"Cadosh gets up at 5.15am as you say, goes to the toilet, on his way back, say 5.17am he hears a *'no'* from next door." Everyone now says a drawn-out, "Yeees?"

"He goes into the house and comes out about three or four minutes later to re-visit the toilet. As he comes out and hears someone bang the fence, as he enters the house again, about 5.25am now. Give or take a minute or two. He leaves the house, and as he passes the church, it is 5.32am. So, his story checks out," Reid stated.

Abberline interjected again. "We all know that, so Long is wrong?"

"No, she is correct also," everyone looked at each other in confusion; Reid smiled to himself, waiting to deliver his explanation.

"Look, whoever it was that Cadosh heard, it was not the killer and Chapman, but another prostitute and client who left at about 5.25am. At 5.30am, or just after, Chapman and the killer meet outside the house. They go into the yard; he kills her at about 5.31 or 5.32am. He takes about four or five minutes to mutilate the body, then leaves at about 5.37am," Reid said with a grin on his face.

"Why didn't we think of that?" Abberline exclaimed.

Chandler then continued with his explanation. "Mrs Long got a look at the man, as she was passing. She says he is about 40 years old, a foreigner with a brown deerstalker hat and a dark coat. She also recognised Annie Chapman, as the woman in the mortuary."

"Did she see the man's face?" Reid enquired.

"No, he had his back to her, he faces towards the market, Chapman faced the other way towards Long," Chandler explained.

"She did well to take in all that from a passing glance. Is she a reliable witness?"

"See, he has a nose for these things, nothing gets past our Edmund," Abberline stated with a smile.

"It is also possible that the man that Mrs Long saw was not the killer. He could have carried on walking down Hanbury Street and then she met the real killer, who may have been following her at a distance. There was time for this to happen, as the body wasn't discovered until nearly six o'clock," Reid added, and everyone had their heads down thinking about Reid's analysis.

"Where does Mrs Long live?" Reid enquired, focussing his gaze on Chandler.

"32 Church Street, Whitechapel, as far as we know."

"Why does she go to the market via Hanbury Street?" Reid asked. "It is simpler to walk down Church Street, and the market is there," he added.

"There is some confusion here as to whether it is Church Street or Church Row. There is a Church Row in Bethnal Green. In which case she'd go down Brick Lane and along Hanbury Street," Chandler stated.

"Check her out," Reid asked.

"There's nothing gets past Reidy is there, Edmund?" Abberline said wryly, smiling and feeling Edmund is taking over the case.

"Right," he continued, "we think the same person committed both murders. They were both prostitutes, and both had their throats cut. They then had their abdomens stabbed or cut open. The doctor thinks it must be a sharp knife six to eight inches long. We are checking all slaughtermen and butchers."

"There was also a fatal stabbing on the 7th of August, that I am investigating," Reid said.

Abberline interjected. "But she didn't have her throat cut, and two weapons were used. These two had a much longer knife used on them."

"Tabram had a deep wound to the chest, through the heart. A dagger or a similar weapon did that wound," Reid stated.

"But they are different, Edmund! The wounds are different!" Abberline painfully explained.

"I'm not so sure, Fred. The killer is gaining experience. There was a stabbing earlier in the year, in White's Row. A woman was stabbed in the throat in Mile End, in March. We need to look at the wider picture here. I don't think several different people are going around stabbing women, in such a short space of time. We need to understand what type of person would do this!"

"A maniac did it, Edmund, a lunatic," Abberline said in a raised tone, without any hesitation.

"Don't you think a maniac, or a lunatic, would be easy to spot Fred? He wouldn't be bothered about being caught."

"You always do this; make it complicated!" said Abberline.

"There's no simple answer here, Fred. We've never experienced this before. This is something else. You mark my words."

Superintendent Arnold interrupted at this point to clarify their next steps. "Edmund, you take charge here and keep Fred informed. Joe, you do the same at J Division. We need to work together on this one before it gets out of hand."

"Yes, sir," they all replied.

"Fred, you have overall control, and you make the press statements, we need to be careful what information we give to the press. We have had two and possibly three murders in a matter of weeks, we need close teamwork on this if we are to crack these cases and catch the criminal or criminals involved," Superintendent Arnold stated firmly.

As they walked out of the office, Reid motioned Fred over to him.

"Can I have a quiet word, Fred? Why are all the cells full? What is going on?"

"I have been locking known villains up who have a record of violence against prostitutes."

"And how long do you think you can keep them locked up, Fred?"

"I was hoping they would come up with something."

"We can't just keep men locked up. Have they an alibi for any of the murders? Fred, we must let them go. We need evidence to lock them up. We also need people and the press on our side."

Abberline looked at Reid, knowing that he was right. "Fine, let them out but keep a watch on them."

The coroner, Mr Wynne Baxter, opened the inquest into the death of Annie Chapman, at the Working Lads Institute. It was convened on five separate days from the 10th of September until its closure on the 26th of September. Inspectors Abberline, Reid, Helsen and Chandler, as well as uniformed officers, were in attendance. Witnesses gave evidence regarding the events of that morning. Doctor Phillips gave the evidence of his post-mortem findings and had also discussed these with the police.

To add to the problems of the police, The Whitechapel Vigilance Committee was also set up on this day. This committee of many local tradespeople and business owners feared that the killings were harming their livelihoods, by driving customers out of the area. The vigilance committee was headed up by Mr George Lusk, a local builder. Its primary focus was that the police needed further resources. All this put tremendous pressure on the detectives leading the hunt for the killer.

Following the recent murders, the police have been interrogating men that were known to be regular users of prostitutes. Men caught with a prostitute were also taken to the police station for questioning. Such men were searched for the possession of a knife, and their clothing was examined for bloodstains.

Also high on the police list of potential suspects were foreign men, people with mental health issues and men known to be violent towards women. Such people were stopped and searched by the police, along with men whose only crime was one of poverty. Such prejudices would later prove to be a great hindrance to the police investigation.

During the police investigation into the death of Polly Nichols and subsequently the death of Annie Chapman, the name John Pizer, also known as Leather Apron, came to their attention while visiting several common lodging houses. Sergeant William Thick had been searching for him and handwritten in his notebook, were several comments, that implicated John Pizer:

"It will be that big-nosed Leather Apron, what done it. He was always pickin' on us and abusin' us if we don't give 'im money," a prostitute called Vicky said.

Her friend and fellow prostitute, Norma backed her up. "His name's John Pizer, 'e's a Jewish bootmaker. That's where 'e got the name, Leather Apron from."

"He is scum, he hates us, he beats us up and tries to blackmail us into giving him money," Anna said in a northern accent.

The women also told Sergeant Thick that they would be prepared to testify against Pizer.

A warrant was out for his arrest since the murder of Chapman. As police searched for John Pizer, people started to believe he had killed both Polly Nichols and Annie Chapman. As a result of these feelings, Pizer was in fear for his life. Fortunately for him, he was found by Sergeant Thick and arrested on the 10th of September. He was kept in the cells until Inspectors Reid and Abberline were available to interview him.

He was interrogated by the detectives and managed to provide an alibi for both murders.

"It wasn't me. I haven't killed anyone. They hate me because I'm a Jew; everyone hates us," the large Pizer said, almost in tears.

"Everyone hates you because you are a big man that goes around beating up women and stealing from them, not because you are a Jew. You are a disgrace to the Jewish people. Now, where were you on the 31st of August and the 8th of September?" said Abberline harshly.

"You can check out where I was. On the 31st of August, I went to sleep at the Round House in Holloway Road. I know this because it was the night of the fire at the London docks. Many people saw me there at the lodgings. Since the murder, on the 8th of September, I was frightened and stayed with my family at 22 Mulberry Street. I never left the house until I was arrested. You have to tell people that I am not the killer, or they will kill me and my family," he pleaded and was visibly scared.

"Look at you, Pizer. You are a bully and a coward. You pick on vulnerable women, and now you are almost in tears. Well, we will check out your alibi, and if it is true, we will let you out tomorrow, when things are a bit quieter. You will need to give evidence at the inquest, to confirm your innocence on Wednesday the 12th, is that clear?" Reid stated firmly.

"I will do anything to clear my name and protect my family." Sweat was running down Pizer's face and into his beard.

"When you have given your statement to the inquest, you had better stay away from prostitutes, is that clear for you?" Abberline shouted while taking hold of Pizer's jacket.

"Yes, officer, sir, I understand," a sorry and rough-looking Pizer said.

September 21st
Police investigations

There were no new leads or sightings of the man that Mrs Long saw just before the murder of Annie Chapman. The two ongoing inquests had failed to produce any solid leads, so far. The press had also whipped up hysteria about the three recent killings and had included Emma Smith's murder to the killer's tally. They had also started deriding the police as incompetent and ineffective.

"Fred, unless we get more resources, there's nothing more that we can do. We have uniformed and plain-clothed coppers on the street. We, or rather you, have exhausted all your contacts; nobody has seen or heard anything in the pubs, the lodging houses, or the churches."

"Edmund, I agree, but I don't hire coppers. I can only keep making the case. Maybe all this bad publicity will help us, as it will put pressure on the Government to do something. The problem is, and I hate to say this, but, if three West-End well-to-do women had been murdered, the Government would have moved heaven and earth by now. But they are only East-End prostitutes and no-one, but us, gives a damn about them."

"We need a different strategy, Fred. We are just chasing our tails from one murder to another. I think it is one man and he will strike again until he is caught. There is a purpose and a pattern here, but I do not see it clearly yet. We usually treat each crime separately, and certain officers just work that case. But what if we miss the big picture of what is really going?"

"Edmund, life is complicated enough, big picture? Patterns? You work this angle if you must but keep me informed." Abberline was having difficulty keeping up with Reid's thinking, it was a different approach to policing than he was accustomed to, and he didn't quite see the relevance of it.

"Fred, I am taking all the possible related crimes that we know of since the start of the year. I may go beyond that later, if necessary. The related crimes include muggings; assaults, particularly on prostitutes; robberies; knife crime and of course murder. Murder like this doesn't start with the first murder; it starts with petty crime and escalates. I am sure the person that is carrying out these killings has been a criminal a long time and will have been in prison at some point. When we interview people, we can cross-check them with prison records of when they were in and out of jail. I think by taking this strategy, I can narrow down our possible suspects."

"Take whoever you need, one way or another we will catch this bastard."

"Understood, Fred."

In the Princess Alice pub, Letty was putting on her hat and coat.

"Right, I am going out for an hour, can you two manage the pub while I'm out?" said the landlady to her nephew and the young fair-haired barmaid. They both answered with a yes. At about 5.00pm the pub was relatively quiet.

"I'm just goin' out a minute, I need some fresh air," the nephew said to the barmaid.

There was no fresh air in Spitalfields, but the nephew wanted his head to clear a bit as he was having quite a bit of head pain. After a minute or two, he saw a young prostitute walking by, and he decided to follow her, forgetting all about the pub. She walked along Wentworth Street and up George Street. She picked up a client there, and they went down a small alleyway just off George Street. The nephew followed and watched them for a while. He then sat down on the ground as the pain in his head was now a stabbing pain. He then seemed to pass out with his body twitching a little.

The Princess Alice pub was now busy, and the barmaid was struggling to cope with the work. While she was a distance from the till serving customers at the bar, someone took money out of the till and ran out with two other men. She had spotted them, but she could do nothing. She was now panicking as she would have to explain this to the landlady. Tears were appearing in her eyes.

"I can only serve one at once; you will have to wait!" she shouted.

The customers were getting impatient and called to her for attention. Suddenly, just after 6.00pm, the noise in the pub dropped for a moment, as the pub door opened and a voice bellowed out.

"What the fuck's goen' on 'ere?" the landlady shouted.

"We're waitin' to be served," a man said.

"Alright, I am 'ere now, who's next?" She began to serve the men at the bar. When the customers were served, she started talking to the barmaid.

"Where is his lordship?" meaning her nephew.

"He said he was only goin' out a minute, but that was just after you left," she said and started crying.

"It's alright love, don't let it bother you."

"It's not that; someone took some money out the till."

"WHAT!" she shouted.

"I was too busy on me own, and me back was turned. I saw who it was, though. I'm very sorry; I'll pay you back," the young woman said, now in floods of tears.

"Don't worry; it's not your fault."

At that moment, the nephew staggered in. "Where the fucken' 'ell 'ave you been?" she shouted, glaring at him and with her hands on her hips.

"I went out for a minute, and then I passed out."

"Passed out! I'll fucken' pass you out, my lad. Someone's nicked some money out of my till, while you were busy passen' out," she shouted, and all the customers heard.

"I don't feel well; I need to lie down."

A few minutes later, the landlady said to the barmaid. "Go and see how he is up there, will ya?"

"I can't do that; he gives me the creeps. I am not bein' alone with him, up there."

"He's alright. Never mind, I'll go." She left the bar for one minute and was straight back down the stairs, at the bar.

"He'll be down in a minute," she said.

She went to check her till, she was good with money and she would roughly know how much there should be there.

"I reckon it is about five or six shillen' down. Did you see who took it?"

"It was one of the three that always stand over there, them grave diggers."

"Oh! It was, was it? Just wait till I get my fucken' 'ands on 'em."

"How much has been nicked?" the nephew asked gently.

"Five or six fuckin' shillen' that's what. I know who's fuckin' done it too. I'll get it back, don't you worry."

An old man asked her for a pint of ale at the bar. She was still seething.

"Two," she said, meaning two pennies. She slammed the pint down on the bar. It wasn't full to start with, and some more was spilt when it was slammed down. The man looked at her but didn't say anything.

"What do you want?" she shouted to another two men stood at the bar.

The old man then said, "me pint's not full."

"Oh, for fuck's sake, give it 'ere!" she filled it up and slammed it down again with more spillage. "'appy now?" she said.

Well 'ave you two made your mind's up then? I 'avent got all fucken' day." She then served them slamming the pints on the bar. The two men said nothing.

"Can I 'ave a whisky?" another man asked rather sheepishly, not wanting to stir Letty's wrath any further.

"It's can I 'ave a fucken' whisky, PLEASE," she shouted,

"Can I 'ave a fuckin' whisky, please?" the man replied.

"Auntie is in a bad mood. If someone starts a fight, she'll fuckin' kill someone," the nephew said to the barmaid.

The three grave diggers returned to the pub sometime later, and the barmaid nodded to the landlady. At that moment, Inspectors Reid and Abberline walked in and were behind the landlady as she walked up to the three men. They watched her knock out the three men very quickly and saw her take money from them. Abberline smiled and had no intention of remonstrating with the landlady. He knew they would have done something wrong.

"Madam, what are you doing? You can't do that! I saw you assault these three men and steal from them," Inspector Reid said firmly.

"These three men stole money out of my fucken' till earlier. I'll do what I fucken' want. Alright?"

"This isn't the way to go about..." Abberline pulled Reid away as Letty moved angrily towards him.

Abberline said calmly to Reid, "let it go; this is how things are done around here. Remember what I have told you."

"What if they are seriously hurt, Fred?"

"Let it go; this is Spitalfields. You must stand up for yourself here; it's the only way you survive," Abberline said to his friend, calmly.

Shortly after, the three men staggered out of the pub and said nothing. They certainly would not go to the police.

Reid and Abberline sat down for one drink before they went home.

"I keep meaning to ask this, as well as the two murders, have there been any other incidents involving attacks on any prostitutes? I checked the arrest books, and nothing was there of any significance," Reid asked.

"Well, we have been checking men for carrying knives or threatening anyone with a knife; nothing new has occurred. As you know, there have been incidents with prostitutes, either they get angry for not being paid, or they have tried to steal from a punter, but nothing with a knife." Abberline paused then said, "except for that one in here, a few weeks ago."

"She said it was a foreigner, about 40 years old," Reid replied.

"But we agreed he didn't use the knife."

"It is a similar description of the man Mrs Long saw, which is curious," said Reid.

"Well we have circulated that description, but no-one has come forward."

Abberline then looked towards the bar and Reid followed his eyes. "The lad behind the bar that was attacked in April was taken in for questioning, with a prostitute, while you were away. He didn't have a knife on him. He was returning home from work when he got into an argument with her. The constable nicked them both and took them in for questioning. No charges were made, and both were let go."

"That is very interesting, Fred... I wonder... yes," Reid mused, not making any sense.

There was a quiet moment between the two friends while Reid pondered.

"He told me that he didn't have anything to do with prostitutes. I wonder if..." Reid paused again.

"What are you getting at? Are you going to let me know what you are thinking?" asked an annoyed Abberline.

"He works in a slaughter yard now; I told you that, don't you remember? He has been in and out prison, but it is probably a coincidence."

"You are still not making any sense," Abberline said, trying to reason with Reid.

"He's not bright and a bit of a loner. I need to think things through a bit," said Reid.

After a moment, Reid sat bolt upright and started talking in a more excited voice.

"These last three murders, all of which involved a knife, have been in the early hours of the morning. All the pubs were closed for the evening. Chapman was murdered after the pubs had opened again, but that was on a Saturday morning."

"I am still not following you, Edmund, not that that is anything new."

"The killer could be employed, Fred!"

"Well, that narrows it down to three-quarters of the population," Abberline said sarcastically.

"The murders so far, have been around the weekends, Fred."

"Tabram's was in the early hours of Tuesday morning."

"Yes, but the Monday before was a bank holiday. It suggests that he works during the day or until about midnight when the pubs close. He could work in a pub Fred," Reid said excitedly.

"Lots of people work in a pub, or stay in one until closing time, Edmund."

"I just have to think about things more, Fred. There are indications here of the killer. I have to think things through."

"Well, you can think things through at home. I think we will catch him red-handed with a knife when he is with another prostitute. We will catch him when he slips up. It is only a matter of time."

"How many more will be killed before he slips up, Fred? He may never slip up. We need another approach."

The two detectives left the Princess Alice pub, and each headed homewards.

In the evening of the 21st of September, Reid is at home relaxing with his wife, Emily.

"You have only been back at work for about two weeks, and you are working all hours on this case; you will make yourself ill if you keep going like this, Edmund."

"Since we have been away, there have been two more killings; both women, like Tabram, were prostitutes. All three of them were killed with a knife. The last two were killed by the throat and neck being deeply cut, causing instant death. The last victim was also horribly mutilated; they found her in the back yard of Hanbury Street. I am certain that these three killings are by the same man. I can't rest while these killings go unsolved."

"Well, it is looking like you were right in linking all these crimes, or most of them. Fred may think they are all different and done by different people. He may be right, but none of the crimes will be exactly the same. The children write stories at school and tell me what they have learned. But as they learn more, they get better at storytelling and writing. Maybe someone who likes killing gets better with each one."

"Yes, of course, I see it now. His killing technique has evolved with each kill; he is getting better at it. But how has he learned to be a better killer? And why is he targeting prostitutes? On these questions, I will think. I want to try to look at the killings from his point of view. I want to understand the killer, and by understanding the killer, I can narrow him down before we have any more murders."

"You need to read what other people have studied concerning similar crimes. There are now doctors that study the mind and how it works, including the minds of criminals. Go to the library, talk to these doctors, and you will find answers, Edmund."

"I do read, as you know; particularly about where new developments could be applied to catching criminals. I know that whatever a criminal does, he leaves us indications as to what type of person he is and why he is doing such crimes. For example, some thieves are opportunists, they see a chance, and they take it, almost on impulse, like pickpockets. There is no real planning on their part; they tend to be younger men who have no life plans; they live day-to-day. Some crimes, however, are more thought out. For example, where a rich person is regularly followed, even to his home; such criminals will plan how best to steal from the man or his home, using some sort of ruse. These criminals tend to be more mature and more intelligent than an impulsive young pickpocket.

"I do not see any plan on the part of the killer; The crime was not concealed in any way. The killer is impulsive, and he takes his chances when they arise. From this, I deduce the killer is a younger man, and impulsive, and lacking in organisational skills. What I haven't worked out is why he does these crimes, and what compels him to mutilate women with a knife?"

"I find people fascinating, Edmund. I like to watch and listen to people and try to work out why they do whatever it is they do. There are many ways of classifying people; some people are quite quiet and are happy being alone for a time. They get great enjoyment from solitary activities such as painting, sculpting, writing music, writing books, reading or sewing etc. A bit like me, for example.

"Then there are people who have to be with other people as much as possible. They need attention and like to interact and talk excessively. They don't like being alone, they need other people and join clubs, spend a lot of time in pubs and have a lot of similar friends; a bit like my sister, she just talks at people and always expresses her feelings to anyone who will listen. She needs a lot of friends and acquaintances. She is also a very insecure person, always concerned about how others perceive her.

"You, however, seem to have a foot in both camps. You like to experience all that life has to offer such as singing, acting, ballooning etc. But you are also a deep thinker, who is also happy working alone and thinking things through. You are an ideas man, always wanting to change things for the better. In many ways, you are like Fred, but Fred is a little more insecure and needs to achieve to feel worthwhile. He has learned to interact with people to get the results he wants, whereas your interactions with people are more natural because of your inner confidence.

"Then there are those people that don't function well on their own or with others. They act without thinking of the consequences. They tend to be more violent and selfish people who only think about themselves. Their lives are full of self-inflicted problems such as alcoholism, prostitution, criminal behaviour, and violence. They find it difficult to exist in normal society. Your killer is in this class, concerned only for himself. Yet something has made these people like they are, they all behave the way they do for a reason. There are reasons why your killer brutally stabs women, and in time you will find out why."

"I see what you mean, Emily. The murderer is from the same class of people, like his victims. He will be criminal, impulsive and immature. Yes, things are coming together. I will have to look into the criminal mind more as you have said, dear."

September 29th
The *Jack the Ripper* letter

On the penultimate day of September 1888, the police received a letter, purporting to be from the killer. The neat, handwritten letter, in red ink, was dated the 25th of September, and was received by the Central News Agency on the 27th of September. After two days they sent it to Chief Constable Williamson. A new name for the killer had arrived.

Dear Boss,   *25. Sept. 1888.*
I keep on hearing the police have caught me, but they wont fix me just yet. I have laughed when they look so clever and talk about being on the right track. That joke about Leather Apron gave me real fits. I am down on whores and I shant quit ripping them till I do get buckled. Grand work the last job was. I gave the lady no time to squeal. How can they catch me now? I love my work and want to start again. You will soon hear of me with my funny little games. I saved some of the proper red stuff in a ginger beer bottle over the last job to write with, but it went thick like glue and I cant use it. Red ink is fit enough I hope ha. The next job I do I shall clip the ladys ears off and send to the police officers just for jolly wouldn't you. Keep this letter back till I do a bit more work, then give it out straight. My knife's so nice and sharp I want to get to work right away if I get a chance.
Good luck.
yours truly
Jack the Ripper
Don't mind me giving the tradename
Wasn't good enough to post this before I got all the red ink off my hands curse it. No luck yet. They say I'm a doctor now ha

Later in the day, Abberline and Reid were discussing the letter that had come down to them from the Superintendent.

"What do you make of this Edmund?" Abberline asked after reading the letter.

"I have a feeling that the killer can't even read properly, never mind write. I think the name is a clever trick; it's used to bait us," Reid replied.

"I think the superintendent wants to know our views on what to do with it; whether to publish it in the press or not."

"Well if you look at the neat, legible writing it shows that it is from an educated person. It is written as a bit of a joke to stir things up for us a bit. It is well set out and generally correct, but with some obvious grammar and spelling errors."

"So, you think it is fake, like me?"

"Yes, probably, Fred, but I am not sure. We don't know it is from the killer. If the next victim has her ears cut off, we know he is the author. I think we are going to be damned if we do and damned if we don't. If we publish it before the next murder, we will never know, unless we keep the bit about the ears from the press."

"I agree. I think the superintendent wants us to discuss it with him tomorrow. I think he will publish it." Abberline said drearily.

"I just hope there isn't going to be another one, but I can't see the killer just stopping," Reid responded.

"What do you think of the name – Jack the Ripper?"

"I think the press will love it, Fred. It is in all probability written by a journalist."

"That is my worry too. Just when you think it can't get any worse. Let's go for a drink," Abberline said.

"Okay, but not for long, I need to see the children before they go to bed. I have been so busy here that I have hardly seen them recently," Reid replied.

September 30th
The killing of Elizabeth Stride

On the Southside of Commercial Road, in the area named St George in the East, there were many rows of two-storey terraced housing. These houses were built in the early Victorian period, primarily for working people. It was a bit less densely populated than Spitalfields; however, it was amply supplied with public houses, small shops and commercial businesses and prostitutes.

Not all prostitutes solicited for business every evening. For some, it may have been when times were particularly hard. For others, it was a part-time occupation for certain evenings with other labour-based employment during the day, when it was available. Elizabeth Stride fell into the latter category. She was registered as a prostitute by the Swedish police in 1865, having been born in Gothenburg. She arrived in London in 1866 and lived for some of the time in the workhouse, in 1877. She regularly told false stories that she has worked in domestic service, ran a coffee house and that her husband and children were killed in the Princess Alice ferry disaster in 1878. She and her husband had actually split up in 1882.

She had an on/off relationship with Michael Kidney, with whom she had lived with for three years, in Devonshire Street. However, she had lived at a common lodging house, 32 Flower and Dean Street, for most weekends over the last 18 months.

She was known to drink and has eight convictions for drunkenness. This evening she had not been drinking, she had however been soliciting with several male clients.

On the evening of the 29th of September, she entered the Bricklayers Arms in Settles Street at around 11.00pm, where she picked up a well-dressed man as a client. She was wearing a dress under a long black jacket, a black hat and a coloured, striped silk handkerchief around her neck. She also visited the George IV public house on the corner of Berner Street and Boyd Street, touting for clients, as well as the Red Lion public house in Batty Street. Liz Stride, at five-foot-two-inches tall, was still attractive for a 44-year-old prostitute. She had a good figure and a delicate bone structure to her face. Liz also had an engaging personality. She knew how to attract men.

There were conflicting reports of what happened in the last hour of Liz Stride's life. It seemed that at midnight she was with a man who bought some grapes from Matthew Packer's Shop and was standing with the man until 12.35am opposite Dutfield's Yard, in the rain.

"You like grape then?" Elizabeth asked the man who bought the grapes. "I like wine, but don't eat grape. I like gin too. Too much, I like gin, but not tonight. I just make money tonight," she said, laughing. She seemed able to pick up better clientele than other women of her age.

They were also seen by PC William Smith, who was on his beat, at around 12.35am. He looked at the pair of them carefully. PC Smith knew she was a prostitute, but they were not doing anything illegal by talking on the pavement. He would be back in Berner Street at 1.00am.

The man with Liz Stride got nervous when he saw the policeman.

"Do not bother about police. I don't like police. In Sveden, they arrest me and put me in cell with other women," Liz stated firmly.

"I have to go," the man said quickly and parted company with her.

"Police, waste of time. Never there when you need them, I look after myself," she said quietly to herself.

At 12.45am, she was assaulted by another man, who was not her usual clientele, but a very rough man indeed.

"I've only got 2d, do it for that, you bitch," the man said.

"No, I will not do it for that, or you. Go away, before I shout for police," Liz said to the man.

"Well an 'and job, then?"

"No, I don't like you. Go away!"

"I'll fuckin' do you bitch!" he said as he held her by the shoulders and threw her to the ground. Liz screamed three times to attract attention.

He then noticed that he had been seen by at least two men.

"What are you lookin' at Lipski?" he shouted to the men across the road, one of which was Israel Schwartz, who later recounted the assault to the police.

Liz got up from the pavement and moved closer to the International Working Men's Educational Club side entrance until he had gone. It was situated at number 40 Berner Street.

She then waited outside the club and saw another man walk towards her just before 1.00am.

"Hello mister, are you looking for business?" Liz asked the man who was dressed in a salt and pepper coloured jacket and a grey peak cloth cap. They stared at each other for a moment; then she recoiled backwards. "It is you! I remember you!" she gasps in horror…

The Whitechapel Murderer, as the press called him, started his evening in the Princess Alice pub as usual. At around nine o'clock, he then moved down Commercial Street and across into Commercial Road. He had decided to stalk an area south-east of his lair for a change.

He sexually abused a prostitute earlier that evening. Rather than have sexual intercourse with her, he forced his fingers into her vagina, until it hurt her. He then squeezed her neck, partly choking her before he let go. For him, prostitutes were for abuse; he has never had a proper relationship with a woman.

He then visited several pubs in the area including the Beehive on the corner of Fairclough Street and Christian Street, the Red Lion on Batty Street and the Nelson Beer Shop on the corner of Berner Street and Fairclough Street. He would follow a prostitute and her punter out of a pub and watch where they went. To launch an attack, he preferred a secluded place, off the beat of the police. He had the peak of his hat pulled over his eyes, to hide his face, although he was not known around this area. The police aided the killer by putting out a description of Annie Chapman's killer, as a 40-year-old, foreigner.

It had been just over three weeks since his last kill. He was a patient killer, waiting for the opportunity to strike. There had been no description of him in the papers, so the woman that saw him in Hanbury Street had not been to the police. It was now going up for 1.00am. He left the beer shop and walked up Berner Street on his way back to Spitalfields.

As he approached a gate opening, a prostitute propositioned him. He looked at her and recognised her as the woman he bumped into when he left number 29 Hanbury Street. He could see that she recognised him, too; he must act fast. She ran for the club side entrance, but he was too quick. He tripped her up, and she fell to the ground mainly on her left-hand side, near to the wall of the club. He then took out his knife, holding his left hand over her mouth; he cut her throat from left to right; blood spurted out from the left carotid artery onto the ground. Her windpipe was cut through, so she could not scream. But he did not finish the cut; someone was coming, he could hear a pony and cart. She fell back a little, he pushed her back onto her left side, out of the way of the cart and then moved to the opposite side of the gate opening and crouched down. As the cart entered the yard, he moved out of it, without being seen and up Berner Street, he then took a left at an alleyway called Batty's Gardens, which led to Back Church Street. He urinated in the alley, before moving Northwards to Commercial Road. The whole kill was made in a matter of seconds, from seeing her to fleeing from the scene. Adrenaline was now pumping through his veins. He was

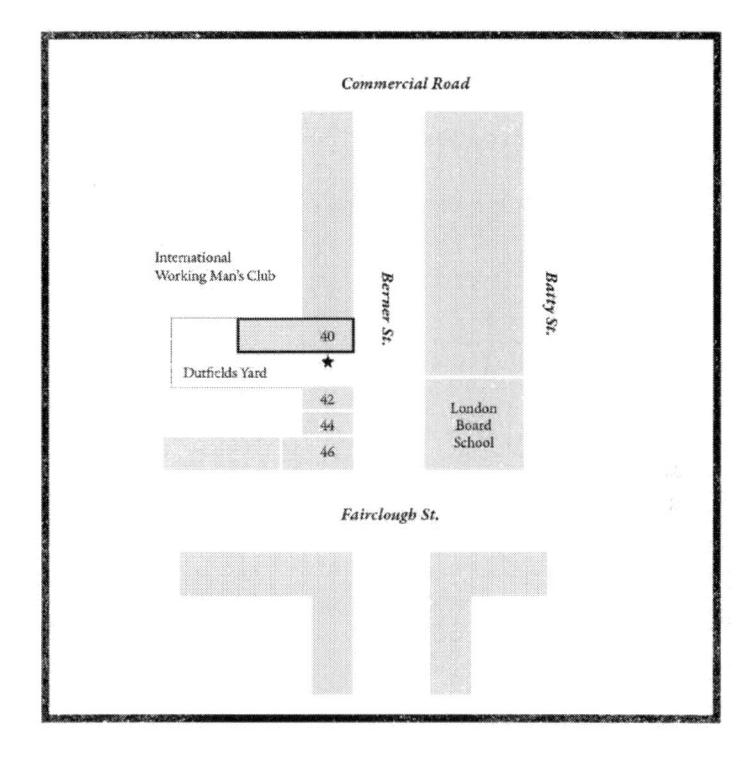

Map 5 – Berner Street
The Lord Nelson Beer Shop was at number 46 and Matthew Packer's Fruit Shop was number 44.

Elizabeth Stride's body was found next to the wall inside of the gates in Dutfield's Yard and is marked by the star. Her body was found at 1am. ★

Normally a killer or a prostitute would likely wish to go to the rear of the yard to escape detection from passers-by. She was killed, where she fell, on impulse without any planning on the killer's part. The Ripper could not mutilate the body where it was found, as the area was still quite busy, as people exited from the club by the side door leading into the yard which is next to the crime scene.

This was an impulsive, but necessary killing by Jack the Ripper.

She was last seen alive at 12.45am, on the pavement next to Dutfield's Yard. She was being attacked by a man who pushed her to the ground; and this was witnessed by two people.

pleased how quickly he reacted; he had become an efficient killer.

The cart that disturbed the killer was driven by Louis Diemschutz, who was a steward of the club at 40 Berner Street. He had arrived back from a day's work, and it was precisely 1.00am. He got down from his cart and struck a match. He could see the body of Liz Stride and blood on the ground. He rushed into the club to inform people, and several members ran out into the surrounding streets to find the police. Louis Diemschutz came out of the club, with a lighted candle, to see the body more clearly. The woman looked dead and was now surrounded by club members, but no-one touched her.

The killer moved onto Whitechapel High Street and drifted Westwards towards Aldgate with no clear plan of direction. He felt excited and elated.

"That's that nosey cow done," he congratulated himself in a quiet voice. "I wasn't expectin' to meet 'er, I 'ad to act quick then."

He walked hurriedly down the road but then slowed down in order not to attract attention. His heart was still beating fast; he was on a high. He kept out of the way of policemen on their beats if he could. In Aldgate, just inside the City of London boundary, he relaxed.

"I was fuckin' lucky wiv that," he said out loud. "anyone could have seen."

Berner Street ran North to South from Commercial Road down to Ellen Street and midway, it was bisected by Fairclough Street. The street was mainly terraced houses on both sides, the main exception to this was the London Board School that had buildings on both sides of Berner Street. On the corner of Fairclough Street and Berner Street at number 46, was the Lord Nelson beer shop, number 44 was Matthew Packers' Fruit shop. Number 42 was a house that is next to Dutfield's Yard. The International Working Men's Club was at number 40 on the other side of the yard. Further along Berner Street, between numbers 30 and 32, was the alleyway called Batty Gardens.

The first constable on the scene was PC 252H Henry Lamb, who was on Commercial Street at the time when he was informed of the murder. He was closely followed by another constable, both running down Berner Street just after 1.00am. "Go and fetch the doctor," PC Lamb said to the other constable. At the scene, PC Lamb tried to keep order.

"You! Can you please go to Leman Street Police Station and inform the inspector, at once?" he says, to a member of the club.

"Can you all please stand back and someone please close the gates," PC Lamb stated, still a little breathless. He then blew his whistle for further assistance.

There were 20 to 30 people now crowded into the yard, eagerly wanting to see the body. PC Lamb felt for a pulse but could not find one. He felt her face, and it was still slightly warm. Edward Johnston, who was Doctor Blackwell's assistant, arrived on the scene at 1.12am with the constable who called for his assistance. At 1.16am Doctor Frederick Blackwell arrived at the crime scene. He began examining the body and declared she was beyond help. He noticed that blood was starting to congeal in the neck wound though the body was still warm. The doctor judged that she had been dead for approximately 20 to 30 minutes. At 1.25am, Inspector Reid was informed to go to Berner Street, closely followed by Abberline. He was met by Inspector Pinhorn and Chief Inspector West who were already there.

The police ushered everyone into the club, and the sergeants and constables began taking all their details and checked everyone's hands and clothing for blood. They made brief statements now and more detailed ones later. At about 1.35am Doctor George Bagster Phillips arrived at Berner Street, via the Leman Street Police Station, who directed him to the crime scene.

Doctor Phillips looked at the corpse with Doctor Blackwell; they both made notes of the body position. Doctor Blackwell explained to Doctor Phillips what he had done when he arrived. Blackwell mentioned that her right hand was smeared with blood as if she had put it up to her throat. He explained the throat incision and asked Doctor Phillips to take a look.

Doctor Phillips examined the body carefully and took a packet of cachous, which were breath freshener tablets, from her left hand and saw that there were also cachous that had fallen out onto the ground. He noted that the body was still warm, but the hand cold. He looked for blood on the adjacent wall but found none.

Inspectors Abberline and Reid gave directions to Sergeant Stephen White and Detective Charles Dolden to start door to door enquiries to ascertain if anyone has heard anything.

Morris Eagle was a printer at 40 Berner Street; he stated to the police: "I entered the club at 12.35am through the side entrance and noticed no dead body lying on the ground. Twenty minutes later, a man called Mr Gilleman, came up and told everyone there was a dead woman in the yard. I couldn't believe it."

William West, who was also a printer at 40 Berner Street, gave the police the following information: "The gates are normally open until late into the night. I left the club at 12.30am and did not notice anything unusual in the yard and the gates were definitely open."

William Marshall, of 64 Berner Street, testified to the police: "I saw the victim and a man talking opposite 68 Berner Street at 11.45pm." However, the police discovered that at the same time, James Brown saw Elizabeth Stride and a man standing outside the Board School on Fairclough Street. He heard the woman say, 'No, not tonight, some other night.' Conflicts of the time were not uncommon, as most people did not possess a watch, so they estimated the time.

PC 452H William Smith, was last in Berner Street, on his beat at around 12.35am. He also saw the victim with a man at that time. Smith gave Inspector Reid a description of the man he saw with Stride.

"He was about 28 years old, and he had no whiskers. He was of a respectable appearance. He was about five-foot-seven-inches tall and had a deerstalker hat on and dark clothes. I also went to the station for the ambulance."

Inspector Reid examined the body and took some notes. He was initially satisfied that death had occurred sometime after

12.35am and before 1.00am based on the witnesses that were present, but he wanted medical confirmation.

"What time do you think she was killed, Doctor?"

"I was there at 1.35am and she had been dead no more than one hour, Inspector."

"Doctor Blackwell arrived at 1.16am and was of the opinion that she had been dead no more than 20 or 30 minutes."

"That is reasonable, Inspector. The victim was found at 1.00am, so those times are possible.

"How do you think she was killed, Doctor?" Reid asked Phillips.

"I believe she will have been seized by the shoulders and placed on the ground and that the perpetrator of the deed was on her right side when he inflicted the cut. I am certain that the cut was made from left to right."

"Would the murderer have blood on him, Doctor?"

"Not necessarily, if the perpetrator were on the opposite side to the wound, the stream of blood, for a stream it would be, would be directed away from him."

"Why do you think he would kill her, here? Near the pavement at this time with people still on the streets and people in the club."

"It is fairly dark here, but I agree he is taking a risk," said Doctor Blackwell.

"Why didn't he take her deeper into the yard, behind that cart? He would not be seen over there, and he could have carried out his mutilations."

"He killed on the pavement at Bucks Row last month," Doctor Phillips stated.

"Yes, but that was about three hours later in a quiet area, without a busy club still open. I think that as he kills, he learns more. He finds more secluded places to kill, to avoid being seen, like the backyard of Hanbury Street, for instance."

"Maybe he isn't too smart. But these are questions for you as a detective, not me, Inspector," Doctor Phillips replied.

At about 2.00am, a young policeman shouted, "Inspector! Inspector!"

"What is it, Constable?" Reid replied.

"There's been another one, sir. In Aldgate; in the City. This one is bad sir. Ripped apart," he said, still breathing heavily.

"What, another murder? He has only just killed here!" Reid said in disbelief.

Chief Inspector West, Abberline and Inspector Pinhorn come over to him.

"There has been another one sir, in the city, not long after this," Reid said in a worried tone.

"We had better get over there," West said, meaning, himself Abberline and Reid. "Inspector Pinhorn you stay here and then ensure the body is taken to the mortuary when the doctors have finished," he added.

"Yes, sir." Inspector Pinhorn replied.

The constable, along with Reid, Abberline and West, headed over to the City of London, walking briskly.

At Berner Street, people started to go home from the club and the street outside. The police maintained a presence there for the rest of the morning. At 4.30am the body was moved to the mortuary which was at St George in the East Church. At 5.30am a constable washed away all the traces of blood and noted that there were no traces of blood on the wall.

September 30th
The killing of Catherine Eddowes

At about the same time that Elizabeth Stride was taking her last breath, another woman was being released from Bishopgate Police Station, in the City of London.

Catherine Eddowes was a 46-year-old prostitute who drank to excess on occasions. She found it difficult to hold down employment. She had one daughter and two sons with Thomas Conway, but she left her family in 1880, as she became an alcoholic. In 1881 she had a new partner, John Kelly and they lived at Cooney's lodging house at 55 Flower and Dean Street, Spitalfields. She then became a prostitute like many women in this area. She was five-foot tall with dark brown hair and hazel coloured eyes.

Earlier on the previous evening, at 8.30pm, she was arrested for being drunk and disorderly, by PC 931 Louis Robinson, in Aldgate. There was a crowd around her, watching her impersonate a fire engine and then trying to sleep on the pavement. She was kept in the cells until she sobered up.

At 1.00am the Station Sergeant James Byfield agreed to let her out. The gaoler, PC 968 George Henry Hutt released her from the cell. He told her she has no business to be that drunk.

She replied, "I'll get a damn fine hidin' when I get 'ome."

"So, you should," PC Hutt replied.

"Goodnight, old cock," she said as she left the station, just at 1.00am.

From Bishopgate Police Station, she turned left to walk down Houndsditch; she should have turned right for Spitalfields. Catherine stopped once or twice, to ask people directions, as she thought she was going the wrong way. She then decided to turn right, into Duke Street and follow it round to the left. Duke Street meets Aldgate at the end; Catherine would know where she was from there. She stopped at the junction with a small alleyway called Church Passage, next to the synagogue. A man was standing there.

"Excuse me mister, 'ave you any money?" she asked casually and smiling...

When Catherine Eddowes was being released at 1.00am, the killer of Elizabeth Stride was making his way towards Aldgate. When he got there he saw a police constable enter Mitre Square from Mitre Street. The policeman then left the square, the same way, a minute later. The church clock chimed the time of 1.30am. He crossed Mitre Street and walked into Mitre Square, which was very dark and quiet. The square mainly comprised of the warehouses of Kearley and Tonge. He then went through the passage on the opposite side of the square and into Duke Street. There he waited a few moments. Three men were coming out of a club on the opposite side of the road. Unexpectedly, a prostitute then asked him for some money.

He replied "no" to the prostitute and tried to move off. She then asked him if he wanted anything, grabbing his testicles. She said she needed some money; he replied with a nod of the head. They walked through the passage towards the darkest corner of the square. These were the last steps that Catherine Eddowes would ever take. In the darkest corner of the square, at about 1.37am, he grabbed her by the throat with both hands. She was a small thin woman, and so she was quickly forced onto the pavement. Before she could react in any way, his knife had cut her throat, not once, but twice. She was dead within a matter of seconds.

In the darkness of the square, he slashed at her body; ripping her open from the sternum to the vulva. As with Annie

Chapman, he proceeded to remove her intestines and draped them over her right shoulder and the pavement. He made little cuts to her face and slashed her mouth open. He felt an enormous thrill as if electricity was rushing through his veins. With his left hand in her abdomen, he gripped organs and cut them out with his knife in his right hand. He took two organs in his hand, which later he finds are the uterus and a kidney. He cut off some of her clothing and wrapped the organs up; he wiped his hands and knife on her clothing. No-one was about; no police were near the scene. The time is 1.42am.

The slayer of Catherine Eddowes exited the square, via another passage into St James's Place. From there he moved in a Northerly direction. He stopped to defecate in an alleyway and calm down a little; he was a little giddy with the excitement. Walking in the general direction of his home he found himself in Goulston Street. Near the top of the street on the right-hand side was a block of flats called the Wentworth Model Dwellings. He found some discarded paper and transferred the organs to the paper. He then flung the blood-stained cloth into a stairwell.

Above the place where the apron landed, was some existing chalk writing. It simply read; *'The Juwes are The men that will not be Blamed for nothing.'* The time was about 1.55am. He then calmly made his way along Wentworth Street, towards the Princess Alice pub. "Two in one fuckin' night," he said, his heart was still beating fast. "I wasn't expectin' that. I need a fuckin' drink now," he said as he entered the Princess Alice.

As the body of Catherine Eddowes was within the City of London boundaries, the case fell under the jurisdiction of the City Police and not the Metropolitan Police.

PC 881 Edward Watkins, of the City Police, was patrolling his beat of 14 minutes, that included Duke Street, Henage Lane, Leadenhall Street, Mitre Street and into Mitre Square, King Street and St James's Place.

At 1.44am, on the 30th of September 1888, PC Watkins observed a terrifying sight. As he walked into Mitre Square, shining his lamp upon every part of the square, he came across the mutilated remains of Catherine Eddowes. There, in the corner of the square, she lay on the pavement. Her insides had been ripped out and draped over her corpse and the ground. Her head was turned towards her left shoulder, and her arms by her sides with the palms facing upwards and the fingers slightly bent. The right leg was bent at the thigh and knee and the left leg straight.

Almost immediately, PC Watkins cried for help, he was in a state of shock himself, but he knew he must get help. He knocked on the door of George James Morris, who was the watchman for Kearley and Tonge.

"For God's sake, mate, come to my assistance!" Watkins blurts out in a manner akin to a stammer.

"Stop till I get my lamp," Morris replied. "What's the matter?" he asked.

"Oh dear, there's another woman cut up to pieces," Watkins replied, almost in tears.

"Where is she?"

"In the corner," the constable answered as he struggled to comprehend the situation.

Morris saw the body and immediately blew his whistle. He then proceeded to run into Mitre Street and then into Aldgate to raise the alarm. Two constables came to his assistance, and he directed them to Mitre Square. PC Watkins stayed with the corpse of Catherine Eddowes.

Very soon, Mitre Square was teeming with police officers. Fortunately, there were not many members of the public about, and it was quite easy to seal off the square from anyone other than the police.

The City of London police officers took charge of the crime scene; PC Watkins was soon assisted by PC 814 Frederick Holland and PC 964 James Harvey. Doctor George Sequeira arrived at the scene at 1.55am. Inspector Collard of the City Police was the senior officer on the scene, and he arrived just after 2.00am, having received the information while at Bishopgate Police Station. He immediately sent a constable to go to Doctor Frederick Gordon Brown's residence. Detective Inspector

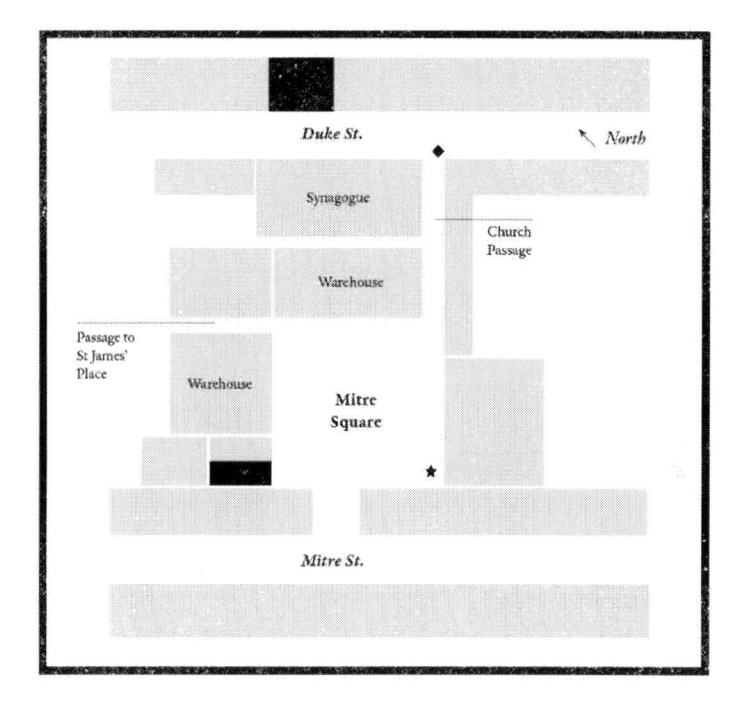

Map 6 – Mitre Square
The shaded block on Duke Street is the Imperial Club from which three men exited at 1.35am and saw the victim with a man at the Church Passage entrance. This was undoubtedly Jack the Ripper. ◆

The killer would have possibly exited the square via the passage to St James' Place at about 1.42-1.43 am

PC Watkins entered the Mitre Square from Mitre Street as part of his beat. At 1.44am he saw the body of Catherine Eddowes in the corner of the square, lying on the pavement. It is marked by the star. ★

PC Harvey was meant to walk up Church Passage to the edge of Mitre Square and shine his lamp into the square at about 1.40am. If he had done so, he could not have failed to see the killer and the victim.

The night-watchman's residence is denoted by the shaded area in the square. Catherine Eddowes would have walked down Duke Street until she stopped at Church Passage and met her killer who would have been on his way back to Spitalfields. ◆

James McWilliam then arrived and took overall charge of the scene and was later assisted by Detective Constables Halse, Outram and Marriot, who were all on the scene just after 2.00am. Doctor Brown, the surgeon of the City Police, arrived at 2.18am and made notes on the position of the body and her injuries. He felt for the temperature of the body, and it was still quite warm. Both he and Doctor Sequeira were sure that she was killed on the spot, instantaneously; and as there was no death stiffening, they conclude that she had been dead for only 30-40 minutes.

Shortly after Doctor Brown arrived, Inspector Reid, Chief Inspector West and Inspector Abberline came and immediately viewed the body; they were very shaken by the sight before them. Inspector Reid explained to Detective Inspector McWilliam and Inspector Collard, that a murder was also committed in Berner Street, just before 1.00am and they think it is the same killer's work. Mitre Square was now very crowded with police officers.

Inspector Collard proceeded to inform the Metropolitan detectives of how and when the body was found.

"There was no dead body in the square at 1.30am, the constable, PC Watkins, is certain of that. As he got to the square at 1.44am, he heard no footsteps of anyone running away. The immediate area is already being searched, and residents questioned."

"I've read the report on Annie Chapman's murder, and this one is eerily similar, not only the neck wounds but the later mutilations. We are looking for the same killer," Reid stated to Collard. "Two murders in less than an hour!" Reid exclaimed with amazement, looking at Abberline. "He has now killed at least four, but possibly five times, since August."

"One of our Constables, PC 964 James Harvey, stated that his beat brought him to the end of Church Passage, over there, at about 1.40am, he saw or heard nothing. He says that he heard the whistle of Morris the watchman three or four minutes later. PC Holland followed PC Harvey to the scene, arriving at about 1.50am," Collard explained.

"Well if that is true, and I doubt it, the murder was committed after 1.40am and completed before 1.44am. There wouldn't be enough time. The murderer and the victim would have to come into the square after 1.40am, he would then kill and mutilate her, then escape before 1.44am, without being seen or heard," Reid stated forcefully.

"I see what you mean Inspector, there isn't the time," Collard said in a puzzled way.

"The woman was already dead at 1.40am Inspector. He must have his times wrong, or he wasn't there," Reid said sharply.

"It may be possible that the lad went to the end of the passage but didn't shine his lamp on the place where the body lay. This killer may have already left by another route," Abberline suggested.

"Well at the moment, from the evidence we have, the murder was committed after 1.30am, but before 1.44am, possibly before 1.40am," Reid replied. "I am not happy about this; it needs further investigation."

"I will have a word with him and check his timings, Inspector," said Collard.

At about 2.30am the body of Catherine Eddowes was removed to the mortuary, accompanied by Inspector Collard and Detective Constable Halse.

There are further developments within the hour, over at Goulston Street, in Spitalfields.

On his regular beat, PC 254A Alfred Long, found a piece of a blood-stained apron and some writing on the wall of the stairwell of 118 and 119 Wentworth Model Dwellings, in Goulston Street at 2.55am. The piece of the apron was taken to the Commercial Road Police Station, and then to the mortuary to see if it matched the clothing, which it did. Police then focussed on Goulston Street and wrote down the message. Superintendent Arnold had been informed and gave orders that no action was to be taken until he got there. Commissioner Warren was also on his way to the scene, having been told at approximately 5.00am.

Several of the detectives of both the City Police and the Metropolitan Police wanted the chalk writing to be photographed when it got light. They were also a bit bemused that Warren and Arnold would come to the scene of some chalk writing, but not make any effort to visit the crime scenes where two women were brutally killed.

"Note down the writing and get it washed off, now. We don't want trouble to be focussed on the Jewish population," Arnold stated.

"I agree entirely. It is too risky to leave for another hour. There will be too many people about. It is my decision, and I take full responsibility. Note the message down and wash it off," the Commissioner stated forcefully.

The words were written down by several officers, but unfortunately, they all wrote it down slightly differently and some with a different spelling of the word *Jews*. Therefore, no-one will ever know the correct version. Some of the detectives were not happy because they wanted to check the writing with the letter received yesterday that was signed by Jack the Ripper.

The post-mortem of Catherine Eddowes took place at the Golden Lane mortuary at 2.30pm on Sunday the 30th of September 1888 and conducted by Doctor Frederick Brown. In attendance were; Doctor George William Sequeira, Doctor William Sedgwick Saunders, who tested the stomach contents which were negative for poisons and narcotics, and Doctor George Bagster Phillips, who knew about the previous killings.

The clothes were removed from the body, and it was evident that there was no blood on the front of the clothes. Doctor Brown recorded the room temperature of 55 degrees Fahrenheit and stated that rigor mortis had set in. Following the post-mortem, Detective Inspector James McWilliam and Inspector Edward Collard questioned Doctor Brown, with Doctors Sequeira and Saunders present.

"What was the actual cause of death, Doctor?" Inspector McWilliam asked.

"The severing of the throat and neck were the cause of death, resulting in a rapid loss of blood. All the arteries on the left side of the neck were severed to the bone, and the throat completely cut through. The wounds on the right side of the neck were less severe. The neck wounds were cut from left to right," Doctor Brown replied.

"Was the woman standing at the time of the throat cut?" McWilliam asked looking at Doctor Brown.

"No, she was on the ground. Her clothes would be stained at the front if she was standing."

"What type of weapon are we looking for?" Inspector Collard asked.

"All injuries were made by a sharp, pointed instrument, like a knife, at least six inches long, and death was immediate. The mutilations were inflicted after death," Doctor Brown replied.

"Would you consider that the person that committed this crime had a great deal of anatomical skill?" Inspector McWilliam asked, addressing all the doctors.

"A good deal of knowledge as to the positions of the organs in the abdominal cavity and the way of removing them," Doctor Brown answered immediately without considering the question.

Doctor Sequeira interjected, hesitatingly, "I don't think there was, GREAT, anatomical skill or that he had any particular design on any particular organ."

"I agree with Doctor Sequeira, that there was no 'great' anatomical skill," Doctor Saunders replied in a friendly tone, trying to amalgamate both opinions.

"The left kidney and the uterus have been removed. Would it require great skill and knowledge to remove these?" McWilliam asked coldly.

"It would require a great deal of knowledge as to its position to remove the kidney as it is covered by a membrane," Doctor Brown answered.

"Would such knowledge be present in someone accustomed to cutting up animals?" McWilliam asked thoughtfully.

"Yes, in all probability Inspector, the anatomy is very similar. Humans and horses are both mammals," Doctor Brown happily answered.

"How long would it take to inflict the injuries, Doctor? Also, is there any evidence that the perpetrator was interrupted?" Collard asked.

"Five minutes at least and he had plenty of time, or he wouldn't bother nicking the eyelids with his knife if he was in a hurry," Doctor Brown said confidently.

"What is the purpose of removing the organs, Doctor?" Collard asked.

"They are of no anatomical purpose; your guess is as good as mine, Inspector."

"Would the person that did this crime, have much blood on him, Doctor?" McWilliam asked.

"No, very little. The victim was killed on the ground with the first wound away from the killer. She was cut from left to right. He would have little blood on his hands as the mutilations were carried out after death," Doctor Brown stated factually, without any doubt.

"Thank you, Doctors, you have been helpful," Inspector McWilliam stated as he shook hands and then left the room with Inspector Collard.

"I will pass the post-mortem report and details to Abberline. It looks very much like the previous murders in Whitechapel and Spitalfields. It seems almost identical to the Hanbury Street murder. They have much more information on the killer than we do. We will help where we can," McWilliam said to Collard.

October 1st
A postcard to the police

The two killings on the last day of September, had put the police under tremendous pressure. Most of the senior officers had not had much sleep, and the stress was telling in their faces.

Superintendent Arnold, Chief Inspector West, Inspectors Abberline and Reid met in Arnold's office at Leman Street to discuss in more detail their thoughts on the two killings and the letter they received two days ago.

"What do you all suggest we do gentlemen? Do you all think this letter is real and from the killer?" the Superintendent asked.

"It may be from the killer, but we don't know for certain. If we publish it, someone might recognise the handwriting," Abberline said.

"I agree, but I am also not sure it is from the killer. It is probably a hoax. It may be done just to goad us," Reid replied.

"We need to use all the leads we have got," West added.

"There's nothing in this letter that has not been in the press. *'I shall clip the ladies ears off.'* That didn't happen, did it?" Reid stated firmly.

"This was sent before these two killings. It could be a hoax, but it could be real," Abberline said, worried as usual.

"It seems a fairly educated hand, with some obvious spelling errors. The press will exploit the name, *'Jack the Ripper',*" Reid reflected.

"Maybe it is from the press; but let us try to identify who sent it." Chief Inspector West said. "However, if we do publish it, we will be inundated with crank letters, you mark my words," he added.

"We will publish, and see if anyone recognises it, in any way," Superintendent Arnold said, then added, "Now what about these two murders? Have we got any leads?"

"Well if we had been allowed to photograph the writing on the wall, we could have checked it with this letter?" Abberline said firmly.

"What is done is done, Fred. We don't even know if the killer chalked on the wall," Arnold replied.

"The writing on the wall is a red herring, Fred," said Reid.

"Well we are certain that both murders were carried out by the person that killed the previous two," Abberline said.

"That's four murders he has done," West stated.

"Five, if you count Tabram and the press will count Emma Smith as well; just to put the pressure on us. Put more plain-clothes officers on the beats, and we will catch him. His luck will run out sooner than later," Reid stated firmly.

A policeman then knocked at the door and entered the room, giving Abberline an envelope that contained a bloodstained postcard, from the Central News Agency, allegedly written once again, by Jack the Ripper.

"I was not codding dear old Boss when I gave you the tip, you'll hear about Saucy Jacky's work tomorrow double event this time number one squealed a bit couldn't finish straight off. Had not got time to get ears off for police thanks for keeping last letter back till I got to work again.
Jack The Ripper"

"This postcard seems to be written by the same hand that wrote the letter. It was posted today and received by the Central News Agency earlier today. He refers to the cutting of the ears, which is in the first letter and that he couldn't finish off the first victim. This information is already out there. I think it is another hoax," said Reid.

"Well, we will publish both on posters and see if anyone recognises the writing. We have enough to do without chasing the authors of these letters. The press are going to batty-fang us on this, using these letters against us. All the headlines will now be Jack the Ripper this, Jack the Ripper that. It will cause unrest if we don't catch him quickly," Abberline said in a raised voice.

"I agree, things are getting worse by the hour. I will get more plain-clothed men on the streets; we must catch him in the act. There is no other way," a worried Superintendent Arnold said.

In the morning, the Inquest into the death of Elizabeth Stride was opened by the coroner, Mr Wynne Baxter, at the Vestry Hall, Cable Street, St George's in the East and attended by Inspector Reid. The body hadn't yet been formally identified.

The post-mortem of Elizabeth Stride was carried out by Doctors George Bagster Phillips and Frederick Blackwell at 3.00pm, at St George in the East Church mortuary, on Monday the 1st of October. After the examination, Inspector Reid asked several questions.

"Can you confirm the actual cause of death, Doctor?"

"Yes, Inspector. Death was due to loss of blood as a result of severing the arteries on the left side of her neck and completely severing the windpipe," Doctor Phillips replied.

Are the fatal injuries identical to the other victims that you have seen Doctor?"

"Almost, except that the arteries on the right side of the neck were intact. However, there were no mutilations, so there are differences with the previous one."

"What else can you tell me, Doctor, about the victim and how she died?" Reid asked politely.

"Well Inspector, rigor mortis is now well developed, and we agreed the time of death previously. She had fallen or was pushed to the ground, largely on her left-hand side; you can tell this by the mud that is matted in her hair. There is bruising on her shoulders and the front of her chest. I believe she was assaulted in the street before being killed. As Doctor Blackwell's site notes confirm, death was due to loss of blood from the left carotid artery and the division of the windpipe."

"Would you say this person is skilled with a knife, Doctor?"

"Well, the cut was clean and carried out with a sharp knife. The vessels of the neck were targeted, so the perpetrator's intention was to kill quickly. I think there is a degree of skill, but I don't think a medical man has done this," Doctor Phillips replied.

"Is there anything else you can tell me about the victim, Doctor?"

"The condition of her main organs was normal, the body was fairly well nourished. Her last meal was contained cheese, potatoes and some flour-based food. She had lost all her teeth in her left lower jaw and she had a deformed right leg; otherwise, she was perfectly normal."

"Would the killer have blood on him, Doctor?"

"As with the other victims, she was killed on the ground, as opposed to standing, so there would be no blood on the killer if he were careful. If the victim had been standing, when her neck was cut, the front of her clothing would be saturated in blood. This was not the case, Inspector."

"Just one last question Doctor, you can confirm for the record, that she was killed where she was found?"

"Definitely Inspector, no doubt of it."

"Thank you, Doctor," Reid said as he left.

While the police were investigating his latest crimes, the killer was out walking the streets. As with the other killings, he took great pleasure going back to the scene of both crimes and listening to what people were saying. He felt powerful and revelled in the fear that had resulted from these two murders. He liked seeing the shock on people's faces and listening to the gossip that went on in the pubs.

"People fink they are so fuckin' clever, but they know fuck all. The mutton-shunters know fuck all, as well," he adds under his breath.

He was delighted with the new name the press have given him. He didn't send any letters, but he basked in the notoriety the media had given him.

To avoid being recognised, he wore different clothes and a different hat. He was relatively sure no-one saw his face, but he knew a Jew was looking at him in Duke Street when he was with the woman he killed.

"Fuckin nosey, four-by-two, cunts. They're all over the fuckin place," he said as he noticed a group of them on the opposite side of the road. He was not particularly anti-Semitic; he just didn't like anyone.

He decided to go back to the Princess Alice pub as he remembered he should be working.

"'ere, where 'ave you been? Thought you were worken' 'ere tonight?"

"I am, I'm 'ere ain't I?" he said aggressively while looking at his aunt.

"Well, you better get to it then." Letty was quite surprised at the tone of his reply, so she didn't push him any further.

"Have people been talkin' 'bout the murders?" he asked in a more conciliatory tone.

"They have been talken' about nothing else. People are all worried now who might be next."

"Well, I don't fink he'll tackle you, Auntie," he said with a rare smile on his face.

"I fink it's another woman that done it, if you ask me," an old man with a long grey beard at the bar said, butting into the conversation.

"Well nobody's asken' you are they? Besides, a woman has got more sense. Women 'ave more important things to do, that goin' around killen' people," Letty said in a raised voice.

"Yea, doin' as they're told. They don't know 'ow to run fings," a rough-looking middle-aged man said with a sneer on his blotchy face.

"Do you see them windows there?" she was very aggressive to anyone who thought a woman's place is in the home and being submissive to a man.

"Well, yea, I sees 'em," the man said; he looked around, wondering what was coming next.

"Do you have a pref'rence which one I fucken' throw you through?" she shouted and moved towards him.

"Well, I didn't mean no offence, like; there's men's work and a woman's work." He was trying to placate her but only made the situation worse; he was now worried.

"Whatever a man can do a woman can do," she shouted at him and bent her head down towards his face.

"Well, it's men that run the country ain't it?" a younger man said, who thought he was clever.

"Yes! And look at the fucken' state of it. Most men can't even run to the fucken' toilet, never mind runnin' the country," the landlady said in a loud voice, and much of the pub began laughing. "You mark my words; a woman will run the country one day. She'll fucken' show you how it's done."

"A woman runnin' the country? Don't be daft!" the old man said, laughing.

"I run this place. I don't need no 'elp from any man."

"Ow's she gonna talk in parl'ament, she won't know what to say!" the middle-aged man said. This made her very angry, and her face had reddened.

"You're right there; she won't know how to talk their shite. She'll tell it 'ow it is, and she won't take any shite from them useless bastards that are in parl'ament now. And any more shite comes out of that fuckin' mouth of yours; my fucken' fist will go in it. Is that understood?" Several men were very close to being hit by her now; she was seething with rage.

"For fuck's sake, Auntie, calm down. They're customers."

"If there's any man 'ere wants a fight with me, you'd better show yourself. Otherwise, I don't want to 'ear any more shite about what a woman can and cannot do. Is that fucken' clear for everyone?"

People could now see that she was furious; they looked down or away from her. The pub had gone silent.

"You need barring, Auntie," he said with a slight smile.

She pulled herself a pint of beer and drank it in about three seconds. She gave a big sigh and began to calm down.

"What are you so 'appy about anyway?" Letty said to her nephew in a quite sharp tone.

"I just am, that's all," he said quietly; he didn't want her to start another argument.

October 2nd
Police investigations

The body found in Berner Street was formally identified as Elizabeth Stride, by several people who had visited the deceased in the mortuary. At Leman Street, Inspectors Abberline and Reid were busy pulling together the information from both murders. They were first discussing the Berner Street killing.

"We have a formal identification, Fred. Elizabeth Tanner, who is the deputy at the lodging house at 32 Flower and Dean Street, formally identified her and knew her for six years. She knew her as Long Liz and that she was Swedish. She last saw Liz alive at 6.30pm on Saturday in the Queens Head public house, on Commercial Street. Catherine Lane and Charles Preston, also from 32 Flower and Dean Street, identified her as Long Liz too, and both saw her at 7.00pm in the lodging house kitchen.

"However her partner Michael Kidney, of 38 Dorset Street, identified her by her correct name. He and Elizabeth Stride had been living together for three years. He last saw her on the Tuesday before her death. He came here to report her missing on the 1st of October. Sven Olsson, who was a clerk to the Swedish Church, also made an identification. He was able to inform us that her maiden name was Gustafsdotter and she was born on the 27th of November 1843. He had known her for 17 years," Reid reported.

"Have we any witnesses to the Berner Street murder, first of all?" Inspector Abberline asked.

"Well, we have several men who saw the deceased with a man at various times," said Reid. "All the descriptions are in effect describing different men," for example:

"Matthew Packer's description of the man is at either 11.00pm or twelve o'clock, the man he saw was five-foot-seven-inches tall with a long black coat, soft felt hat, broad-shouldered and 25-30 years old.

"William Marshall's description of the man seen with the victim at 11.45pm was about five-foot-six-inches tall, with a small black coat, and dark trousers, a round peak cap, stout and middle-aged.

"PC Smith stated that at about 12.35am; he saw a man five-foot-seven-inches tall, dark coat and trousers, hard felt deerstalker hat and about 28 years old.

"Most interestingly, Israel Schwarz saw the victim with another man outside 40 Berner Street at 12.45am. He came in to give a statement yesterday, through an interpreter. He stated that he was walking past Dutfield's Yard, on the opposite pavement, when he saw the victim. She was being assaulted by a man who threw her onto the pavement. He said that there was a man opposite looking over, and lighting a pipe. The man who assaulted Liz Stride, shouted to the man opposite, who we believe to be a Jew, *'What are you looking at Lipski.'* Both Schwartz and the man ran off. He describes the man as five-foot-five tall, dark coat and trousers, black peak cap, broad-shouldered and about 30 years old.

"At the same time as Schwartz saw the victim on Berner Street, James Brown, who lives at 35 Fairclough Street, saw a man in the said street, next to the board school, with the victim, five-foot-seven-inches tall long coat to the heels, unsure of a cap, stout build, no age. Brown says he heard the woman say, *'no, not tonight.'* He then says he saw someone in the street, about 15 minutes later, shouting for the police and stated it was one o'clock."

Reid then went on to add. "We haven't got one good description of a face. But they have all identified the woman as the victim."

"So, he kills at about 1.00am in Berner Street. He then comes down to Aldgate, finds a prostitute, goes to a remote location, kills her then makes his escape before 1.44am. Is that possible?" Abberline asked.

"Just about Fred. It is about 12 minutes from Berner Street to Mitre Square, depending on what route you take. He could be around Aldgate by 1.15am, giving him 20 minutes to find a woman to kill. It's possible," Reid explained.

"Let's stay on Berner Street, Edmund. Someone found a knife, didn't they?"

"Yes. Thomas Coram, who lives at 67 Plummer's Road, Mile-end. He was on Whitechapel Road going towards Aldgate, at about 12.30am. He crossed over the road and saw a knife lying on the doorstep of number 252, a laundry business. A blood-stained handkerchief was wrapped around the handle. He called over to PC 282H, Joseph Drage, who confirmed the time etc.

"The constable confirmed it was a long knife, sharpened on one side and was about nine-or-ten inches long," Reid explained. "He is also fairly sure it was not there 15 minutes previously, but he can't be certain," he added.

"We need to get Doctor Phillips to look at the knife, to give us an opinion as to whether it is the murder weapon. It is unlikely due to the time it was found, but we need confirmation," Abberline said.

"Let's take this knife to Phillips. I would like to ask him one or two more questions," said Reid.

So, the two inspectors walked over to number two Spital Square to Doctor Phillips' surgery and fortunately, were able to see him immediately.

"Good afternoon Doctor, thanks for seeing us," Abberline said politely.

"Could you confirm as to whether she ate any grapes just before her death Doctor? One witness said he had sold her some grapes on the night of her murder." Abberline asked.

"There were no grapes in her stomach, Inspector."

"Doctor Phillips, do you think this is the work of the same hand that killed Chapman three weeks ago," Reid enquired.

"There is a great dissimilarity. In Chapman's case, the neck was severed all round down to the vertebral column, the vertical bone being marked, and there had been an evident attempt to separate the bones."

"Both victims had their necks cut from left to right, Doctor. Maybe he was disturbed before he could complete the cut," Abberline said.

"It is possible, Inspector."

"We found this knife, a short distance from the scene. Could this have been the knife used to commit the murder?" Reid enquired.

"It is like a knife used in a chandler's shop, a slicing knife. Such a weapon could have produced the neck injury. However, it has recently been blunted, and the edge turned by apparently rubbing against a stone. It is not the weapon I would choose. If she was killed on the ground, it becomes an improbable weapon."

"Would the injury take long to inflict, Doctor?" Reid asked.

"Only a matter of seconds, maybe two."

The two inspectors then thanked the doctor and left his surgery.

"It is like getting blood out of a stone, Fred. I think he a bit out of his depth with these killings, don't you?"

"I think we all are. I certainly am, Edmund. We have the times of death from the witnesses though, and Doctor Blackwell was useful in narrowing the time down."

"Yes, that is true, but we have no clear description so far. Do you fancy a drink, Fred?"

"That is the best question of the day."

Meanwhile, sometime after 9.00pm, John Kelly, of 55 Flower and Dean Street, entered Bishopgate Police Station and stated that he thought the Mitre Square murder victim was his wife. He was then taken to the Golden Lane mortuary, where he identified the body as Catherine Eddowes. John said that she and he had cohabited for seven years, but they were not legally married.

John Kelly told the police that he last saw her at 2.00pm on Saturday in Houndsditch. She was going to see her daughter in Bermondsey for money. She promised to be home by 4.00pm. He said he was told later by two women, that she had been locked up at Bishopgate Police Station for drunkenness.

Catherine Eddowes was also identified by her sister, Eliza Gould, who lived at number 6 Thrawl Street. She stated that she had not seen her sister for three or four months and that her sister lived with a man called John Kelly.

The police then called at 55 Flower and Dean Street, where the deputy manager of the lodging house, Frederick Wilkinson, confirmed he knew the deceased and John Kelly for seven or eight years.

The final identification witness was her daughter, Anne Phillips, who gave police an overview of her mother's life.

In the relative safety and obscurity of the Princess Alice pub, the man now termed, *Jack the Ripper,* was amazed at the sensation of the two killings that he had carried out on the last day of September. He was not good at reading, but he listened to other people reading the newspapers out loud.

"They are all fuckin' idiots. I wasn't plannin' on doin' any killin' on that night. It just 'appened. I was goin' home when the Stride woman saw me, and if the other woman hadn't grabbed me bollocks, she would still be alive," he says quietly to himself when he is alone.

He had visited many pubs to listen to the conversations about *'The Ripper.'* For the first time in his miserable life, he felt a sense of pride. He never expected his killings to give him such feelings. This notoriety spurred him on to carry out further attacks.

He was slowly regaining aspects of his memory. He now knew the attack on him was not by a gang, he thinks it was by a prostitute, but he doesn't remember why the attack happened.

"I'll find that fuckin' bitch if it is the last fing I do. If only I could remember." The attack on him was always in his mind, and he was full of revenge.

Later in the day, he worked happily at the slaughter yard. He recalled the mutilations of the women when he was disembowelling a horse. He worked fast, building up his experience and killing proficiency. He had become quite skilful with a knife, making him a very dangerous adversary. An unarmed policeman would have had no chance against him.

"We're goin' to the pub, you comin'?" asked two of the slaughtermen.

"Yea, I'll come for one, I'll just clean up 'ere."

Bill and an older slaughterman called Alf, went into the pub with the man now named, *Jack the Ripper*. They each purchased a pint of porter ale and sat down in the reasonably crowded pub.

"Jack the Ripper is in all the newspapers," Bill said excitedly.

"They'll not catch him, 'e's far too clever for the coppers," Alf stated.

"What makes you say that Alf?" he asked out of self-interest.

"Well, he's not been caught after all this time. Five he has done, and the police don't have a clue," replied Alf.

The Ripper thought to himself *'It was luck more than anything. If only they knew the facts.'*

"Do you fink 'e will do anovver one, Alf?" Bill asked.

"Definitely, he won't stop."

"How do you know what 'e will do?" the Ripper said, angrily.

"Wew, I would if I were Jack the Ripper!" said Alf.

"But you're not though, are ya? Nobody knows, wot's gonna 'appen; Maybe the Ripper doesn't know 'imself?" the Ripper responded.

"Let's not keep talkin' about Jack the fuckin' Ripper, the blokes a wanker. I would cut him in two with me knife if I met him," said Bill.

"Maybe you will meet him, Bill, one day. He's killed five times, how many 'ave you killed?" the Ripper said calmly.

"Let's change the fucking subject," said Alf.

"Well, I'm off now, I'll see you both later," the Ripper said abruptly.

When he had left, Bill commented, "maybe 'e's Jack the Ripper?" and then laughed.

"Don't be fucking daft Bill; 'e's only a young pup. The Ripper is a big fucking foreign bloke; that's what the papers say!"

Everyone had a different opinion of whom Jack the Ripper was. So far, only one person knew for sure, but things may change soon.

October 3rd
The Ripper and a woman

'The doctor was right; the headaches are lessening, and the seizures are not as bad,' he thought to himself. What had not changed were the voices of his mother shouting at him and verbally abusing him. He hated prostitutes because he hated her. If he could only be free of her, the attacks would stop. The attacks were her fault. As much as he tried, he could not get his mother out of his head; she was driving him crazy.

Some of his memory was also returning but he couldn't remember any other details about the woman who attacked him. His feelings for revenge had never subsided; if only he could remember something about her. The Ripper walked the streets day and night looking for his attacker. There was some clue of his nemesis, there in his head, but it would not come out.

As adrenaline pumped through his veins, he became more and more dangerous. He sometimes felt that he could attack anyone, just to satisfy his anger. The only way for him to release his sexual lust was for him to kill and mutilate. He knew these were not normal feelings. He knew that he was on the road to destruction, but could he satisfy his feelings for revenge first?

"It's all your fuckin' fault, I wouldn't be in this mess if it weren't for you," he said, pacing up and down his room. "I can't 'elp fings, I'm tired of you, I wish I could forget you." It is as if his mother was there in the room with him. "I need to escape from this place, but where do I go?" he said, still pacing up and down with his fists clenched.

His words and his thoughts were not coherent; he didn't have the mental capacity to understand his thoughts and feelings. He then stopped pacing, and sat down, holding his head in his hands. The Ripper was getting a throbbing pain in his head now, so he laid on the floor and breathed heavily. His agitation had made his headache worse, so he decided to go for a drink or two at the bar to help him relax.

"You don't look so well, are you alright?" the landlady said, looking concerned for her nephew.

"Not really, I still get pains in me 'ead."

"Well sit down and 'ave a drink, 'ere get this down you."

"I fought me 'eadaches were getting better, but I just 'ad a bad one, like."

"It's when you get worked up about your mother; I hear you talken' to yourself about her. What is done is done, you can't change that."

"I know, but she is just there in me 'ead, givin' me grief."

"You need to stop feelen' sorry for yourself, that's your problem. Everyone has a hard time, that's 'ow it is. Pull yourself, to-fucken-gether."

"I need somefink to eat; I feels better when I've 'ad somefink."

"Go and get somethen' then, I'm not your fucken' servant."

He felt very miserable now; lacking a good sleep and being in pain would make anyone unhappy. He knew that the beer would help him forget things. After some food and drink, he ventured out once more, stalking between pubs. He saw people stopping to pick up small pieces of food from a street gutter; it did not bother him, seeing people do that. He did not feel any pity for them.

A frail old man, who was sat on the pavement, asked him for a penny for some food. His response was, "fuck off," and a kick.

An old woman was walking the streets with a baby wrapped up in a blanket. She was not begging to anyone. She just kept walking and talking to the baby. He saw her put the baby down on the ground near the workhouse infirmary and leave. The baby started to cry, but he just walked by with no regard for the child whatsoever.

Near to his previous murder site of Bucks Row, some children were begging in the street and asked a reasonably well-dressed man for some money. "You can each have a penny if you suck my dick," was the reply, then he started laughing when the children ran away.

He followed the man down Bucks Row and onto Brady Street. In the darkness, he attacked the man with his fists, knocking him to the floor, quickly. He kicked the man several times and stole his money and watch. "Fuckin' pervert," he said. It was clear that he had a strange moral compass of what was right and wrong. The pervert he had just beaten up was wrong, yet he, the killer of women, was somehow not a pervert. He was delighted with the amount of money he has acquired. He will buy some more good food, clothing and ale. He now felt happy with himself and was energised by his newly acquired bounty.

He spent the rest of the evening in the public houses on Brick Lane. He followed prostitutes out of the pubs and watched them covertly. There were people asleep in an alley, he emptied the contents of some of the bins onto them and moved the bins away so that a policeman would move them on.

He moved on to the Princess Alice pub, ordered a pint and sat down alone. A woman came over to him.

"You work in 'ere don'tcha, I've seen you at the bar." She was a young woman, about his age; but unlike him, she exhibited a lot of self-confidence.

"What of it?" he snarled aggressively.

"I work at the market, we 'ave a grocer's stall. I'm called Lucy," she said, smiling and trying to form a conversation with him.

"I fought you were anovver of them," he said with a stern face. He didn't pick up on her friendly body language.

"What! I'm not a whore, you cheeky bastard!" Though her words were harsh, she said them with a smile on her face.

"Sorry then, do you want a drink?" He didn't know what else to say; his communication skills were poor.

"Okay, I'll 'ave what you're 'avin'. Can ya afford it?" Lucy said confidently, still smiling and with her head back and her hands on her hips.

"Yea, course."

He bought her a pint, and she sat down with him. He looked a little uncomfortable and waited for her to say something.

"What 'appened to your boat, if ya don't mind me askin'?"

"I was attacked, and when I find her that did it, she will 'ave more than a damaged boat," he said this with real anger. She read his body language and quickly changed the subject.

"Sorry to 'ear that. You got a girlfriend?"

"No, never 'ad one and I don't fink I will 'ave now," he replied with regret in his voice and held his head down so she could not see his mournful expression.

"Don't be like that; you're awright. Do you want me to show you how to do it?" Lucy replied confidently.

"What?" He was slow to understand people and read a situation like this.

She leaned into him and said in a loud whisper "Do you fancy a shag?"

He was drinking at the time, and the beer went all over the place, while he was spluttering. His face had also gone red.

"How old are you?" he said, attempting to compose himself.

"Twenty-one, and you?"

"Twenty-five, nearly six."

"Wew then, are we 'avin' a shag or not?" she said as she moved closer and pushed her face into his.

"We can go up to me room, up the stairs, like," he said, very nervously.

They went upstairs to his small and basic bedroom. Lucy quickly got undressed and was completely naked, revealing a slim figure and firm round breasts. She had a couple of front teeth missing, yet she was still attractive. He slowly removed his clothes, and immediately she knelt to perform oral sex on him. He ejaculated almost immediately.

"You were ready for that, weren'tcha," she said after spitting the semen out.

"Come on," she says as she lies on the bed with her legs wide open. "Lie on top of me, and I will put your cock inside me, you'll soon get the 'ang of it."

He did as Lucy commanded, and they had sexual intercourse.

"When you fink you are coming, pull it out, and I will wank you off, I don't want a fuckin' kid."

He complied with the instruction, just in time, he thought.

"Well, did you like that?"

"Yes, did you?"

"Yea, we can do it again sometime, now that you're no longer a virgin. You will get better in time."

"You're not a shy gal, are ya?" he laughs.

"You don't say much, do ya?"

"I get bad 'eadaches."

He had just had sex for the first time, yet he still appeared miserable. He could not express himself verbally and rarely showed his feelings. Lucy read that he was uncomfortable, so she quickly made a move to go.

"I'm gonna go now, but we can see each over again. I don't wanna to be out late wiv that fuckin' killer out there."

"Ok, but you'll be safe," he said this with a smile; he could quickly respond on this subject without giving himself away.

"'ow do you know?" she turned to him with a serious expression; it was the first time she had said something without smiling.

"Cos, you're not a whore, are ya?" For once, he had made a smart response and looked more confident than he had done in a long time.

"Wew, you fought I was one."

"Yea, but not many come over and talk to me, except them who want money."

As she left him alone in his room, he felt alive for the first time in his life. He was not bothered as much about his mother or revenge. He had tasted new fruit and liked the taste. He slept well for the first time in a while.

October 5th
A missed opportunity

Inspector Collard of the City Police had just interviewed two key witnesses who saw Catherine Eddowes with a man, just before her death. The first one was from Mr Joseph Lawende, who was a commercial traveller. He stated to Collard that on the night of the murder, he and two colleagues, Joseph Levy and Harry Harris, rose to leave the Imperial Club in Duke Street at 1.30am. Inspector Collard wrote down their statements in full.

"The Club clock struck the half hour and my two colleagues and myself rose to leave. We put on our coats and hats then went down the stairs, we were still talking so it must have been three or four minutes later that we opened the door to go outside. As we walked down Duke Street we saw a man and a woman outside Church Passage, on the opposite side of the street. I couldn't see the woman's face but she had a black bonnet and jacket on."

"So you can confirm that the clothing that we have shown you, is the same as that on the woman you saw." Collard asked.

"Yes Inspector."

"What can you tell me about the man she was with?"

"The man was taller than the woman by about five inches, Inspector, and had on a grey cloth peak cap. He had on a loose pepper and salt coloured jacket and a reddish handkerchief tied in a knot around his neck. He was about 30 years old, five-foot-seven or eight-inches tall, with a fair complexion and fair moustache, and medium build.

"Would you be able to recognise the man again, Mr Lawende?"

"I doubt it, Inspector."

"Did you hear the couple say anything?"

"The couple were not arguing and she put her hand on his chest. We did not like the look of them, so we moved off quickly."

"What time was it, when you saw these two people?"

"It must have been 25 minutes to two o'clock, Inspector."

"Thank you Mr Lawende, that is all."

His friend Mr Hyam Levy gave a similar story to the Inspector.

"We left the building three or four minutes after 1.30am and we saw a man and woman across the street, on the corner of Church Passage."

"What can you tell me about them, sir?"

"I didn't take much notice, Inspector. The man may have been three inches taller than the woman."

"Can you confirm anything else about them, such as what they were wearing? Or what time it was."

"I don't know what they were wearing, Inspector, but it must have been about 1.35am, because we rose to leave the club at 1.30am."

"Could you see if the woman was in trouble in any way, sir."

"No Inspector, they seemed to be just speaking."

"Thank you, sir."

Detective Inspector James McWilliam led the investigation for the City Police. He and Inspector Edward Collard were discussing the witness statements of Mr Lawende and Mr Levy.

"If these two men are telling the truth, then she was killed after 1.35am and before 1.44am. Given that Doctor Brown says it would take five minutes to carry out all the mutilations, and the killer would need a minute or two to get her from Duke Street to the murder scene, and a minute or two to leave the scene, then she was probably killed and mutilated from 1.37am to 1.42am. This is what Inspector Reid said, so there was no way PC Harvey could be at the end of Church Passage, he would have seen the murder taking place, Jim," Collard commented.

"You are correct Ted, it is just as Reid has said. The woman was already dead at 1.40am. Harvey must have been somewhere else. If he had been there at the end of the passage, we would have caught Jack the Ripper. Damn the man!"

"Reid and Abberline will not be happy that our man was not on his beat and missed the Ripper," Collard said.

"I'm not bloody happy, Ted!"

"We need to get Harvey in for questioning, as soon as possible, Jim.

"Send the statements to Abberline and Reid; but ask them to keep the man's description back from the press and the inquest. This description of the man is the description of the Ripper, mark my words, Ted."

In the evening of the 5th of October, the Central News Agency, received a letter at 8.55pm that evening. This was immediately forwarded to Chief Constable Williamson of the Metropolitan Police, CID. It was another letter claiming to be from Jack the Ripper. Williamson then wrote out a copy of it and sent it onto the City Police. The tide of Ripper letters was now in full flow.

October 6th
Another letter and a glimmer of hope

Early in the morning, in Reid's office in Leman Street, Reid and Abberline read the latest letter from Jack the Ripper.

5 Oct.1888

Dear Friend
In the name of God hear me I swear I did not kill the female whose body was found in Whitehall. If she was an honest woman, I will hunt down and destroy her murderer. If she was a whore God will bless the hand that slew her, for the women of Moab and Midian shall die and their blood shall mingle with the dust. I never harm any others or the Divine power that protects and helps me in my grand work would quit forever. Do as I do and the light of glory shall shine upon you. I must get to work tomorrow treble event this time yes three must be ripped. Will send you a bit of face by post I promise this dear old Boss. The police now reckon my work a practical joke as well Jacky's a very practical joker ha Keep this back till three are wiped out and you can show the cold meat.
Yours truly
Jack the Ripper

"The letter came in late last night. Another idiot claiming to be Jack the bloody Ripper," an angry Abberline said.

"Well the text is like the first letter, but there is no evidence he knows anything about the killings that we have kept back. It is another press hoax," Reid stated.

"I agree, Edmund. I have thought about this since we published the first letter. It sells papers and scares people, which puts us under pressure. We have enough to do without some joker pedalling this shite out to everyone."

"If there are three next time, and I don't for a minute think there will be, then this letter writer may be true or just lucky at guessing," Reid said.

"It's time we pulled all our resources and the City Police together. We have four, possibly five, murders by the same hand. We are getting pressure from all sides now; this can't go on, Edmund." Abberline sat down heavily with a sigh, his face looking tired and stressed.

"I agree entirely, Fred, but something inside me tells me that there is worse to come. It isn't over yet. We must understand the type of person who is doing this, to have a chance of catching him. If we can do that, we can narrow down who we are looking for and where he may be."

"I have never experienced this sort of crime before, but the crimes I do know about, it is always local knowledge that solves them, but not in this case. It is as if the killer were a ghost. It worries me greatly that at the back of my mind, I have a nagging doubt that keeps coming back saying that we may never catch him. But I have been awake most of the night; I can't sleep properly. Sometimes I can't eat. Sometimes, I get very negative about the whole case, and then other times I am ok and believe we will succeed. I wish it was over Edmund."

"I have never heard you express your feelings like that before, Fred. The case has really got to you, hasn't it?" said Reid, totally understanding his colleagues state of mind.

"We need to go through everything again, step-by-step to make sure we have the right information. Otherwise, we are, as you say, chasing ghosts.

"I am as frustrated as you Fred, but I haven't lost hope, nor have you. There are clues to the killer in every one of his attacks, that put together, will reveal him. Now, the picture of him is still vague, but we must start looking at the case differently, from his perspective. If we can understand him more, the clearer the picture will become."

"Eh? You might as well have said that in Chinese, Edmund. That's about as clear as mud on the banks of the Thames. You do the thinking, Edmund, I need a drink. I should have stayed making clocks in Dorset. I used to sleep then, and Dorset is such a lovely place, why did I move?"

Around mid-morning, a constable came in with a letter from the City Police. Abberline took the letter.

"It's from McWilliam, of the City Police; they have two witnesses to the Eddowes murder."

Reid and Abberline read the contents of Inspector McWilliam's letter, which included a description of a man, and more importantly, the time this observation took place.

"I was right Fred; the murder was committed before 1.40am. The constable who should have been at the end of Church Passage was not there. He has missed the Ripper. We should have had him there and then," Reid retorted while pacing up and down the floor.

"Of all the bloody luck! Just one break we need. The PC was probably talking to someone or taking a piss somewhere, or even worse shagging a prostitute somewhere. He wants a bloody good talking to," Abberline shouted.

"I don't think all our men were in the right place at the right time. I think one or two were round at the slaughter yard in Winthrop Street, having a brew and a chat, when the Bucks Row murder took place. The Ripper is the luckiest bastard that ever lived," Reid said with great annoyance written all over his face.

"Well, at least we have some sort of description this time. There isn't time for someone else to come along. This was the Ripper at Duke Street at 1.35am," Abberline stated more calmly.

"Given she was discovered at 1.44am. This is probably, the best description of the murderer," Reid added enthusiastically.

"And he isn't like any of the descriptions from Berner Street," Abberline added in a loud voice.

"It also means, that he must have killed her between 1.36am and 1.43am, when he must have exited Mitre Square," Reid stated firmly.

"I am going to nail this bastard, Edmund!"

"We are going to nail this bastard, Fred," said Reid, emphasising the We.

"Let's get this information circulated to all our men on the streets. We are going to get him! Get more uniforms into plain clothes. I will get more drafted in from other divisions and talk to the chiefs upstairs."

"The case is becoming clearer, Fred. I can see the light at the end of this tunnel."

"Will you just bloody stop it with your ridiculous bloody clichés. What the bloody hell does that mean? On second thought, don't tell me. Just speak simple, plain, bloody English, Edmund, for fuck's sake."

Following the publication of the first letter signed *Jack the Ripper*, the police had become inundated with other similar messages, false confessions and false claims by members of the public, about Jack the Ripper. Jewish men of Whitechapel and Spitalfields were under suspicion. This may have been because the murder at Berner Street was next to a Jewish club. Jewish premises were targeted for searches; in particular, butchers, slaughterhouses and barbers.

The police were also guilty of giving too much credence to the eye-witnesses, who were near the crime scene, at the time of the murders. The eye-witnesses Elizabeth Long on Hanbury Street and Israel Schwartz on Berner Street, both led police to look for a middle-aged foreign-looking man, even though the two descriptions did not match. Both witnesses only briefly saw the potential killer as they passed the man by.

Later in the same day, work was underway trying to deal with all the letters and statements following the double killings a few days ago.

"How are we going to sort all these letters out as well as all the witness statements?" Detective Constable Charles Dolden asked Inspector Charles Pinhorn.

"All those that seem to have useful information go in that box there; the other box is for the rest," Inspector Pinhorn replied.

"I know that sir, but how do we know what is useful and not? Most of these letters are hoaxes and made up by people, but one of them may be true, but how will we know, sir?"

"I will see what Inspector Reid wants us to do."

"There is getting too many of them, sir; we will need more men to go through them all. More letters are coming every day, sir," Dolden said.

"You just get on with it son, I will see Inspector Reid, as I have said."

Inspector Pinhorn then met up with Abberline and Reid, in Reid's office.

"What is it Charles, you wanted to see me?" Reid said politely.

"We are getting flooded with letters and people wanting to give statements about all sorts of things. We can't cope unless we get more men."

"Fred, see if we can second some men from other divisions."

"There is something else, Edmund. We are having difficulty knowing how to sort through this information to know what is genuine and what is a hoax."

"I have been thinking about this, and we need some sort of system. For example, we need to collate, all the descriptions of the killer, once the witnesses have been checked out. Then…"

Abberline interrupted, "How long is that going to take? There are hundreds, maybe thousands; I suppose we are going to arrest all the false statement writers also?"

"Fred, Charles, we have to be thorough, eye-witnesses take priority once they have been checked out. Secondly, statements and letters that support the eye-witness descriptions need to be investigated. We need someone else working on the information, querying the whereabouts of family members or people that have seen blood on someone else's clothing," Reid stated.

"I knew this would happen when we released the Ripper letters," Abberline said, shaking his head.

"The press would have released them anyway, Fred. They are probably the authors of many letters; it sells papers. We need to visit every slaughter yard, butchers and all properties surrounding the murder sites. Boots on the ground are required, even if it is for the next month or two. Somehow, we then need to collate any statements with each murder, and maybe something common to each murder will stand out. We will need more space also, Fred."

"This is getting out of hand; we are not office workers; we are policemen. The men need to be out there to catch him," Abberline shouted.

"We need *both* Fred; we must explore all routes. Someone may recognise a family member as the killer, but they want to remain anonymous, so they send in a letter. We have no option; if we catch him and it turns out that relevant information in a statement or letter has been overlooked, then we will be blamed. We need every resource on this until he is caught," Reid said, looking at Abberline and Pinhorn; both of whom looked tired and dejected.

Inspector Reid had re-visited the crime scenes after the last two killings in the same night. It appeared to him that if a scream or noises were made, that possibly someone would have heard them. Reid concluded that the last four women were silently killed before they could cry out. They were all killed by a severe cut to the neck and throat. However, he was uneasy about the Tabram killing and the two attacks of Millwood and Wilson. In the two early attacks, the victims screamed, and the attacker fled. The Tabram murder worried Reid because she was not killed instantly and so she must have screamed, in which case, someone may have heard her. He wanted to talk through it again with Abberline, but before he did, he tried to put some of his thoughts by his wife, Emily, first. Reid was concluding that

Abberline was being cynical about his methods, and so he wanted some independent confirmation first. Emily was a good listener and thought deeply about issues; this made her an ideal companion for Reid.

After dinner and spending time with the children, Reid started to explain the necessary details of the Tabram murder, but without giving too much of the gory details away. Emily listened attentively with several nods of her head while he explained.

"What I don't understand Emily, is that if a man is struggling with a woman, which he undoubtedly was with Martha Tabram, some noise must have been made. In which case, why didn't someone come to her aid, or shout for the police? He hadn't learned to kill quickly yet; there was no throat-cutting of Tabram, so surely she would have made a noise, wouldn't she?"

"I agree, you would think so, unless he had one hand over her mouth; in which case she would have two hands to defend herself against the knife in the murderer's other hand," Emily said while moving her hands to deflect an imaginary knife. "Maybe someone heard something but ignored it. Maybe noise is common, even at night."

"I thought that too, so I went and checked. I made some noise in George Yard Buildings, and usually, someone was aroused to come and look. So somehow, he must have killed Tabram without any noise, which seems to rule out that a struggle occurred. This then conflicts with the injuries that suggest it took a while to kill her. Given the first two attacks involved the victim screaming; so, what if in this case, he gagged her somehow, then stabbed her to death?"

"It is possible. He wanted to stab, but he did not want any noise. It is a possibility, Edmund."

"Then this suggests that the killer had done some pre-planning if he took some sort of gag with him. He must have decided that his next attack would be quieter and thought of the gag. More importantly, he hadn't thought about cutting the throat as an alternative. So how did he get the idea about throat cutting?"

"Someone must have told him?" suggested Emily.

"What if he learned it as part of a job as a butcher or slaughterman? We can narrow our search down to slaughtermen in the area."

"It makes sense when you think about it. Although she could have passed out from being partially strangled and she wouldn't be able to cry out if she was being throttled."

"Yes, Emm, but there would then be no struggle; he was unable to kill her quickly with his clasp knife, so he used a dagger. If she was unconscious, he could have cut her open until she bled to death, so there would be no need for the dagger in the heart."

"I see what you mean. She was therefore conscious and was struggling, in which case some noise must have been made."

"Which leads me then onto a different set of questions; why did he not strangle her first to make it easy for himself? The only thing I can think of, is that he did not consider that it would be quite so difficult to kill with a clasp knife. I think it was because he was unskilled at killing. This then points to a younger person with little previous experience, who is showing a general progression from just stabbing to attempting to kill someone, but without any real thought."

"I see you have given this a lot of thought, Edmund, and your analysis seems cogent. So, what you are saying is that the Ripper is a younger person who has only recently started killing and that his killing technique has improved as he has progressed. You, therefore, think that he has obtained the killing skill from a slaughterer or butcher recently."

"Yes, Emily and that is how we can narrow him down."

"So, Edmund, you must have the courage of your convictions to discuss this with Fred and explain your thoughts in detail to him. If he rebuffs you, then you have done all you can. I think there are only a few men in Spitalfields that fit your criteria for the killer, so get after them."

Reid smiled. "Emily, you are, as always, a good listener and you have an open mind. I wish Fred were as open-minded. He is a good copper, the best in fact, but his methods don't work in this particular case; the worst of it is though, he just can't see it."

October 19th
The Lusk kidney and the *From Hell* letter

On the 16th of October at around 5.00pm, George Lusk, chairman of the Whitechapel Vigilance Committee, received a package and a letter. Not expecting a package, Mr Lusk carefully opened the small box to find it contained what appeared to be part of a kidney. A letter explained the contents to a degree. In a very rough, scrawled handwriting and blood staining the page; it read as follows:

From hell

Mr Lusk
Sir
I send you half the
Kidne I took from one women
prasarved it for you tother piece I
fried and ate it was very nise. I
may send you the bloody knif that
took it out if you only wate a whil
longer

Signed   Catch me when
you can
Mishter Lusk

George Lusk thought this was a sick joke, as he had received earlier correspondence. After consulting two members of the vigilance committee the following day, the kidney was eventually taken to Doctor Openshaw, curator of the London Hospital Museum. He declared it to be half of a left kidney from a human. The letter and kidney was subsequently taken to the police. Inspectors Abberline and Reid saw the letter at Leman Street Police Station.

"What do you think of this letter, Edmund?" Abberline asked, "it was sent with a kidney, of all things, to George Lusk." Inspector Reid considered the letter and its wording carefully, reading it several times.

"I think this is another hoax, written by someone who is making deliberate errors to give the impression of a disturbed and more illiterate hand. People with poor writing skills tend to write phonetically; that is, how the words sound. It is very easy to spell words like *piece* and *fried* wrong, but these two words are correctly spelt, as are the words *signed* and *half*. Similarly, you would expect the word *knife* to be spelt as *nife*, and not *knif*. The same with the word *while*, phonetically it would be spelt *wile*, but here it's spelt *whil*. *Kidney* would be spelt *kidny* not *kidne*. So, this letter is written by someone who can write correctly but is deliberately misspelling certain words and missing more obvious ones to misspell. Also, although there are spelling and grammar errors, the structure of the letter is correct. The address is written top right, the addressee top left, and it is signed at the bottom," Reid explained.

"So, you think this is nothing more than a sick joke Edmund?"

"Yes, it is an offal joke, Fred."

"Your jokes are offal. What about the kidney did it come from the Eddowes woman?"

"The doctor says that it is a human left kidney, but not much more than that. We just don't know if it belonged to the victim. If it did belong to Catherine Eddowes, then this letter is from the murderer," Reid stated firmly.

"Everything that has been in the letters has been in the press, including this one."

"As you have said before, Fred, we can only publish and see if someone recognises the handwriting."

"We are already getting inundated with false leads and claims, and we won't have the manpower to deal with them. Meanwhile, there is a killer still out there, waiting to strike again." Abberline was worried. The more he thought about the case; the more overwhelmed he got.

"I fear that unless we catch him in the act, he's not going to stop. We can't put a plain-clothed policeman on every prostitute in Whitechapel and Spitalfields. Even if we could, I feel the killer would just move further afield; we must find another way," Reid said firmly.

"We have checked and interviewed all the people that use the lodging houses. We have checked and interviewed all the workers at all the slaughterhouses. We have sent out 80,000 leaflets and been to all the properties near all the murder sites. We have drafted in officers from other divisions, and there are more plain-clothed officers about. What else can we do, Edmund?"

Abberline knew he was repeating himself, and that his words were painful, but he had to vent his feelings.

"I agree, Fred. Our best hope is that someone else who knows the killer gives him up. Someone must have suspicions about certain relatives or workmates or clients. Yet, we may not have asked the right questions, because we haven't got a clear picture of what the Ripper is like. Once we have that, we can narrow our searches and ask the right questions."

"If there are any more, we are going to have rioting on our hands," Abberline said while pacing up and down, he was agitated, and Reid wasn't helping.

"His luck will run out soon, Fred. We will catch him. I am sure of it."

"I wish I had your confidence. What I don't understand is why here? Why kill in this area? Why now? We haven't had anything like this before. So, what makes someone start killing like this, in Whitechapel, at this time?"

"Well, it is funny that you say that. I have been reading a book by Richard von Krafft-Ebing, that was published a couple of years ago called *Psychopathia Sexualis*. He talks about a *psycho-sexual lust murderer*, where murder and mutilation are part of the sexual act. If the Ripper is one of these lust murderers, as Ebing states, then he doesn't have normal sexual relations. Sex alone isn't enough for him. He needs to mutilate to get sexual excitement."

Reid was in his element talking about this topic; he loved new approaches and people who thought differently about things. His expressions and body language demonstrated his energy for the case.

"And does that help us catch him, Edmund?" Abberline sounded cynical and despondent; it didn't fit in with his local knowledge policing.

"I don't know Fred; I will have to think about this. It may help us narrow down who we are looking for. Before you asked why Whitechapel, and why here? In all probability, it is because he lives and works in this area. It is his home. I have several ideas on how we may narrow this down. His crimes tell us something about him."

Abberline interrupted with a sharp "what?"

"Hear me out, Fred. The doctors think that it is someone that is used to using a knife, but not a surgeon. We have a description of someone of average height and build, aged mid-twenties to 30 or thereabouts. He is easily angered, probably a criminal and been in prison. He possibly lives alone and near the crime scenes. These factors narrow it down. If we now employ these criteria to say, slaughtermen or butchers, we will get a much smaller number. We can search these men specifically, interrogate them deeply, check where they were on the nights of each attack to see if they have an alibi. It is now only a matter of time. If we don't get him, then we can watch a smaller number of suspects until we do get him."

"We don't know for certain he is a slaughterman, Edmund," Abberline painfully replied, bending down slightly and placing his hands on the desk.

"Correct Fred, or a butcher, but we can narrow it down. For example, we can narrow it down by recent prison records of who fitting these criteria and has been let out of prison in the past year. It will be someone with a criminal record. Someone who has been a delinquent. Someone violent. What I am saying is this, it's a new concept of mine: If we have a list of potential criminals, we can crossmatch them to a list of slaughtermen and butchers and cross-reference them to our known criteria. We will find that with all these different variables, only one name will match. I am sure of it. We need a lot of people to make a lot of records and match them up. It is the only way, unless we get lucky at the next attack."

"Edmund, he might not be on any list you draft up. He could be a sailor, or a foreigner or a transient worker." Abberline was negative and not willing to consider any approach, other than the one he was comfortable with and had served him well.

"Possibly. What I am talking about is a process of elimination. I am sure that he lives in Spitalfields, that excludes sailors and passing foreigners or transient workers. Someone born, living and working in Spitalfields. I will bet my life on it!

"There are only so many men, in their mid-twenties, that have been criminals, living in Spitalfields; he is one of them. I have thought about this, again and again, reading the reports, putting it together in my head. This is the way to solve it. I even have a few possible suspects, just by the chance of knowing them. I haven't thoroughly checked them out with the two recent murders, but I am trying to ascertain their whereabouts on the key dates."

October 26th
Inspector Reid's deliberations

On the walls of a large room in Leman Street Police Station, a series of separate notice boards had been placed in chronological order, with the date and name of the victim as the heading for each board as follows:

>*February 25 Annie Millwood*
>*March 28 Ada Wilson*
>*April 3 Emma Smith*
>*August 7 Martha Tabram*
>*August 31 Mary Ann Nichols*
>*September 8 Annie Chapman*
>*September 30 Elizabeth Stride*
>*September 30 Catherine Eddowes*

Each board had the following information:

>*Details of the victim*
>*Descriptions of the attacker*
>*Method of killing or attack*
>*Post-mortem mutilations*
>*Time of the murder or assault*
>*Witnesses*
>*Map of the location of each crime scene*

There was also a separate map of the whole area with each crime scene pinpointed.

Inspector Reid explained the boards to Abberline.

"What we have done Fred, is to try to pull all the information together from each crime, and it gives us some indications of the killer, which we can put on this board," he said, pointing to one board headed *Jack the Ripper.*'

Reid moves to the first two boards.

"These two crimes are stabbings, and both women survived. Ada Wilson was apparently a robbery. Both offences were impulsive and not planned. Not what a mature criminal would do. Not what a particularly intelligent criminal would do, also. These may have been his first attacks with a knife, for all we know.

"The next six victims were all prostitutes all living in common lodging houses in Spitalfields. Emma Smith may not have been killed by the Ripper. She stated that she was attacked by a gang and died due to the rupture of her peritoneum. Someone else was savagely assaulted at the same time, but with a hammer. Again, it could have been a gang; we don't know.

"The remaining five victims were killed by a knife. Tabram stabbed 39 times, one of the wounds was a deep wound to the heart, by a dagger or similar weapon. A struggle ensued before the victim died.

"The remaining four victims were all killed by the neck arteries and throat being cut. Can you see the pattern, Fred? The killings are getting more clinical; the killer is learning to kill more efficiently as he gains experience."

"Okay Edmund, I see that."

"So, what do we have so far? Someone who is immature in some ways, late teens, but more likely early twenties, and his killing is improving with time. So, he's not a mature killer. An older person who is accomplished would not make the mistakes with the first three stabbings. So, on this board, we can add something about his age, possibly mid-twenties." Abberline nodded as Reid continued his explanation.

"Now, all the victims, except Wilson, lived in Spitalfields. This includes the first attack and the first killing. Let us assume the killer lives or works in Spitalfields and knows the area well. So, we can add *'Spitalfields'* to the board. He stalks them from pubs in Spitalfields or from their common lodging houses. As he gained confidence, he moved further afield from his home.

"His early attacks are with a clasp knife and are immature stabbings; his later attacks are with a longer stiffer bladed instrument and his attacks are lethal. He, therefore, has had some practice or instruction with a knife. Cutting the neck is the quickest way to kill an animal at a slaughter yard. Maybe he works as a butcher or a slaughterman?"

"Well if that is the case, why did he kill with a clasp knife earlier?"

"Good question Fred, the answer is that he didn't work at such places then, he has obtained such employment between Tabram and Nichols."

"So, we can add in something for the use of a knife and occupation," Abberline said with conviction. He is now beginning to understand Reid's method.

"Now, if you remember, I did mention that this killer may have been in prison and therefore has a criminal background. The level of criminality will also have increased with age. Started with shoplifting, then burglary, then robbery, you get the picture?" Reid asked, looking his colleague straight in the eyes. "I don't know of anyone that lives a blameless law-abiding life until their mid-twenties then just starts cutting up women on the streets."

"Agreed. He's a wrong un. Once they start with crime, they don't get better."

"So, we can add that he almost certainly has a criminal record."

"Do you see what this is doing Fred? By looking at all the evidence together, to obtain a pattern of behaviour, it starts to narrow down the criminal. I am not looking for a foreign 50-year-old sailor or a law-abiding printer in his twenties.

"There is some debate amongst the doctors, whether the Ripper has any anatomical knowledge or not. But he did remove a uterus from Chapman and a uterus and kidney from Eddowes, so even though he is clearly not a medical man, he has some knowledge. This fits with a slaughterman or a butcher, for example.

"With the other criteria, I will have to speak to some eminent doctors first. I have a few ideas, but I need some confirmation." The two inspectors are quiet for a few minutes as they studied the part completed board, headed *'Jack the Ripper'*.

> *Description?*
> *Height and build?*
> *Where does he live/work? Spitalfields*
> *How old is he? Mid-twenties*
> *Criminal Record? Almost certainly*
> *Ability to use a knife? Yes, accomplished*
> *Some anatomical knowledge? Yes, but basic*
> *Background?*
> *Occupation? Slaughterman or butcher?*
> *Personal characteristics?*
> *Evidence of abuse?*
> *Evidence of severe injury?*
> *Personal relationships?*

"You have a different way of looking at things than myself, Edmund. I see the logic in your approach and the principle of narrowing down the suspects, but it doesn't tell us who he is."

"That is correct, Fred, but we now need only slaughtermen in their mid-twenties for example, rather than interviewing all slaughtermen."

"How do you come up with this idea?"

"I have read various reports on criminals and their behaviour. I have read examples of similar cases that have been cited in multiple publications. I have had discussions with professionals that have an interest in such matters. But I naturally just like things to be ordered and all the evidence presented logically. Once I have the correct evidence; I can then evaluate it."

November 2nd
Revelations in the Ten Bells

There hadn't been a murder now in just over a month, but it had not stopped people talking about it. The press had stirred up a frenzy about the man called Jack the Ripper.

The Ten Bells, on the corner of Church Street and Commercial Street, was a popular public house. The pub itself was quite a feature on the corner and opposite, Christ Church. It was four stories high and built from facing brickwork as was much of Spitalfields. Originally the pub was called the Eight Bells Alehouse in the 1750s and changed its name to the Ten Bells in the 1790s. The pub was quite ornate both inside and out.

A frequent customer in the Ten Bells was Mary Jane Kelly, she was a 25-year-old prostitute, originally from Ireland. She was an outgoing person who made friends easily. She was known to be a heavy drinker, and she could be quite violent when drunk. She was drinking in the pub with two female friends, who were also prostitutes. They had been talking quite loudly about the double murder that occurred on the 30th of September.

"Well I didn't know either of them girls, but that bastard needs hanging for what he did to them," Mary said in her Irish accent.

"I am afraid to go out with anyone I don't know now; it might be the Ripper," Katie, her tall blonde friend, said.

"We should go in two's so that we ain't on our own," Frances, the older dark-haired companion, said.

"He'll just kill boaf of us then," Katie replied.

"Wew, it's only my suggestion, innit."

"Don't be like that with her, she is trying to help, aren't ya love," Mary said, putting her arm around Frances. "I also know something else that helps an' all," Mary said, bringing a hammer out from her bag."

"Watcha' doin' wiv that?" Katie asked.

"Protection," Mary said, boasting in a loud voice. "I've already used it once, to hammer some bastard with a knife, in Angel Alley one night. I've also threatened to use it again, I have, and they had the sense to fuck off," Mary said cockily.

Unknown to Mary and her two companions, her conversation was being overheard since she brought out the hammer. The eager listener was the landlady of the Princess Alice public house. She was with one of her friends, Elsie, having a drink. Both saw the hammer and heard Kelly's boast of using it.

"Ere, wasn't your nephew hit wiv an 'ammer?" Elsie asked.

"Yes, but it was a gang, at least he said it was," Letty said.

"Well she said it was in Angel Alley, and that's where 'e was attacked, wasn't it?"

"You're right. I'll ask 'im when 'e gets 'ome. Do you know her name, Elsie?"

"Kelly, Mary Kelly, lives on Dorset Street somewhere, I fink."

"Come on. Elsie, we're leaven', drink up."

In the Princess Alice pub, Letty asked her nephew about the attack in April. He maintained it was a gang. She told him that there is a woman in the Ten Bells called Mary Kelly, who had a hammer and she used it on someone in Angel Alley. The nephew was very quiet but very interested.

Later that evening, the lone killer of women now known as Jack the Ripper entered the Ten Bells on several brief searches and stalked the streets around the pub. Eventually, Mary Jane Kelly came in and talked to someone at the bar that she knew.

"Are you goin' to buy me a drink and all?" she said with her Irish accent.

The Ripper recognised her voice immediately. It was as if a light had switched on inside his head. From now on, the killer had the scent of his prey. It was now only a matter of time before the kill. He was patient and bided his time. He satisfied himself with the sweet thoughts of revenge. He felt that he would happily die after his attack was complete. Stalking her next week would be an absolute joy. The Ten Bells was a popular pub with both the locals and travellers alike; hence, it was quite noisy. The Ripper covertly kept an eye on Mary, from a distance, to make sure that she didn't recognise him.

November 9th
The killing of Mary Jane Kelly and the police investigations

Mary Jane Kelly was born in Limerick and had lived some of her life in Carnarvon, where she married a miner around 1879. Unfortunately, he was killed two or three years later. She moved to Cardiff in 1883 and became a prostitute, then came to London in 1884 and worked in a West End brothel. She met Joseph Barnett in April 1887, and they lodged together until the 30th of October 1888, when they split up.

He left Kelly because she was using their room for prostitution and had other prostitutes staying there. Mary had long, dark, reddish-brown hair. She was attractive with a curvy figure, so had no problem in obtaining clients and she could be quite selective if she needed to be. Although she ate well, most of her earnings went on drink, and she was in rent arrears. She could be quite loud and violent when drunk and was known to be able to drink large quantities of alcohol, which fuelled her aggression.

Mary was living in a rented room at 13 Miller's Court, Dorset Street. This room was on the ground floor and accessed via the courtyard. The room was only about 12 feet by 10 feet and was partitioned off from the rest of number 26 Dorset Street, which may well have been the roughest street in London. It was inhabited by criminals and prostitutes, and it had some of the worst common lodging houses in Spitalfields. Alcoholism and violence were rife in this area. A stranger was likely to be mugged here, and no-one would have seen anything.

Miller's Court was accessed via an archway between numbers 26 and 27 Dorset Street. Inside it was a small, dingy, damp and dismal courtyard that gave access to 13 little tenement hovels, on either side. It also contained a filthy reeking toilet and a basic waterpipe stand. Dorset Street consisted of approximately 20 terraced houses on each side, of three stories in height, leading to Commercial Street at one end and Crispin Street at the other. It was littered with rubbish, horse droppings, vomit and had a stench of urine. On the same side as Miller's Court, and only four houses away, was the Britannia public house on the corner with Commercial Street. At the other end of the street, and still on the same side as Miller's Court, was the Horn of Plenty beer shop, on the corner with Crispin Street. These two pubs were basically a second home for the doss house residents. At numbers 16-19 Dorset Street and directly opposite Miller's Court was Crossingham's Lodging House, which was a hive for criminals, prostitutes and drunkards. Number 35 Dorset Street on the same side as Miller's Court was another Crossingham's doss houses.

On the evening of the 8th of November and the early hours of Friday, the 9th of November, Mary Kelly had been selling herself and spending the money in the pubs around Commercial Street. These were usually the Ten Bells, the Britannia, the Horn of Plenty and the Queen's Head. At 11.45pm on the 8th of November, she returned to her lodgings in Miller's Court, in a drunken state, with a man in his 30's, as witnessed by Mary Ann Cox. She was heard to be singing from midnight to 1.00am by several of her neighbours.

Sometime later, she was back in Commercial Street. At about 2.00am, and roughly between Thrawl Street and Flower and Dean Street, Mary Kelly stopped George Hutchinson, whom she knew, and asked him for sixpence. He stated that he had no money left. She replied, "good morning, I must go and find some money," and set off towards Thrawl Street. A man walked towards Mary and stopped her. He asked her something, to which they both burst out laughing. Hutchinson heard Kelly say "alright" and he heard the man say, "you will be alright for what I have told you."

Hutchinson stood outside The Queen's Head public house and watched the couple walk past him. The man had a small parcel with him and kept his head down with his hat over his eyes. The man tried to avoid being seen by Hutchinson. The couple went into Dorset Street, and Hutchinson followed. He looked intensely at the man and his appearance.

The couple then entered Miller's Court, and Hutchinson again followed, but he could not see them. He waited outside Crossingham's, directly opposite Miller's Court for about 45 minutes and no-one came out, so he left. Hutchinson was the last known person to see Kelly alive, apart from the killer.

The Ripper had now been stalking Mary Jane Kelly for one whole week, noting her movements and habits. He knew that she could only open the door to her room by reaching through the broken window. He was watching her in Commercial Street as she picked up a well-dressed gentleman. He decided that he would move into position tonight and deal with Mary Kelly once and for all. Just before 2.00am, he walked into Miller's Court and placed his arm through the window to open the door. There were not many places to hide in the room; he needed to observe her and strike when she was alone.

At just after two o'clock in the morning, Kelly and her client entered the room. The man did not want sex with Kelly, he wanted to lie on the bed in an undressed state with Kelly and for her to pretend that he was a baby. The man kept making baby noises, and Kelly acted as his doting mother. He paid her one shilling and sixpence. All this time, the Ripper was close by and getting impatient. He felt like killing the bloke as well, but he waited for him to leave. Eventually, Mr baby man left at 3.00am, and Kelly stayed in bed and turned onto her right side, facing the wall. After a few minutes, she was asleep.

Slowly and very quietly, the Ripper eased himself from his hiding place under the bed. His heart was beating faster and faster. Revenge was coming; he has never been without pain since her attack on him. He slowly slipped off his overcoat, revealing his leather slaughterman's apron that he had brought especially for tonight.

He took his sharp, long dagger in his left hand, this time. He gently knelt on the bed; she was still asleep. His right-hand reached over towards her mouth. His left hand had the knife close to her neck.

He put his hand over her mouth; then she opened her eyes. He looked at her face.

"Remember me, bitch," he said quietly to her.

For a moment, her eyes widened as she remembered him. But before she could move, her neck was cut deeply from right to left. Arterial blood spurted onto the partition wall. The last second of Mary Jane Kelly's life was looking into the eyes of Jack the Ripper. Within a second, another deep cut was made through the neck, again from right to left, and Mary Kelly lived no more. What happened next, turned a killer of women, into a legend that will last forever.

"Hit me face, with a fuckin' 'ammer, will you, bitch? Well, see, what I'm going to do to yours, you Irish slag," he whispered to himself.

He was very agitated; adrenaline was rushing through his veins; he couldn't keep still with the excitement of what came next. He laid the body on her back then took his dagger and started peeling the skin off her face. He threw the slices of flesh onto the table and sliced off her nose which was then thrown somewhere in the room.

"Not too pretty now, are you?" he whispered. More, much more was to come, before he was satisfied.

He took his knife and cut through her underclothes and spread them wide. He cut her from the breastbone to the groin. He then made semi-circular cuts around her abdomen, on each side. He placed the abdominal skin onto the table. His excitement increased with every cut. He then lifted out the intestines and placed them by her right side; he made a circular cut around each breast and removed them both. One of her breasts was placed under her head, along with her uterus and kidneys. He got enormous sexual pleasure from cutting off her breasts. Mary's other breast was thrown towards her right foot. He was so excited now, he masturbated and ejaculated almost immediately. He lifted out her liver and placed it between her feet. Her spleen was cut out and placed by the right side of the body.

He made several jagged wounds to the inside of her arms. The skin around her groin, including her vulva, was removed and placed on the table. Both of her inside thighs had the skin removed. Her right thighbone was exposed. There was a deep jagged cut through her left calf muscle. He was in a state of elation and was just about holding himself together. The pericardium, which contained the heart, was cut from below and the heart removed. Her heart was placed with other viscera from the body. The bed was soaking in blood, urine and faecal matter, which in turn was dripping onto the floor.

Panting heavily, he stood back to admire his work. He placed Mary's left arm over her abdomen, and he spread her legs wide with the knees bent. He then urinated all over the corpse of Mary Kelly. He would have loved to scream out with sheer joy, but he knew he couldn't. He wiped his knife and hands clean. He also wiped down his leather apron, which he then removed and rolled up. He placed his coat back on and exited the room, pulling the door shut and the latch engaged. The time was approximately 3.35am. The court was now quiet. The Ripper carefully made his way back to his residence.

One of the most shocking discoveries in the annals of crime was made on the morning of the 9th of November 1888. This crime scene rocked the police to their very core. The image of the disfigured and disembowelled body of Mary Kelly, lying on her bed, was permanently burned into the mind of anyone who saw that scene, on that cold November morning.

Thomas Bowyer, of 37 Dorset Street, was an employee of John McCarthy, a landlord situated at 27 Dorset Street. At 10.45am,

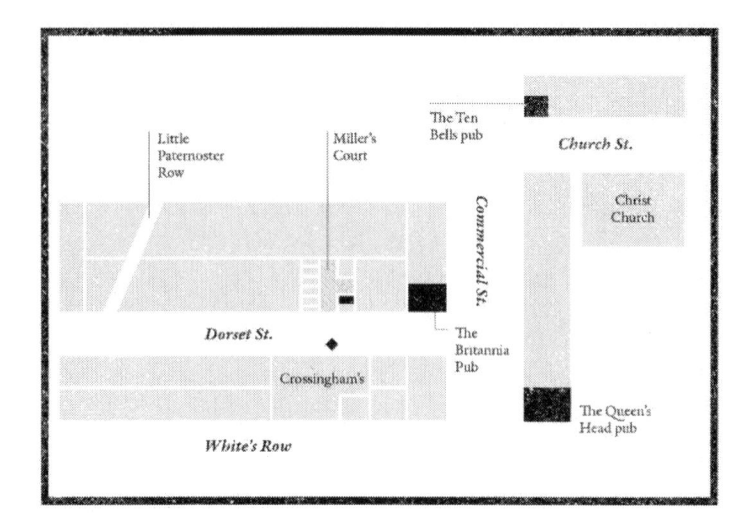

Map 7 – Miller's Court, Dorset Street

Mary Kelly's room was in Miller's Court with the black shading. The court was between number 26 on the right and number 27 on the left which was John McCarthy's shop. Kelly's room was number 13 and directly behind number 26 Dorset Street.

Opposite Miller's Court was one of the Crossingham's lodging houses. George Hutchinson stood from 2am until 2.45am on the morning of 9th November. Hutchinson saw Kelly with a man as they passed the Queen's Head pub in Commercial Road, just before 2am. ◆

Miller's Court contained 13 separate rented rooms. Adjacent to Dorset Street was White's Row where Annie Millwood was attacked on the 25th February 1888, at number 8 Spitalfields Chambers.

The movements of Kelly would have been under observation by the Ripper and he struck while he had the chance, when she was alone.

he was ordered to go to Kelly's room at 13 Miller's Court to collect some of the outstanding rent, which stood at 29 shillings. Having heard no response from knocking on her door, he moved around to the side window. He pulled back the curtain covering the broken windowpane and looked inside. He saw piles of flesh on the table next to the bed. In shock, he took a second look, and his eyes fell upon the mutilated corpse of Mary Kelly. He almost passed out; he felt faint; he almost vomited. He managed to steady himself and then rushed back to John McCarthy's shop and told him of what he had just seen.

John McCarthy went to Miller's Court to look for himself and wished he hadn't. He threw up immediately. He and Bowyer then rushed to the Commercial Street Police Station. There, at about 11.00am, a pale-faced and ill-looking, McCarthy spoke to Inspector Walter Beck, and they returned, along with Detective Constable Walter Dew, to Miller's Court. McCarthy was sure it was Mary Jane Kelly, as he had known her and her partner Joseph Barnett for about ten months. Inspector Beck of H Division immediately sent for the doctor and secured the court to all persons. On their return to Miller's Court, both Bowyer and McCarthy were still shaking.

Doctor Phillips, of number 2 Spital Square, was called by the police at approximately 11.05am, to visit Miller's Court. He arrived at 11.15am and ascertained very quickly through the window that all life was extinct and that there was no-one else in the room that needed help. Even though he was a doctor, he had never seen anything as horrific as this, and he was visibly shocked. He remained at the scene until access to the room was made.

Inspector Abberline and Inspector Reid arrived at the scene at 11.30am, Abberline was especially shocked, he could not comprehend the scene. Reid was visibly upset but had some understanding of the criminals' behaviour. They began taking statements of witnesses, residents and the two men who discovered the body. The door was kept locked because there was a suggestion of using a bloodhound, but this idea was later discounted. Superintendent Arnold arrived at 1.30pm and ordered the door to be broken open. Doctor Phillips quickly ascertained that death was caused by the severance of the right carotid artery, due to the saturated condition of the sheets on the top right-hand corner of the bed and that death occurred while she was lying down.

After some general discussions with other officers and witnesses, the police took statements from the following people during the morning and early afternoon:

Mary Ann Cox lived at number 5 Miller's Court and was a prostitute. She gave her statement to Inspector Reid:

"I know Mary Jane, and I last saw her alive about midnight. She was in front of me and very elephants. She was wiv a short, stout, shabbily dressed geezer, he had a longish coat and wore an 'ard billy cock hat. He was carrying a pot of ale and 'ad a blotchy face and a full carroty moustache, like. They then went into 'er room, and she started singin' *'a violet plucked from my mother's grave.'* I left the court about 15 minutes later and returned at one o'clock; she was still singin' then. I then went back out on the streets and returned home at free o'clock. Her light was out, and there was no noise. It was then rainin' 'ard, and I didn't go to sleep and 'eard no furver sounds, except men going in and out as usual in the court."

Reid then interrupted, "tell me about Mary Kelly; what was she like?"

"Well, she was awright, if you know what I mean. She liked a drink and a good time."

"Was she violent? Did she have a weapon?" Reid asked.

"She could 'andle 'erself, but I don't know nuffink about no weapon."

"Did you hear a cry of murder at about 4.00am? Because someone else did," Reid asked.

"I would've 'eard a cry of murder, but I 'eard nuffink and was awake," she said firmly.

Elizabeth Prater gave her statement to a constable with Abberline listening on impatiently.

"I live at number 20 Miller's Court, directly above Mary Jane Kelly's room. I had been out for a while and returned at one o'clock. I stood on the corner of Mr McCarthy's shop for about 20 minutes, waitin' for a man that I live with. Me husband deserted me five years ago. The man did not come, so I went up the stairs to me room. On the stairs, I could see a glimmer of light through the partition into her room. I did not take notice. I could have heard her movin' if she moved about. I put two tables against the door and went to sleep at once, as I'd been drinkin', and slept soundly. Me cat woke me at about half past free to four o'clock, and I heard a faint cry of murder. It's not uncommon to hear cries of murder, so I ignored it. I slept until five o'clock and then went to the Ten Bells for a rum. I was there at about a quarter to six. I then went back 'ome and slept until eleven o'clock. I didn't hear any singin' from her room."

"So, you saw nothing or heard anything about Kelly or her murderer?" Abberline retorted.

"Well, it's like I said…" Abberline cut her off abruptly and walked away, annoyed.

Inspector Reid interviewed Caroline Maxwell in Miller's Court:

"I live at 14 Dorset Street, me 'usband, Henry Maxwell, is the lodgin' 'ouse deputy. I knew Mary Jane for about four months and Joe Barnett. I only spoke to her twice. I took a good deal of notice of the deceased this mornin', seeing her standin' at the corner of the Court on Friday from eight o'clock till 'alf-past."

"You saw her this morning? She was dead at eight o clock; you can't have seen her." Reid shouted.

"I am positive the time was between eight and 'alf-past; I said to her 'why Mary what brings you up so early?' she said, 'oh, I do feel so bad! Oh, Carry, I feel so bad!' She knew me name. I asked her to have a drink. She said, 'oh no, I have just had a drink and brought it all up'. She was hungover, so I then left her, then about 20 minutes to 'arf an hour later, at about quarter to nine, I saw her outside the Britannia, talking to a man. The man had dark clothes on. Mary Jane had a dark skirt, velvet body and a maroon shawl and no hat," she said.

"Madam, you are telling me you saw Mary Kelly twice this morning when she had been dead several hours! Are you sure it was this morning, and not another morning, or someone who looked like her?" Reid said firmly.

"Wew, if you say she was dead, it must be someone else," she replied.

Sarah Lewis gave a statement to one of the constable's, with Abberline present:

"I live in number 24 Great Powell Street, Spitalfields. I went to visit the Keyler's at number 2 Miller's Court, on the 9th of November at half past two in the mornin'. There was a man opposite the court, next to the lodgin' 'ouse. He wasn't tall but stout. He wore a black wide-awake hat, and I couldn't see his ovver clovves. He kept lookin' up the court as if waitin' for someone to come out. At the Keyler's, I remained awake and 'eard no noise. I may have dozed for a little while but woke up at half past free. A little before four o'clock, I 'eard a female shout murder, but I took no notice of it. I've been 'ere ever since, can I go now?"

"You heard a cry of murder at 4.00am, are you sure?" Abberline asked.

"Yes, sir, I fink I did," she replied.

"What else can you tell me about the man you saw at 2.30am?" Abberline asked.

"Nuffink really, sir, I couldn't see his face. He was just standin' there," she replied.

"Well, you're a lot of help as well," Abberline said loudly and sarcastically. Reid could tell Abberline was angry and not helping the situation. He went over to his colleague.

"Fred, why don't you give yourself a break? Either at the Commercial Street Station or in one of the pubs. I will finish off here; then we can discuss things."

"Right. I am wasting my time with this lot. I will go to the station and see you later," Abberline said, grudgingly.

Reid went over to Sarah Lewis. "My colleague has had a difficult day as you can imagine, madam. Were you going to say something else?"

"Wew there is anovver fing, now you ask, sir. On Wednesday at eight o'clock, on Befnal Green Road, I was wiv anovver woman, when a gentleman spoke to us and asked us to follow him down a passage, to which we both refused. He was a short man with a pale face and a black moustache and aged about 40 years. He had a bag with him and a round hat on. He had a long brown overcoat and salt and pepper trousers. The funny fing is that I saw him this morning, at 2.30am, with a woman near the Ringers public house. He 'ad the same clovves and bag but no overcoat."

"Have you got all that constable?"

"Yes, sir."

"Well, thank you, madam," Reid said courteously.

Julia Venturney gave a brief statement to a police officer and Inspector Reid, at Miller's Court:

"I live at number 1 Miller's Court. I'm a charwoman and live with Harry Owen. I know the woman at number 13. She was a married woman, and her name was Kelly. She lived with Joe Barnett and both of them frequently got elephants. I last saw her on Fursday at about ten o'clock, 'aving breakfast with anovver woman in her room. I went to bed about eight o'clock Fursday night but couldn't sleep. I only dozed but 'eard no singin' or scream."

"So, you saw or heard nothing of any value, madam?" Reid said firmly.

"I can only say what I know, sir."

Maria Harvey, also a prostitute, gave the final statement to a constable who wrote it down as follows:

"I live at 3 New Court, Dorset Street. I knew Mary Jane Kelly and slept with her on Monday and Tuesday night. I am a laundress, and we were together all Thursday afternoon. I was in the room when Joe Barnett called. I then went and left some laundry in the room. I didn't see her again."

Shortly after 4.00pm, Mary Kelly's remains were removed from the room and conveyed to the mortuary in Shoreditch. The police padlocked the door and boarded the windows up. It took a while to clear people from the court and Dorset Street. The police spoke to Joe Barnett at length and checked out his alibi. Barnett was visibly shocked and distraught. He identified the remains on behalf of the police, as she had no known relatives.

Later that day, when Abberline and Reid were more composed, and the shock of the mutilation was beginning to subside, they started to discuss the crime and the witness statements. Both looked weary and fell into their chairs.

"Who would do such a thing, Fred? I have never seen such a foul thing in all my life!"

"I don't know Edmund. These killings are by some sort of madman."

"We are dealing with another kind of killer here. This person kills one after another and continues until he is stopped somehow. This is someone who wants to kill and feels compelled to kill."

"Why, though, what is the reason?" asked Abberline.

"Some people are born that way; some people become like that because of abuse or neglect, possibly. The killings are getting worse. There is an escalation of violence. There is also evidence that the killer is learning from each kill and refining his technique."

"I can't see it, Edmund, it makes no sense to me. The killer is someone that I have never come across before. I am tired Edmund, shocked, tired and worried."

"He is a criminal, Fred, that has evolved into an efficient killer. He enjoys the killing and mutilations. Let us both go and speak to Doctor Bond tomorrow."

"What about these witness statements, Edmund, have you been through them? Do they tell us anything of value?"

"Mary Cox confirms Kelly was alive and singing at 1.00am. She went out and came back at 3.00am and heard no noise or cry of murder."

"Who's next?"

"Elizabeth Prater returned home at 1.30am, directly above Kelly's room. She heard nothing, no singing. But she heard a cry of murder about 4.00am. Sarah Lewis also visited the Keyler's, at 2 Miller's Court, also heard a female cry murder at about 4.00am."

"What else have we got?"

"This next one is strange, Fred; Caroline Maxwell saw the deceased at about 8.30am and again at 8.45am. We know she was long dead by then. The doctor says she had been dead for about 12 hours. Then, Julia Venturney, at number 1 Miller's Court, heard nothing and was awake most of the time. That's it, several people have identified her.

"There was another thing, Sarah Lewis saw a man opposite Miller's Court at 2.30am in a black wide-awake hat, and he looked like he was waiting for someone. She also said she saw, at the same time, a man with a woman near the Britannia. He was about 40 years old, well dressed and carried a small bag."

"So, all we know is that she was alive at 1.00am. Two people heard a cry of murder at 4.00am. Kelly couldn't cry murder as her throat would have been cut before she knew what was going on. This Maxwell woman must be mistaken. So, we have nothing again," Abberline said angrily.

"We need to ask people in Commercial Street and the pubs, if they saw Kelly early this morning," Reid suggested.

"We need a bloody miracle!"

"We will go to Doctor Bond tomorrow, to find out about the post-mortem and get his views on the case. He is a bright man, very knowledgeable," Reid said.

"Well, you should get on well with him. What is he going to tell us that we don't already know?"

"I don't know, but we have to explore all possibilities, something may come up."

"My lunch is going to come up. I have had all I can take with this case."

"I thought that I did the jokes, Fred."

"Shut up Edmund, shut up." Abberline was despondent and down. He was looking quite ill and pale.

The despair that is seen in many people in Spitalfields, especially the homeless and destitute, was there in Abberline's face. He has been on the case since the death of Polly Nichols. He had spent sixteen hours a day working since the beginning of September when he received the call about her death. It had only been ten weeks, but to Abberline, it seemed like ten years.

"Let's get you something to eat and drink; you will feel better then," Reid suggested.

"I can't get that image of her out of my head, lying on that bed like that. I have seen all five victims. Their dead faces are burned into my memory," Abberline said, almost in tears.

Reid helped Abberline to his feet and helped him put on his overcoat. "Come on, let's get you fed and watered."

Abberline followed Reid with his head down, too tired to say anything.

November 10th
Doctor Bond's profile of the killer

The day after the traumatic events of the 9th November 1888, was a difficult one. Everyone was still in shock at the scale of the murder in Miller's Court. A much less shocking, and a much less critical event yesterday, was that Charles Warren's resignation was accepted. He had resigned as Commissioner of the Metropolitan Police on the day before the murder.

Inspectors Abberline and Reid arrived at Doctor Thomas Bond's, surgery; he had performed the post-mortem on Mary Jane Kelly, earlier in the day.

"Good afternoon Doctor, is there any light that you can shed on this mysterious case, as to who may have committed this latest crime, and the other murders of women in the Whitechapel area?" Abberline enquired.

"The post-mortem revealed that she died of blood loss due to her throat being savagely cut, then extensive mutilations of the body were all carried out after death. Although many organs were removed from the body, they have all been accounted for. You also asked about the other murders, and coincidently I have been asked by the Home Office to review the cases as to the murderer and the amount of surgical skill and anatomical knowledge he may possess. I am sending the report today, so I will also furnish you with my opinions.

"I have looked at the post-mortem notes on the murders at Bucks Row, Hanbury Street, Berner Street and Mitre Square and

I have conducted a post-mortem on the body found yesterday at Miller's Court, Spitalfields.

"I believe that all five murders were committed by the same hand. In the first four cases, the throats appear to have been cut from left to right. In the last case, owing to extensive mutilations, it is impossible to say in what direction the fatal cut was made, but arterial blood was found on the wall to the right of the victim's head.

"I believe that in all five cases, the women were lying down when they were murdered, and in each case, the throat was first cut.

"Concerning the first four murders, I cannot form a very definite opinion of the time that had elapsed between the murder and discovery of the body. In the case at Berner Street, it appears that the discovery was made immediately after the deed. In the other three murders, it seems from other reports that only several minutes could have elapsed between the murder and the discovery. However, from a medical point of view, only three or four hours could have elapsed maximum.

"Concerning the fifth murder, I saw the body at 2.00pm, and rigor mortis had set in and increased during the progress of the examination. rigor mortis can vary from 6-12 hours, and the remains were comparatively cold. Her stomach contents show a partially digested meal. I am therefore confident that the woman has been dead about 12 hours and death took place three or four hours after the food was taken. So, one or two o'clock in the morning would be the probable time of the murder," Doctor Brown explained.

"Sorry to interrupt Doctor, you said she had been dead about 12 hours, so that places the murder at about 2.00am, but you say it could be an hour earlier at 1.00am. Could it also have been an hour later at 3.00am?" Inspector Reid enquired.

"It is possible; it does vary with the temperature of the body and the room. It could be an hour on either side of 2.00am. The food was partially digested, so that gives us three or four hours. If you can find out what time she ate a meal, we can then fix a more accurate time of death," replied Doctor Bond. He then resumed his narrative:

"In all five cases, there appears to be no evidence of a struggle and the attacks were sudden and made in a way that the women could neither resist nor cry out. In Miller's Court, the sheet to the right of the woman's head was cut and saturated with blood. This could indicate that the face may have been covered at the time of the attack.

"In the first four cases, the murderer attacked from the right-hand side of the victim and in the last case it was possibly from the left-hand side. The murderer would not necessarily be splashed or deluged with blood, except for his hands and arms, and some of his clothing would have been smeared with blood.

"The mutilations all showed the same characteristics, which demonstrated that mutilation was the main objective of the murders. In each case, the mutilations were inflicted by a person who had no scientific nor anatomical knowledge. In my opinion, he does not even possess the technical expertise of a butcher or horse slaughterer or any person accustomed to cutting up dead animals."

"Interesting that you say that, Doctor, because Doctor Phillips has said that there were some anatomical knowledge and skill," Reid said quickly.

"Yes, I am aware of that Inspector, but I find none."

"I concur with the other doctors that the instrument used must have been a strong knife, at least six inches long, very sharp, pointed at the top and about an inch in width. It may have been a clasp knife, a butcher's knife or a surgeon's knife. I think it was no doubt, a straight knife.

"In terms of the type of man that committed these crimes, I am sure he must be a man of great physical strength and great coolness and daring. There is no evidence that he had an accomplice. He must, in my opinion, be a man subject to periodical attacks of homicidal or erotic mania. The character of the mutilations indicate that the man may be in a condition sexually, that may be called, *satyriasis*. It is, of course, possible that the homicidal impulse may have developed from a revengeful or brooding state of mind, or that religious mania may have been the original disease. But I do not think either hypothesis is likely.

"The murderer, in external appearance, is quite likely to be a quiet, inoffensive looking man; probably middle-aged and neatly and respectably dressed. I think he must be in the habit of wearing a cloak or overcoat, or he could hardly have escaped notice in the streets if the blood on his hands or clothes were visible.

"Assuming the murderer to be such a person as I have just described, he would probably be solitary and eccentric in his habits, also he is most likely to be a man without regular occupation, but with some small income or pension. He is possibly living amongst respectable persons, who have some knowledge of his character and habits, and who might have a suspicion that he may not be quite right in his mind at times. Such persons would probably be unwilling to communicate doubts to the police for fear of trouble or notoriety, whereas, if there were a prospect of reward, it might overcome their scruples."

"You mentioned the term satyriasis, Doctor; I presume you have read Richard von Krafft-Ebing's work, *Psychopathia Sexualis*. Would his term of *a 'psychosexual lust murderer'* be applied in these cases?" Reid enquired.

"Most definitely. I am familiar with that publication. *The mutilations are part of the sexual act'*. They are what he derives pleasure from."

"Is he mad Doctor, is he insane?" Abberline asked sharply.

"Not in the legal sense no. He knows what he is doing, he knows right from wrong, but he feels driven to do these things."

"Do you think he will stop these killings?" Reid enquired.

"I think it is highly unlikely, Inspector. He will carry on until you catch him."

"Doctor, I have been thinking about these killings, and I have wondered why someone would do such a thing? For example, do you think the person would have had a traumatic childhood, or suffered from some sort of injury to the brain?" Reid asked intelligently.

"That is a fascinating and intelligent question, Inspector," the doctor said. "Yes, either of those may be a primary cause of this man's crimes. As a result of neglect or abuse or brain injury, he is more likely to be criminal in nature. He is likely to have a criminal record if that helps."

"You have been really helpful to us, Doctor, I will study your reports carefully," Reid said, shaking the doctor's hand.

"Thank you for all your work, Doctor," Inspector Abberline said gently.

"You seem very happy. Do you know someone who has had a traumatic childhood and a brain injury and is a criminal to boot?"

"As a matter of fact, Fred, I do," Reid answered and smiled. "I have a few possible suspects. I will begin interviewing them on Monday, while you go to the inquest."

"I can't take much more of this case, Edmund. My head is going to explode." Abberline said gloomily.

"Do you remember when we were in the pub in January, and we caught those two thieves? Those days will be back, give it time. This case will be over soon, Fred."

"I have forgotten what happiness is. It is like someone has drained all the energy from me."

"We are near the end; I am sure of it. It is all fitting together for me, after speaking to Doctor Bond," Reid said confidently.

"Tomorrow is Sunday Fred, a day of rest. So, rest man, rest. Have you thought of going to church, it seems to help some people?"

"What? And pray to a God that watches five or six women be butchered and does nothing," Abberline said angrily.

"Sorry, Fred, it was a stupid suggestion, I feel the same, but Emily keeps asking me to go. Your Emma doesn't go to church either; that's something to be thankful for."

For the first time in a while now, Abberline laughed. "Well, there is that."

"See, we are feeling better already," Reid said, smiling.

November 11th
The Ripper's demise

Since overhearing that Mary Kelly attacked a man in Angel Alley, which she thought was her nephew, Letty had been pondering as to whether he was responsible for these killings. She had been telling herself that it is all a coincidence and berated herself for thinking such things, but the thoughts wouldn't go away. If Kelly attacked her nephew, he had a good motive for revenge. But why kill the others? Did he hate prostitutes because his mother was one? The more she thought about this, the more nervous she got.

"He has a knife," Letty said to herself while pacing up and down. "He cuts up animals for a living," she added. "He is always going out late at night. Oh my God, what do I do?" she said in a terrified and worried tone.

Letty sat down for a moment, in her kitchen. "Think, woman," she said out loud. "The killer has taken body parts, they may be here," she said, startled and horrified by her own thoughts. "They could be in this pub."

She moved to the bar area of the pub and had a large brandy. Just as she was thinking about the events, the Ripper entered the pub and sat down in the bar area; it was just after closing time.

'What do I do now? Do I go to the police? What then happens to me? My business and home?' Strange thoughts are now in her head. *'I will sort this out myself,'* she thought, coming to her senses. She was

a strong-minded woman; she always does what needed to be done.

'I'll break his fucken' neck and make it look like an accident, I will,' she thought to herself. *'I have had to kill animals on the farm, I can do him too.'*

When everyone was out of the pub, Letty went over to him with a bottle of whisky.

"Here get that down you," she said, pouring him a considerable measure which he drank in one.

"Fanks for lookin' after me Auntie," he speaks very drunkenly. He rarely said thanks to anyone.

"I need to ask you somethen', and I need the truth, is that clear?"

"What do you mean? What trufe?"

"You killed that Kelly woman, didn't you? After I told you about her," Letty asked in a clear tone.

"Look what she fuckin' did to me. Yes, I fuckin' killed her, I fuckin' loved it. She fuckin' deserved it."

"You stupid bastard, they will hang you for that! They know someone attacked you. I have put things together, so will the police."

"They don't know nuffink."

"Don't be too sure of that; that Inspector Reid and his mate Abberline are not stupid. Reid has been asking me about you since you were in the 'ospital. You have been talking to him as well. He is a smart one that one, he ain't as stupid as he looks."

"He was only askin' 'bout me 'ealf, that's all."

"He's on to you; you fucken' brainless twat!"

"'ere get that down you." She poured him another large whisky and one for herself.

"They know you work at a slaughter yard. They know you can use a knife. They know you have been in and out of prison. They know you were attacked and have had a head injury. They know you can be violent. Reid probably knows that you hate prostitutes as well. He is a cunning one, that one."

He sank down in his chair with his head down, and his legs were shaking. Guilt was all over him.

"And the other four that were killed, did you do them as well?" she asked.

"Five others not four. Yes, I did all of them; they were all whores and got what they deserved."

"They don't deserve to be killed, just because they are prostitutes, you stupid bastard!" Letty's voice was low and full of hatred. She paused for breath and composed herself a little.

"So, you're telling me that you're the Ripper, aren't you?"

He looked her directly in the eyes, "It's me, you 'appy now? Take me in; I've 'ad enough of this shit life anyway," he says flippantly and drunkenly.

"What is all this about? Tell me? Get it off your chest. I know you have 'ad a shit life, but so have most of the poor bastards around here, but they don't go killen' and rippen' womens' bodies up, do they?"

"Awright, I'll tell you, but I'm sayin' nuffink to no coppers. Me movva was a whore, a drunken whore. She abused me and let men abuse me. She hated me, and I hate her. No-one 'elped me, then. So, I looks after meself and gets arrested for fievin' and the like. I gets sent to prison and gets more abuse. Fuckin' coppers; fuckin' prison; fuckin' everyfink! All I have known is a beatin' or abuse. I fuckin' 'ate finking about it, so I drink a lot. I keeps gettin' angry, so I takes it out on someone. Prostitutes are easy game, that's all. I'm not like ovver people. They don't 'ave my problems. They 'ate me and I 'ates them."

"So, what made you start killen'? When did it start?" his aunt asked.

"I 'ave been robbin' a long time and fret'nin' people wiv me knife. I was goin' to rob a woman I saw walkin' 'ome. I knocks on her door, but I just started stabbin' 'er instead. I enjoyed it and wanted to do it again. That was in Feb'ry. I stabbed anovver woman in the froat 'cause she wouldn't give me no money. That was in March. But I wasn't wantin' to kill no-one, not yet. I wanted to kill after me attack in April. I wanted someone to pay for it.

"I started followin' women and watchin' them 'ave sex un fings. But I finks that was what me movva was like, so I wished to attack 'em, in 'er place. I beat one or two of 'em up when I gets a chance, but me 'eadaches are bad and I 'ave angry foughts about me movva. She is in me fuckin' 'ead, goin' on at me, all the fuckin' time. I had a few drinks and went out lookin' for a woman to do. I saw this fuckin' fat bitch." Letty looked across at him angrily, and he backtracked somewhat.

"No offence to you Auntie, I don't mean you are fat, er... or a bitch. She was loud, you know." The aunt looked at him again.

"I don't mean loud like you were... are... I mean. You're not loud, all the time, she was annoyin'. You're not annoyin'. She was gettin' drunk and laughin'." Letty was nearly exploding by now, and he noticed her anger.

"I know you drink and laugh as well, but she was diff'rent if you know what I mean." If there were awards for keeping calm under extreme provocation, the large landlady would have surely won one. Her face was red, and her eyes wide.

"I wasn't feelin' well, and she was gettin' on me nerves. Can I 'ave anovver drink please?" He was shaking even more now; he couldn't keep his arms or legs still. "I followed her to George Yard Buildings and waited while she was alone. I was just so fuckin' angry, so I took it out on 'er. I kept stabbin' and stabbin'. It was hard to kill her; she kept fightin' me. I stabbed her frough the 'eart wiv me dagger." He started to calm down a bit, and the shaking became less.

"I felt relieved after, and calm. I then gets a job, slaughterman and learns to kill quick, like. I like the job. I fought next time I will cut the froat, like the 'orses. So, there is no strugglin', like. Me fuckin' movva keeps appearin' in me 'ead, and so I drinks to forget her, but I get angry. So, I does anovver one, in Bucks Row. Then I do anovver and anovver, till I found that Mary Kelly bitch. I am glad what I done to 'er. I hated 'er; I didn't 'ate the ovvers the same if you know what I mean."

Getting this secret off his chest was a big relief, even though he knew it was the end for him. He took a big sigh and calmed down even more, and the shaking reduced further.

"You've made quite a name for yourself, 'avent you? You didn't think of me when you were doing this, did you? What will 'appen to me when they find out you are the fuckin' Ripper?"

"That's the only fing I am sorry for. It's not your fault. What 'appens now, you 'andin' me in?" He was not really bothered what happened next. His life has been one of pain, and he will be glad when it is over.

"You're going nowhere me old china. Where are the body parts?" she asked.

"Cellar," he replied. "What are you goin' to do then?"

"What I have always done, what's fucken' necessary."

"I'll go away if you want: I'll not be no trouble to ya."

"That won't be necessary. Let's get you upstairs."

Letty helped her nephew to make the short journey, as he was too drunk to stand on his own. At the top of the stairs, she took hold of his jacket lapels.

"I'm sorry about this, but there is no other way," Letty said, as she lifted her nephew up and threw him down the stairs. There were several cracks heard and his body fell into a heap at the foot of the stairs. The landlady went down the stairs to check if he was dead, which he was.

Letty took his knife off him and noticed a cord around his neck; it has two brass rings on. She remembered one of the victims had two brass rings taken from her. She wrapped the knife and rings up in some cloth and hid them in a waste bin outside, at the rear of the pub.

Next, she descended the stairs to the beer cellar. There was one gaslight and two oil lamps in the cold, damp cellar. She looked for hiding places.

"What would he store body parts in? Old pickle jars," she deduced.

She looked around for places that were less likely to be disturbed. There was a steel cabinet with some old barrels in front of it. She easily moved the barrels and could see marks on the floor where they have been disturbed before. Letty opened the metal cabinet, and in front of her, there was a large pickle jar.

She lifted it out and brought it into the light and saw that it contained something like flesh; she turned it around and saw a kidney, which was unmistakable.

"The dirty, sick bastard!" she said, nearly dropping the jar. She went back up the stairs to the kitchen and threw the flesh from the jar onto the fire in the stove, Letty then ran out into the street for someone to fetch a doctor, as someone had fallen down the stairs.

Approximately ten minutes later, the doctor arrived and pronounced him dead, due to falling down the stairs. The doctor could smell alcohol strongly on the deceased.

"We will have to do a post-mortem, and I will inform the police," the doctor said.

November 12th
Inspector Reid's final investigations

The inquest into the death of Mary Jane Kelly was held at Shoreditch Town Hall for one day only. The coroner was Mr Roderick McDonald. The first witness was Joseph Barnett, who was a labourer and resided at a common lodging house at numbers 24 and 25 New Street, Bishopgate. He identified the body in the mortuary and confirmed that he had lived with the deceased for 18 months. He outlined for the court the life history of Kelly, as he knew it, based on what she had told him. He last saw the deceased on Thursday afternoon at around 4.00pm when Maria Harvey was present.

The other witnesses called, were those people that gave information regarding knowing Kelly or finding the body and had given statements to the police. Doctor Phillips was called, as was Inspectors Abberline and Beck from the police. Surprisingly, Doctor Bond, who carried out the post-mortem was not called.

While the inquest was underway, Inspector Reid turned up at the Princess Alice pub during the morning.

"Good morning, madam. I would like to speak with your nephew, please," Reid asked.

"Haven't you 'eard. He died last night. He was drunk and fell down the stairs. He broke his neck," the landlady said, looking a little upset.

"What? When?" Reid shouted.

"I've just said, last night," she replied.

"I apologise, madam, please forgive me. I am sorry for your loss," Reid said in a more composed manner.

"Did he have a room here by any chance?" Reid quickly asked.

"Yes, upstairs," she replied.

"Could I possibly go and have a look please, madam?"

"Yes, I will come and show you. What's this all about?"

"Just enquiries madam. It's just an idea I have," Reid replied excitedly.

In the small room was a single bed, a wardrobe and a table. It was a sparse room, with not many clothes or belongings.

"Is this all that he had madam?" Reid asked, looking in the wardrobe.

"Yes, he didn't 'ave much."

"Has he any other belongings?" Reid asked her while looking under the bed.

"Not to my knowledge, Inspector. Had he done somethen'?" she enquired.

"I don't know, madam. He was badly injured a while back, wasn't he?"

"Yes, he nearly died and had terrible 'eadaches, that's why he drank a lot, for the pain, you know."

"Do you mind if I look in the other rooms, please?"

"Fine," came the sharp reply.

Reid looked in the other rooms, including wardrobes and cupboards. He made a very interesting discovery in one of the wardrobes.

"What is it you are looking for, Inspector?"

"Evidence madam. I had an idea that your nephew was involved in something, but I can't say what exactly."

"Well if you find what you can't say exactly, you will let me know, wont ya?"

"Where did he keep his knife? He used one at work."

"Well, could it be at work, Inspector?" she said sarcastically.

"Can you account for his whereabouts at night, madam?"

"No, why should I? It ain't up to me to watch him all day and night. Can your wife account for all your whereabouts, Inspector?"

"Very well, madam, that will be all, thank you," Reid stated as he left the room and the pub. He didn't want to get on the wrong side of the landlady.

"Damn it! I thought I was onto something," Reid said to himself.

Reid rushed to the mortuary to see the body and obtain a photograph. He told a constable to take a message to the Imperial Club, that he needed to speak to Mr Lawende and Mr Levy.

Inspector Reid then took a Hansom cab to Mile End; he wanted to see Ada Wilson, as soon as possible, at her home in Maidman Street. He didn't have an appointment, but he was hoping she would be in. As he alighted from the cab, he saw that someone was just leaving the very same house. The Inspector approached the front door and knocked on it.

"Excuse me, my name is Inspector Reid; I wanted to see Mrs Wilson about the attack on her a while ago."

The tall attractive woman at the door introduced herself. "I am Ada Wilson you had better come in."

"I was wondering if you could still remember the face of your attacker, I would like to eliminate or confirm a person who may have attacked you. I have details that you said he was a fair-haired young man with a small moustache."

"Yes, that is correct, Inspector."

"Well, if I show you a photograph, could you tell me if it is the face of the man that attacked you?"

"Very well."

The inspector showed her the photograph of the man's face, that was taken in the mortuary.

"It could be him, but his face is a little different. Is he dead?"

"Yes, he met his death falling down the stairs and had a facial injury earlier this year."

"Well, I hope he suffered, the bastard. It could be him Inspector, but if he is dead, why are you asking me?"

"Well, I have another witness I want to show the photograph to. This man is a suspect in a much bigger investigation, and I wanted to confirm whether he attacked you also."

"A much bigger investigation? You don't mean Jack the fucking Ripper, do you?" she shouted.

"Your attack was a stabbing, so there may be a link."

"Oh, fucking hell, I never expected that," she said as she sat down.

"I didn't mean to shock you, at all."

"It's alright Inspector. I can't say for certain he is, but I can't rule him out either. He may be the one that attacked me. I need a drink; do you want one?"

"No thank you, madam."

"Is he the Ripper then?"

"I don't know, madam, I haven't got enough evidence. Even if you were certain that he attacked you, he still might not be Jack the Ripper. I am just exploring all leads."

There was a knock at the door, and Ada got up to answer it.

"I'll leave you now, thank you for all your help," Reid said as he left. He walked up to Mile End Road to get a cab back to Whitechapel.

Reid then managed to visit the slaughterhouses in the area to ascertain the whereabouts of men aged around 25 years old with a criminal record. He took their names and addresses, and as it turned out, there were not many men fitting his requirements. He asked police officers to check their whereabouts and alibis on the key dates.

In response to the message he sent to the Imperial Club, Mr Lawende turned up at the Leman Street Station, in the afternoon, and asked for Inspector Reid. He was taken up to the inspector's office.

"Mr Lawende, thank you for calling. I wanted to show you a photograph of a man. I want to know if the man in the photograph is the same man that you saw with Catherine Eddowes."

The well-dressed Mr Lawende looked closely at the photograph. "It is possible, Inspector, but I cannot be certain as it was dark at the time, and I was a good few feet away. He was a younger man, just like in this photo, but his face is a little different."

"He has had some facial damage since you saw him, due to a recent accident, He is about the height that you said, take another look."

"The man I saw looked a rough type, and he does too. If he wasn't the man I saw, it was someone very similar, but I can't say I recognise him, Inspector. The man in the photograph is dead, did you kill him?"

"No, we don't kill suspects now Mr Lawende," Reid said sarcastically. "He died in an accident, thank you for coming in," he said with a smile and a handshake.

"Thank you, Inspector. I am only too glad to help. My colleague, Mr Levy, didn't get a good look at the man's face. He is now away on business for a few days."

"Thank you, Mr Lawende."

Lawende then paused and walked back to Inspector Reid. "Inspector," he said in a drawn-out, querying tone, "the man in the photograph... is that Jack the Ripper?"

"I honestly don't know. I haven't got any direct evidence unless you and another witness are certain. As he is dead, we will never know. It is a possibility, but we will know he isn't the Ripper if there is another murder in a month or so."

In the Princess Alice pub, a young girl called Lucy walked up to the bar and asked the landlady, where her nephew was.

"He's not going to be around anymore, dear, 'e 'as 'ad a nasty accident."

"I wanted to see him, we 'ave met a time or two recently and I 'avent been wiv anyone else."

"What are you on about, luv?"

"I'm 'avin his kid, that's what."

"I'm sorry to 'ear that deary, but 'e's gone, kicked the bucket, brown bread. Is that clear enough for you?"

"Sorry to bovver you, then," she left the pub and faded into obscurity. Whether she was pregnant, no-one will ever know. The landlady was not interested in the woman's plight. She thought it was better for the child and the mother to have no knowledge of the potential father.

The pub was already quite full of people, who were mainly just sitting down, keeping warm. It is in effect the day doss house for many people. "Another fucken' day at the zoo," the landlady said to someone else at the bar, who smiled.

Later in the day, at 6.00pm, Mr George Hutchinson walked into the Commercial Street Police Station. He voluntarily gave a statement to Inspector Ellisdon, and Sergeant Badham, of seeing Kelly at 2.00am on the 9th of November. The movements of Kelly and Hutchinson had already been stated previously. Inspector Abberline then decided to have a few words with Hutchinson.

"Why did you wait until the inquest finished? You should have given evidence to the court today," Abberline retorted.

"I don't know. I didn't think it was important, as I thought Mary was killed much later," Hutchinson responded.

"How do you know what bloody time she was killed?"

"I heard about her death in that afternoon, so I thought she was killed much later than when I saw her."

"The doctor said she was killed between 1.00am, and 2.00am."

"That can't be right because I saw her at 2.00am. She was alive then. She must have been killed after that."

"And don't you think that information should have been given at the bloody inquest?"

"Yes, I am sorry, Inspector, but I did see the man she was with," replied Hutchinson, cowering a little at Abberline's sharp tone.

"Well, what is he like then? And don't you waste my time, or I will make your bloody life a misery."

"I understand Inspector; Mary was my friend; she didn't deserve this. And I want the bastard that did it as much as you. The man was about 34 or 35-years-old, five-foot-six-inches tall, pale complexion. Slight moustache curled up at the ends, dark hair and very surly looking."

What was he wearing?"

"He wore a long dark coat, collar and cuffs, and a dark jacket. He also had on a light waistcoat with dark trousers and a dark felt hat, turned down in the middle. He had button boots and gaiters with white buttons. He also wore a very thick gold chain, white linen collar and horseshoe tie pin. Respectable and Jewish in appearance."

"So, he was some sort of toff; is that what you are saying?"

"That is what he looked like."

"You have made a detailed statement of the man she was with, including details of his clothing. How can you take in so much detail, from a quick look as they went past you, while you were stood on the pavement?"

"I don't know; I just remember that's all. I saw both on Commercial Street, they passed me, and I followed them to Dorset Street, so I had a while to look at him."

"Would you recognise him again?"

"Yes. I am willing to come around with you, to look for him, Inspector. I just want to help you catch who did this, Inspector. I'm sorry to come late with the news," Hutchinson said, genuinely.

"What were you doing out at this time?" Abberline asked.

"I had just got back from Romford. She spoke to me at 2.00am then went off to Miller's Court with the gent I mentioned. I went into the court, but I could not see them. I waited outside of Crossingham's, opposite the court, until about a quarter to three, then I left. No-one came out of the court."

"Well, thanks for letting us know. We now know she was killed after 2.00am," Abberline said formally.

November 13th
Inspector Reid's analysis

Early in the morning at Leman Street Police Station, Inspectors Abberline and Reid were discussing the case and the latest developments. Reid had all his notice boards on show, with the key information circled. Abberline however, started off the discussion.

"Yesterday evening, a man called George Hutchinson gave me a description of a man that was with Kelly at two o'clock. 30-35 years old, moustache and dark hair, surly-looking and a toff. He said he could be a Jew.

"Well, why was he not at the inquest?" Reid queried.

"I have asked him that. He thought Kelly was killed much later and not just after he saw her. We have his statement. We must bring him to justice, Edmund. He is out there, and we will get him. We are going to take Hutchinson out, to see if he can spot this man that was with that Kelly woman. We have the description of the man that was with Eddowes, just before she was killed. We will find him."

"But, Fred, these are two different descriptions, Hutchinson's man and the man Lawende saw at Mitre Square. They can't both be right. I think Mary Kelly was killed after this man that Hutchinson saw, had left her."

"Well, what do you suggest, Edmund?"

"Have you checked Hutchinson out, Fred? What was he wearing? Was he the man Sarah Lewis saw at 2.30am?"

"I don't know Edmund. I am tired. I will get someone to look into these points you raise," Abberline said dejectedly.

"Let me tell you, Fred. I have formed an image of this killer, by critically looking at his crimes and reading about similar crimes, as well as talking to people like Doctor Bond and asking pertinent questions. From the evidence of the crime scenes and the weapon used, it is possible to narrow down our suspect. I have developed criteria that match the evidence. Let me explain:

"These crimes are rage murders and are done by someone who is very angry. The level of violence tells us that it is overkill. The mutilations are the killer's way of expressing his anger by shocking people, and it may sexually excite him. In other words, he derives pleasure from the killing and the mutilation; a lust murderer. If you remember, I asked Doctor Bond about the killer. If he didn't derive any sexual pleasure, why do it? Remember there was no evidence of rape or robbery, except one, but I will come to that.

"He didn't just start killing efficiently; he has had to learn that. So, where does this start? He will have been a delinquent, a young criminal, becoming more violent with age. He has not matured normally into adulthood.

"So, we are looking for someone who has had a traumatic childhood, possibly time spent in prison. Someone who has perhaps been injured or disfigured in some way that it affects his personality. Someone not quite normal but does not stand out as mad – someone strong and adept with a knife that has learned to kill quickly. We can narrow our searches down. It's someone who has lived and worked in Spitalfields, Fred."

"What you say may be true, but we don't know that for certain. They are educated guesses, Edmund."

"I'm not making sense Fred, am I? And I probably have not got things in the right order, but my view of the criminal fits the evidence. Think about this, Fred. In February, just a few streets away from here, a woman called Annie Millwood is stabbed with a small knife in the abdomen repeatedly, but she survives. There was no robbery or rape motive. The main organs were not touched, so there is no clear evidence of a purposeful kill. A month later in Mile End, another woman, Ada Wilson, is stabbed in the throat by a man who wanted money, she also survives. Now, what do these two attacks mean? What do they show of the killer? Knocking on a door and stabbing a woman is not something a mature criminal would do, even if robbery was your motive. The assailant could easily overpower or threaten the woman if he only wanted money, but this was not the case. They were acts of impulsive behaviour. Younger people are generally more impulsive than mature people."

Abberline was sat deep in thought and didn't respond.

"Are you still with me, Fred? Speak up if you need to."

"I see the immaturity angle, and I get that these are early attempts at crime," Abberline commented.

"Well done, we will make a policeman out of you yet!"

"Now don't be so fucking cheeky, Edmund. That remark is several rounds of drinks alone."

"Sorry, Fred, you know I'm only joking."

"Get on with it, and no more of your so-called bloody humour."

"Where was I? Yes, the two stabbings. They are criminal and abnormal. This man has grown up without proper parental control and discipline. He has been neglected and has had to fend for himself. He has not been educated and does not know how to behave normally.

"If he has been neglected or abused, then anger will form quite quickly. He will have a hatred of the abusers and possibly society in general. Now, and I was taking a leap of faith with this one, and it proved correct: What if the person responsible for the abuse and neglect was his own mother? Possibly disowning him or even hating him, leaving him in the workhouse or orphanage. Now here is the big one, what if she was a prostitute and an alcoholic, just like our six victims? Six murder victims. Do you see where the anger is going to come in, Fred?

"Now, the killings. The victims were overpowered easily, except for Tabram," Reid anticipated Abberline's interjection here and raised his hand to stop him, then quickly added, "before you butt in, I will explain that. He was, therefore, strong and agile, so he is not a teenager; he is a fully developed male, say mid-twenties. An immature male mentally, not smart, doesn't get on well with people, prefers to be alone because that's how he was brought up. He doesn't seem to want normal sexual relations; he sees sex and violence together; they are the same to him. Why? Because he has been the victim of sexual abuse."

"Go on Edmund, this is fascinating, but for now carry on, I will ask some questions later."

"He follows prostitutes; he watches them from a distance. He may have started to be violent towards them rather than having sex with them. He hates them because his mother was one. He can't take it out on her; she is dead. So, he takes his anger out wherever he can, and who are the most natural victims? Prostitutes.

"Now, in April Emma Smith was attacked and sadly dies, but she says it was a gang and that she was robbed. So, she may not be a related victim. Our killer works alone, and he kills quickly.

"Now let me explain something at a tangent to all this. In April, the same evening that Emma Smith was attacked, someone was attacked in Angel Alley. Not a prostitute but a man – mid-twenties by the way – he was attacked savagely with a hammer, which left him unconscious for a week with a fractured skull and possible brain damage. He was left with crippling headaches. Are you still with me, Fred?" Abberline responds with a slight nod of his head.

"In a few months, he makes a recovery, but his face is a mess, and he is in pain. He is now angrier than before, now he wants revenge, but he can't remember much of the attack or who attacked him. He probably drinks to ease the pain, but this fuels his aggression."

"Are you sure you are a policeman and not one of these mind doctors or something?"

"I do the jokes, Fred, you know that."

"I know where my fist will be as well."

"Now then, on the 7th of August, Martha Tabram is attacked and repeatedly stabbed 38 times with a clasp knife and once through the heart with a long-bladed knife. She struggles with the attacker, so he uses a dagger to kill her by stabbing her in the heart. This has the hallmarks of someone who is killing for the first time. He doesn't know how to do it quickly, so he gets into a fight, and he is struggling because Tabram is a large woman. He is stabbing her repeatedly in an angry manner, but she doesn't die quickly. He remembers he has a dagger and stabs her in the heart. He now knows it takes too long to kill with a clasp knife, which is what he started the attack with, and that he needs to target specific parts of the body.

"Now, what if, between the killings of Tabram and Nichols, he learns how to kill by becoming a slaughterman. What does he learn? I went to a yard to find out how to cut the neck arteries; specifically, the carotid arteries and death occurs in seconds due to excessive blood loss. Now – and I apologise for keep saying *now*, I sound like a teacher – if you stand on the opposite side of the neck, you don't get any blood onto you or your clothes.

"Now the next victim, Polly Nichols, Bucks Row, 31st of August, is killed on the ground by her throat being severely cut from left to right. Being on the ground lessens the arterial blood spray. If the victims were standing at the time, the whole front of their clothes would have been covered in blood. So, we know they were all led down when killed."

"Amazing, I sit here in awe," Fred said, genuinely impressed.

"Then her abdomen is stabbed and slashed, but someone is coming so he cannot fully mutilate the body. A slaughterman has to disembowel the horse or animal. What if the act and sight of disembowelling gave the killer sexual excitement?

"A week later, 8th of September, Annie Chapman, is killed by the same method of throat-cutting, on the ground from left to right, two deep cuts to the neck again. Then because he had time, he disembowelled her, within five minutes, not one hour like that idiot, Doctor Phillips, claimed; he also thought she had been dead two hours."

"Got that, but the next victim, Elizabeth Stride in Berner Street, is not mutilated," Abberline interjects.

"Yes, the consensus was that he was disturbed before he had time to mutilate her. However, her throat was also cut from left to right. Now, what if he wanted to kill her because she had seen something and was a threat to him? I have been worried as to where she was killed. It would be more sensible for him to be picked up by Elizabeth Stride and go to the back of the yard to kill her, out of sight of everyone. He wasn't going to mutilate her near the gate; he only needed to silence her. She must have recognised him, and he had to act quickly, on impulse," Reid responded.

"Fascinating Edmund, it makes sense to me. Well done."

"Now, later that same early morning, on the 30th of September, about 45 minutes after Stride is killed, Catherine Eddowes is killed in Mitre Square. Again throat-cutting first, left to right, like Stride and the two others. Then he disembowels her, like Annie Chapman."

"Why would he kill again instead of just going home as soon as possible?" Abberline asked.

"Well Fred, I think because an opportunity arose and he took it. He's impulsive if you remember."

"Now, where was I? Timings, yes, I have missed timings. Going backwards. Kelly was probably killed between 2.00am and 4.00am. Eddowes was killed between 1.36 and 1.43am FACT. Stride was killed just before 1.00am, FACT. Chapman was killed between 5.30am and just before 6.00am; most likely 5.31 or 5.32am. Nichols was killed between 3.30 and 3.40am FACT. Tabram was killed sometime between 2.00 and 3.30am. So, we know he kills in the early hours of the morning. Therefore, he will not have an alibi for these times. So, wherever he lives, he comes and goes without suspicion. Consequently, he is probably not in a relationship. Do you see Fred, this helps to build up a picture of the killer?"

Fred nodded.

"We have only one credible sighting of the killer, and that's the man standing with Catherine Eddowes at the entrance to Church Passage at 1.35am, moments before she was killed. I wrote down what the City Police sent us, precisely as they put it."

"He is described as; 30 years old, five-foot-seven or eight-inches tall, fair complexion, fair moustache, medium build, salt and pepper loose jacket,

grey cloth cap with a peak, a reddish handkerchief tied around the neck, He has the appearance of a sailor. He doesn't think he would be able to recognise him again, though'.

"There is only one other known sighting of a man attacking a woman with a knife. That is the attack on Ada Wilson in March when she was stabbed in the throat. He was seen by both Ada and Mrs Bierman, and they describe him as *'Age about 30 years, five-foot-six-inches tall. He had fair hair and a fair moustache; he also had a sunburnt face. He wore a dark coat, light trousers and a Quaker type hat.'*

"My suspect fits those descriptions as well as other criteria, but I have no direct evidence.

"Five weeks later, we are here, Miller's Court, Mary Kelly. The killer has even more time to mutilate, but the victim is killed first by her throat being efficiently cut. He is now a very efficient killer.

"But there is something else. This last one, Mary Kelly. This was rage – real anger – at her. He cuts her entire face off. He mutilates her beyond recognition. What if she has crossed him somehow, or injured him? What if the man injured in Angel Alley in April was attacked by Mary Kelly? Kelly was known to carry a hammer. The attack on Mary Kelly was revenge Fred, pure and simple revenge."

"It's all speculation though, Edmund! There is nothing here to convict anyone!"

"You're right, Fred. I thought I had an excellent suspect who fits Doctor Bond's view of the killer and the image that I have formed of him, but he has just been killed in an accident. I have no evidence, no knife, no human organs that the killer took, no brass rings from Chapman. But he fits. He lived with his aunt at the Princess Alice pub in Spitalfields, since he was let out of prison in January. He was convicted of theft and violence; he had several other convictions. He was the man injured in Angel Alley. He was a slaughterman who started the job just after the Tabram killing. He liked killing and mutilating. His mother, the aunt's sister, was a prostitute, an alcoholic, and do you know Fred, she used to rent him out to men for sex, as a young boy. The boy was mentally damaged, irreparably, by this abuse. As he got older, he got more violent.

"You remember the board that relates to the killer, which was partly completed, well after speaking to Doctor Bond, I can complete the board to a greater degree." Reid went over to the notice boards and amended or completed most of the information concerning the Ripper.

Jack the Ripper

Description? Two eyewitness description – Fair hair, fair moustache and possibly a pale complexion

Height and build? Between 5'5" and 5'7" He is a medium build

Where does he live/work? Spitalfields, probably

How old is he? Mid-twenties – possibly up to 30 years of age

Criminal record? Almost certainly Yes – for a range of crimes, including theft and violence

Ability to use a knife? Yes, accomplished – through his occupation

Some anatomical knowledge? Yes, but basic – he is a slaughterman

Background? Traumatic and neglected childhood, the workhouse, the orphanage and prison

Occupation? Slaughterman or butcher? Yes, for a brief time

Personal characteristics? Criminal, sexually abnormal, accomplished liar, unreliable, violent

Evidence of abuse? Probably physical, sexual and mental abuse as a child

Evidence of a severe injury? A head injury causing permanent facial damage and possibly brain damage

Personal relationships? Probably none, likely to be alone. Maybe one close relative

"I have been to the asylum, the jail, the workhouse, the orphanage. What I found was that many criminals had been neglected or abused in childhood. They are mentally damaged people. These people must learn to survive by stealing, fighting begging etc. They don't know any different life. We will find the Ripper's life to be the same. He may have some relative, but many of these people have no-one. I specifically mentioned to Doctor Bond about the Ripper being a sexual deviant, and he agreed. He said the mutilations are part of the sexual act for him.

"There is no evidence, Edmund!" Abberline badly wanted to believe in Reid's summary but knew that they need cold, hard evidence.

"Yes, I do know, Fred. But he had a convenient accident yesterday; falling down the stairs and breaking his neck, killed instantly. I searched the pub and his room and no sign of a knife or brass rings or female body parts. But I did find something: a grey cloth cap, a black wide-awake hat, a dark suit, a salt and pepper jacket, a dark overcoat. They were all the aunt's late husbands. He has been borrowing them. What if someone was onto him first and disposed of the evidence?"

"It's all —what if this? —what if that? There's no bloody evidence, Edmund," Abberline said while shaking his head slowly.

"Did I tell you that this man has had terrible headaches and fits, since the accident? He is our man. There won't be two of them living in Spitalfields that meet all my criteria. Also, the Princess Alice pub is central and very close to the first attack, Annie Millwood, and the first murder, Martha Tabram. He widened his net, so to speak, as he got more confident.

"When I discovered the likely age and possible occupation of the Ripper and that he had likely been in prison, I went to the local slaughterhouses and butchers. How many men do you think fitted those characteristics? Well, I will tell you, four possibly five men. I talked to them, and ruled them out because they had an alibi, they had no criminal record, or they were stable and had a long work record, except one man. He had these other characteristics and fitted the description of the man seen with Catherine Eddowes. I wanted to find out if he had an alibi for any of the murders. All I have done is narrow down who we should be looking for, but I don't know if I am right."

"Without firm evidence, we will never know. Your theory won't stand up in court," Abberline interrupted.

"I went over to see Ada Wilson the other day, and I also spoke to Joseph Lawende. I showed them a photograph of his face; they could neither confirm nor deny that it was him. He was a possibility to them both, Reid said excitedly."

"Edmund, all that means is that he may have attacked her! It does not mean he is Jack the Ripper. Even if he was the Ripper, we can't try him because he is DEAD," Abberline shouted.

"Well, if there are no more murders, it will convince me that I am right and that he will not be brought to justice. It will go down as unsolved. If only we had some sort of blood test or fingerprint test. In time we will, but it will be too late for this case. I am certain there will be no more murders, but I can't prove it," Reid said confidently.

"This case is taking its toll on me, Edmund. I can't relax or sleep properly, and I'm drinking too much. It's wearing me down."

"I know what you mean, Fred. I have found this case hard, too. But I have learned to think more about crime and why it is done. I am not a doctor or a specialist in the criminal mind; I will have gotten things wrong and missed things out, but in time detectives like us, will be more sophisticated in their investigations than I could ever be, but I do have this feeling that it is over. I am sure the man we are looking for is now dead, but I can't prove it. Let's wait and see. We can't do any more than we have done." Reid noticed for the first time just how tired Abberline is looking; he seems to have aged years during this case.

"Take some leave Fred; I can look after things here."

The two friends looked at each other, saying nothing. Both were exhausted with the prolonged investigation.

"Let's go and have a drink. I'm buying for insulting you," Reid said, smiling as usual.

As time slowly progressed, Hutchinson never managed to see the person he identified with Mary Kelly, even after several nights trying. The police had no other leads or sightings of Mary Jane Kelly on her last evening alive. The killer left no clues. Also, the police could not confirm where and when Kelly ate her last meal of fish and potatoes. It was as if she was invisible. She was buried at Leytonstone Cemetery on the 19th of November.

The coroner of the inquest of the man that fell down the stairs, at the Princess Alice public house while intoxicated, declared that it was an accident and death was due to a broken neck. The post-mortem also revealed brain damage to the frontal lobe. He was buried in a minimal ceremony, in an unmarked communal grave.

As the weeks went by without another Ripper kill, the police started to wonder if the Ripper had moved onto somewhere else, or simply decided to stop, after the last one in Miller's Court. They were still actively looking and took any attack on prostitutes seriously. On the 20th of November Annie Farmer claimed that she had been attacked in her lodging house in George Street. The wound was found to be a very slight cut to the neck and probably self-inflicted. The following month, on the 20th of December at Clarke's Yard, High Street, Poplar, Rose Mylett was found dead with no evidence of a struggle or signs that she was attacked. However, a post-mortem revealed that there were signs of strangulation, and a murder verdict was given. The marks on the neck were slight, and an examination by another doctor found no signs of strangulation and that death was due to natural causes. Any future attacks on prostitutes are naturally linked to the Ripper by the press, but such crimes lacked the severe and deep throat-cutting of the Ripper and the post-mortem mutilations.

Only one person knew for sure that there would be no more Jack the Ripper attacks and Letty would take her secret to the grave. She became friendly with the Glaswegian landlord of the White Swan on Whitechapel High Street. She remained in the Princess Alice pub and lived a long, happy life.

The anonymous killer, Jack the Ripper, would take his place in history, as being part of the most infamous unsolved murder case the world had known.

Detective Inspector Edmund Reid retired in 1896 aged 49 years old. He died on the 5th of December 1917 aged 71 years old.

Detective Inspector Frederick Abberline retired in 1892 aged 49 years old. Throughout his career, he received 84 commendations and awards. He died on the 10th of December 1929 aged 86 years old.

The End

Appendix 1
Translation aid

From Glaswegian into English

"Get the fuck oot of 'ere an' donnae cam back, ye self-righteous twat."
Means – Go out of here and don't come back, you self-righteous twat.

"Af ye donnae like it, ye can fuck off an all, am nae bothered."
Means – If you don't like it, you can go as well, I am not bothered.

"Am gaein' as fest as aye ken, A need mare ale oop 'ere."
Means – I am going as fast as I can, I need more ale up here.

"A've ainlae wen pair of honds, af ye just gav' us a manit."
Means – I have only one pair of hands if you just give me a minute.

"I'll be wath ye in a manit, hen."
Means – I will be with you in a minute, dear.

"Whet's ye two gentlemen heving, mare of the porter, as it?"
Means – What are you two gentlemen having, more of the porter is it?

"Yer the poliss ain'tcha? I knows the poliss were aim fro."
Means – You're the police, aren't you? I know the police where I'm from.

"Nae problem at ail, wa needs sam lae 'n' erder a roond 'ere."
Means – No problem at all, we need some law and order around here.

"De ye wanna a whasky tae?"
Means – Do you want a whisky too?

"Cam 'ere yae bastards."
Means – Come here, you bastards.

"At was ham wath tha bag sideburns."
Means – It was him with the big sideburns.

"Nae problem, ye deserve a drank on the 'oose, baethe of ye."
Means – No Problem, you deserve a drink on the house, both of you.

"Am just gaein' for a pash!"
Means – I am just going for a piss.

East End Cockney Speaking
Replacing the 'th' for 'f'.
Usage: thief becomes *fief*, think becomes *fink*, thing becomes *fing*, thugs becomes *fugs*, throat becomes *froat*, thought becomes *fought*. Nothing can be written *nuffin'* (as it sounds), but it is also pronounced and written with *nuffink*. (See below). Thursday becomes *Fursday*.

Replacing the 'l' with 'w'.
Usage: girl becomes *girw*, help becomes *'ewp* (h dropped as well), old becomes *owd*, well becomes *wew*, will becomes *wiw*.

Replacing the 'th' in the middle or the end of some words for 'v'.
Usage: brother becomes *bruvver* or even, *bruvva*. Northern becomes *norvern* or even *norvan*. Also; another becomes *anovver* or even *anovva*, with becomes *wiv*, and without becomes *wivout*. other becomes *ovver* or clothes becomes *clovves*.

Replacing weak consonants with the glottal stop.
Usage: water becomes *wa'er*, cottage becomes *co'age*.

Replacing 'g' at the end of <u>some</u> words for 'k'.
Usage: nothing becomes, *nuffink*, something becomes *somefink*.

Dropping the 'er' at the ends of words and substituting an 'a'.
Usage: Mother becomes *movva*, (v replacing th as well), butter becomes *butta* or even *bu'a* (the two 't''s also dropped for the glottal stop).

Dropping the 'h' at the beginning of words.
Usage: horrible becomes *'orrible*, hospital becomes *'ospital*, hang becomes *'ang*.

Dropping the 'g' altogether at the end of <u>some</u> words.
Usage: singing becomes *singin'* trying becomes *tryin'*.

Contractions

Ain't meaning am not, is not, are not or isn't.

Ain'tcha and *arn'tcha* meaning is you not and aren't you.

Don'tcha meaning don't you.

Weren'tcha meaning weren't you.

Wasn'tcha meaning wasn't you.

Whatcha meaning what are you (doing).

Some Victorian East End Cockney Phraseology

Back slang. Means – to go out of the back door.

Bags of mystery. Means – sausages.

Bangtail. Means – an unfortunate woman forced into prostitution.

Batty fang. Means – to beat someone hard.

Done a bunk. Means – to abscond.

Guv. Means – short for governor (pronounced *guv'na*) or boss.

Mutton shunters. Means – the police. (sheep shagger's, basically)

Nicked. Means – stolen or someone arrested by the police.

The word for **my** is *me* pronounced *mi* and not *mee*.
Usage: where's **me** purse. The *'i'* sound is the same in words like sit, fit, bit. If the emphasis of me or of ownership is used, then '<u>my</u>' is used. That's <u>my</u> purse, not yours. They don't 'ave <u>my</u> problems.

Double negatives are also used in the Cockney dialect. i.e. *I didn't do nuffin'*, Meaning - I didn't do anything. *He doesn't know nuffin'* Meaning - He doesn't know anything or something. *Not be blamed for nothing* Meaning Not be blamed for anything or something.

East End Cockney Rhyming Slang used in the book

Apples and pears – stairs. Usage: He fell down the apples.

Boat race – face. Usage: What's wrong with your boat?

Brown bread – dead. Usage: He's brown bread (always both words).

Brahms and Liszt – pissed. Usage: He's Brahms again.

China plate – mate. Usage: me old china.

Elephants' trunk – drunk. Usage: I got elephants last night.

Four by Twos – Jews. Usage: It is full of four by twos around here. (both words)

Half-inch – pinch. Usage: He tried to half-inch me wallet. (both words)

Hampstead Heath – teeth. Usage: I'll knock your Hampsteads out.

Plates of meat – feet. Usage: Me plates are killing me.

Shovel and pick – nick (jail). Usage: He's just got out of the shovel.

Tea leaf – thief. Usage: It is full of tea leafs around here. (both words).

Tomtit – shit. Usage: He's just gone for a tomtit (always both words, as 'tom' means tomfoolery i.e. jewellery).

Some dialogue of Kent; where Aunt Letitia is from

Words ending in 'ing', like running, the 'g' is dropped to make *runnin'* (same as Cockney).

However the 'i' is replaced with an 'e' to make *runnen'*, for example. Doing becomes *doen* and is pronounced dooen.

Many words with an 'u' sound as in Tuesday, tune and dew, sound like *Toozdy, toon and doo*.

Similarly, words with an 'o' sound are also pronounced with an 'oo' sound. Such as go, road and boat become, *goo, rood and boot*.

Generally, words are pronounced more correctly than the cockney dialect. It is nearer to the standard English of the middle classes. Letty now has some sort of hybrid accent.

Appendix 2
Inspector Reid's noticeboards of the victims

Criteria	Annie Millwood
Age	38
Occupation	A laundry worker and widow
Address	A rented room at number 8 Spitalfields Chambers, White's Row
Place of attack	At the front door of the above
Date of attack	25th February 1888
Time of attack	Sometime in the late afternoon
Witness descriptions of the attacker	A man that was taller than her with a large hat on. She didn't see his face
Sustained injuries	Stab wounds to the lower abdomen and legs. There were also cuts to the arms and hands. The wounds were not deep, and none of the major organs were targeted. She recovered from these injuries.
Reason for attack	None given, the attacker did not speak

Criteria	Ada Wilson
Age	Possibly 39
Occupation	A seamstress and possibly a prostitute
Address	19 Maidman Street, Mile End. Her own house
Place of attack	At the front door of the above
Date of attack	28th March 1888
Time of attack	Possibly just after midnight
Witness descriptions of the attacker	The victim stated that it was a man of about 30 years of age with fair hair and a small moustache. He was around 5' 6" tall and had a tanned face. He wore a dark coat with light trousers and a Quaker style wide-awake hat.
Sustained injuries	Two stab wounds to the throat, maybe with a clasp knife. She made a full recovery.
Reason for attack	Robbery was the motive. The victim was stabbed for failing to provide the attacker with money.

Criteria	Martha Tabram
Age	39
Occupation	Prostitute
Address	19 George Street, a common lodging house, Spitalfields
Place of attack	First-floor landing of George Yard Buildings, Spitalfields
Date of attack	7th August 1888
Time of attack and possible witnesses	Between 2.0am and 3.30am. Found by John Reeves at 4.45am. The body was seen at 3.30am by Alfred Crowe, who ignored it.
Throat injuries and cause of death from post-mortem descriptions	38 stab wounds to the neck chest and abdomen, with a clasp knife. One stab wound to the heart with a long-bladed knife.
Other injuries after death from post-mortem descriptions	No other injuries or mutilations
Doctors performing the autopsy	Dr Timothy Killeen
Doctors opinions on the perpetrator.	Two weapons used a clasp knife and a dagger type knife
Witness descriptions of the perpetrator	None
Burial	Not Known

Criteria	Mary Ann Nichols
Age	43
Occupation	Prostitute
Address	Lodging at Wilmott's, 18 Thrawl St and The White House, 55 Flower and Dean St. Both are common lodging houses in Spitalfields.
Place of attack	Bucks Row, Whitechapel, on the pavement of the gateway entrance to Brown's stable yard.
Date of attack	31st August 1888
Time of attack and possible witnesses	Approx. 3.30am - 3.40am Found at approx. 3.40am by Charles Cross and seconds later by Robert Paul. Body seen at 3.45am by PC John Neil.
Throat injuries and cause of death from post-mortem descriptions	One 4" long cut to neck, 1" below the left ear. 1" below this cut and 1" in front of it, a circular cut of about 8" long terminating about 3" below the right jaw. All neck tissues severed down to the vertebrae.
Other injuries after death from post-mortem descriptions	A large and deep jagged wound to the left lower abdomen. Several deep cuts to the lower right abdomen, running downwards from left to right. No organs removed from the body.
Doctors performing the autopsy	Dr Henry Llewellyn

Doctors opinions on the perpetrator	The murderer seemed to have some rough anatomical knowledge. The crime could have been executed in four or five minutes.
	The murderer likely attacked from the front, probably by strangling, then cutting the throat when on the ground. A long sharp knife was used.
Witness descriptions of the perpetrator	None
Burial	Little Ilford Cemetery

Criteria	Annie Chapman
Age	47
Occupation	Prostitute
Address	Cunningham's Lodging House, 35 Dorset Street, Spitalfields
Place of attack	The rear of 29 Hanbury Street, next to the rear doorsteps, Spitalfields
Date of attack	8th September 1888
Time of attack and possible witnesses	5.30am or just after. Albert Cadosch heard someone in the yard of number 29 at about 5.20am and about 5.25am. Elizabeth Long saw the deceased outside number 29 at 5.30am. Body discovered by John Davies at about 5.55- 6.00am.
ThroatiInjuries and cause of death from post-mortem descriptions	Two deep jagged incisions were running right around the neck, running from left to right.
Other injuries after death from post-mortem descriptions	Large scale mutilations to the abdomen and the intestines lifted from the body and placed over the right shoulder. Some organs removed from the scene, possibly by the attacker. The uterus and two-thirds of the bladder had been entirely removed.
Doctors performing the autopsy	Dr George Bagster Phillips

Doctors opinions on the perpetrator	The victim was partially strangled, held by the chin and throat cut from left to right. A thin-bladed knife 6-8" long.
	He thought that some anatomical knowledge was demonstrated in consequence of haste. The injuries would take 15 minutes to perform.
Witness descriptions of the perpetrator	Elizabeth Long who saw a man at 5.30am with the victim. She described him as a little taller than the deceased who was 5' tall. He appeared to be both dark and a foreigner, about 40 years of age; he had a shabby-genteel appearance about him. His height was possibly 5' 3" to 5' 5".
Burial	Manor Park Cemetery

Criteria	Elizabeth Stride
Age	44
Occupation	Prostitute
Address	Lodging House at 32 Flower and Dean Street, Spitalfields
Place of attack	Close to the sidewall near the entrance to Dutfield's Yard, 40 Berner Street, St. George's in the East
Date of attack	30th September 1888
Time of attack and possible witnesses	Probably between 12.55-12.59am. Found at 1.00am by Louis Diemschutz
Throat injuries and cause of death from post-mortem descriptions	One clean-cut incision on the neck 6" in length, commencing 2.5" below the left jaw angle, all left-sided arteries and tissues were cut through. The left carotid artery was not entirely cut through. The cut was more superficial on the right-hand side of the neck.
Other injuries after death from post-mortem descriptions	No other injuries to the body
Doctors performing the autopsy	Dr George Bagster Phillips and Dr Blackwell

Doctors opinions on the perpetrator	The throat was cut while the victim was on the ground or falling to the ground. No evidence of strangulation. The victim was seized by the shoulders and forced to the ground. From a position on her right side, he cut her throat left to right. The perpetrator seemed to have some knowledge of where to cut the throat to kill quickly, It took two seconds. A knife maybe 6" long such as a shoemaker's knife could have made the cut.
Witness descriptions of the perpetrator	PC Smith sees Stride with a man at 12.30am on Berner Street opposite the Working Men's Club. The man is described as 28 years old, dark coat and hard deerstalker hat. Israel Schwartz sees the victim and a man at 12.45am. He describes the man as about 30 years old, 5' 5" tall with a fresh complexion, dark hair and small brown moustache. He is dressed in an overcoat and an old black felt hat with a wide brim.
Burial	East London Cemetery

Criteria	Catherine Eddowes
Age	46
Occupation	Prostitute
Address	Lodging House, 55 Flower and Dean Street, Spitalfields
Place of attack	Mitre Square, on the pavement in the darkest corner of the square, Aldgate, City of London
Date of attack	30th September 1888
Time of attack and possible witnesses	Approx. 1.36-1.43am Found by PC Watkins at 1.44am Joseph Lawende, Joseph Hyam Levy, and Harry Harris see the deceased with a man at 1.35am at the corner of Duke St and Church Passage.
Throat Injuries and cause of death from post-mortem descriptions	The neck and throat were cut from left to right. The cut commenced under the left jaw for about 6 "or 7" to the right jaw. All tissues and arteries on the left side were cut through.
Other injuries after death from post-mortem descriptions	Large scale mutilations to the abdomen and the intestines lifted from the body and placed over her right shoulder. Some organs removed from the scene, possibly by the attacker. Left kidney carefully removed and part of the uterus. Mutilations and cuts to the face.

Doctors performing the autopsy	Dr Frederick Gordon Brown. Also, present, Dr William Sedgwick Saunders, Dr George William Sequeira and Dr Phillips
Doctors opinions on the perpetrator	The victim's throat was cut first when she was on the ground. He had considerable knowledge of the position of the organs in the abdominal cavity and the way of removing them. It required a great deal of medical knowledge to have removed the kidney and to know where it was placed. The attack would have taken at least five minutes. A 6" long sharp-pointed knife must have been used.
Witness descriptions of the perpetrator	Joseph Lawende, saw the victim with a man at 1.35am, which is just minutes before her murder. He was 30 years old, 5' 7" tall, fair complexion and moustache with a medium build.
Burial	Little Ilford Cemetery

Criteria	Mary Jane Kelly
Age	25
Occupation	Prostitute
Address	13, in Miller's Court, Dorset Street, Spitalfields
Place of attack	In the room of 13 Miller's Court, Dorset Street, Spitalfields
Date of attack	9th November 1888
Time of attack and possible witnesses	Probably between 2.00-4.00am. Body not discovered until 10.45am by Thomas Bowyer. Sarah Lewis and Elizabeth Prater hear a faint cry at 4.00am. George Hutchinson saw the victim and the man enter Miller's Court at 2.00am he waits till 2.45am and no-one leaves.
Throat injuries and cause of death from post-mortem descriptions	Several deep cuts to the neck, from right to left, severing all tissues of the neck and throat. The attacker stood at the left-hand side of the bed and victim.
Other injuries after death from post-mortem descriptions	Very, large-scale, mutilations to the face body and legs. Many internal organs cut from the body and placed in the room. No organs were apparently removed from the scene by the attacker.
Doctors performing the autopsy	Dr Thomas Bond. Also present was Dr George Bagster Phillips

Doctors opinions on the perpetrator	Dr Bond's view was the perpetrator was a man of physical strength, great coolness and daring, but no scientific nor anatomical knowledge, not even the technical knowledge of a butcher or horse slaughterer. This view extends to the four previous killings also.
Witness descriptions of the perpetrator	George Hutchinson described the man he saw with the victim at about 2am, as having a pale complexion, a slight moustache dark hair, dark eyes, and bushy eyebrows. He was 5' 6" or 5' 7" tall and about 35 or 36 years old and very smartly dressed.
Burial	St Patricks Cemetery Leytonstone

Appendix 3
Police officers and officials

Some of the key Police Officers involved in the Jack the Ripper case	
Whitechapel H Division	
Superintendent Thomas Arnold	Head of Whitechapel H Division on leave for the Nichols and Chapman murders
Chief Inspector John West	Acting Superintendent for the Nichols and Chapman murders
Detective Inspector Edmund Reid	Local CID Inspector for H Division on leave for the Nichols and Chapman murders
Detective Inspector Joseph Chandler	The first officer on the scene of the Chapman murder
Detective Inspector Charles Pinhorn	Involved with the Stride murder
Detective Inspector Walter Beck	The first officer on the scene of the Kelly murder
Detective Inspector Walter Andrews	Seconded from Scotland Yard
Divisional Inspector Ernest Ellisdon	Involved with Tabram murder and George Hutchinson
Detective Sergeant William Thick	Arrested John Pizer
Sergeant 31H Edward Badham	Took George Hutchinson's statement
Detective Sergeant Eli Caunter	Found Mary Ann Connolly, who had gone missing for a while

Police Sergeant Stephen White	Involved in Stride murder
Detective Constable Charles Dolden	Involved in Stride murder
Detective Constable Walter Dew	Involved in Kelly murder. He knew Kelly
PC 262 Thomas Barrett	Found Tabram's body
PC 55H Jonas Mizen	Involved in Nichols murder
PC 252H Henry Lamb	Found Stride's body
PC 452H William Smith	Involved in Stride murder
PC 282H Joseph Dragge	Found a knife just before the Stride murder
PC 12HR Albert Collins	Involved in Stride murder
PC 385W Walter Stride	Identified Stride who had previously been married to his uncle. Drafted from W Division
PC 254A Alfred Long	Drafted in from A division. Found the apron in Goulston Street
Central CID Scotland Yard	
Assistant Commissioner Dr Robert Anderson	In overall charge from 6th October when he returned from sick leave
Chief Inspector Donald Swanson	In overall charge of the murders from 1st September to 6th October
Detective Inspector Henry Moore	Liaison between Abberline and Swanson
Detective Inspector Fred Abberline	In charge of detectives on the ground during the murders

Bethnal Green J Division	
Detective Inspector Joseph Helsen	Local CID Inspector for J Division, therefore involved in the Nichols murder
Inspector John Spratling	Involved with Nichols murder
Detective Sergeant Patrick Enright	Involved with Nichols murder
Detective Sergeant George Godley	Involved with Nichols murder
Sergeant 10J Henry Kirby	Involved with Nichols murder
PC 97J John Neil	Found Nichols' body
PC 96J John Thain	Involved with Nichols murder
City of London Police	
Detective Superintendent Alfred Foster	Present in Mitre Square soon after the discovery of the body
Detective Inspector James McWilliam	Head of CID for the City police therefore involved with the Eddowes murder
Inspector Collard	Involved in the Eddowes murder
Detective Sergeant John Mitchell	Involved in the Eddowes murder
Station Sergeant James Byfield	Put Eddowes into the cells
Detective Constable Robert Outram	Involved in the Eddowes murder
Detective Constable Edward Marriot	Involved in the Eddowes murder
Detective Constable Baxter Hunt	Involved in the Eddowes murder

Detective Constable Daniel Halse	Involved in the Eddowes murder
PC 881 Edward Watkins	Found Eddowes' body
PC 968 George Hutt	Let Eddowes out of the police station
PC 964 James Harvey	His beat took him to the end of Church Passage; he said that he did not see a dead body
PC 931 Louis Robinson	Arrested Eddowes
PC 922 Richard Pearce	Lived in Mitre Square
Other Officials	
George Collier Whitechapel Deputy Coroner	Tabram Inquest
Wynne Baxter Whitechapel Coroner	Smith, Nichols, Chapman and Stride Inquests
Samuel Langham City of London Coroner	Eddowes Inquest
Roderick McDonald Shoreditch Coroner	Kelly Inquest
Doctor George Hellier	Conducted the Smith post-mortem
Doctor Timothy Killeen	Conducted the Tabram post-mortem
Doctor Rees Ralph Llewellyn	Conducted the Nichols post-mortem
Doctor George Bagster Phillips	Conducted the Chapman and Stride post-mortems. In attendance at Eddowes and Kelly post-mortems
Doctor William Blackwell	In attendance at the Stride post-mortem
Doctor Frederick Gordon Brown	Conducted the Eddowes post-mortem

Doctor George William Sequeira	In attendance at the Eddowes post-mortem
Doctor William Sedgwick Saunders	In attendance at the Eddowes post-mortem – Tested the stomach contents
Doctor Thomas Bond	Conducted the Kelly post-mortem. Profiled the killer

Appendix 4
Sources of information and permissions

The two quotations from; *Psychopathia Sexualis*, by Richard von Krafft-Ebbing (1886)

The following National Archive records have been accessed via the *Jack the Ripper Sourcebook*.

The folio records are as follows:

MEPO 3/140, folios 9-11, 15-31, 34-59, 204-216, 227-232 235-241

MEPO 3/142 folios 491-492

MEPO 3/3153 folios 1-4, 10-18

HO 144/220/A49301B folios 179, 299

HO144/221/A49301C folios 6-11, 13-21,42-46, 78-79, 110-118, 128-134, 136-145, 147-159, 162-199 and 217-223

Other publicly available sources of information have been accessed from *The Jack the Ripper Sourcebook* are as follows:

Elizabeth Stride inquest; *The Times* 2 October 1888 page 6 (pages 137-177)

Catherine Eddowes inquest; number 135 Corporation of London Record Office (pages 199-238)

Mary Kelly inquest; MJ/SPC, NE1888 Box 3, Case paper, 19, London Metropolitan Archives. (pages 363-379)

Acknowledgments

My thanks to my dear wife, Carol, for all her proof-reading, editing and layout skills.

Thanks to my lovely daughter, Natalie Chester for all her thorough and constructive comments and also her assistance with marketing on social media.

A major thank you to my son-in-law and Graphic Designer, Adrian Newell, for his excellent graphic design skills for the front cover and the maps. www.adriannewell.co.uk

The primary source of information used to compile this book was *The Ultimate Jack the Ripper Sourcebook; An Illustrated Encyclopedia. By Stewart P. Evans and Keith Skinner.* This reference work has transcriptions of the actual Metropolitan Police records from the National Archives at Kew, London.

Appendix 4 contains the archive records referred to, with kind permission from the National Archives.

There are two small quotations used from the book *Psychopathia Sexualis,* with kind permission from Skyhorse Publishing.

Note: If anyone does know where the missing Metropolitan Police file on Emma Smith is, please return it to the police or the National Archives at Kew, London. Anonymously if you wish, it belongs in the archives. File evidence from other Jack the Ripper case files are also missing. These files need returning as vital evidence may be present in them.

ABOUT THE AUTHOR

Paul Kenny was a university and college lecturer for 31 years, until his retirement in 2018. He is married to Carol and has two grown-up daughters and two grandchildren.

After studying the case for 30 years, he now publishes his views in the form of this novel. He finds the case fascinating not only because it is unsolved, but because it is intriguing as to the type of person the Ripper was and why he committed such crimes.

Printed in Great Britain
by Amazon